C000138586

THE UNITED FEDERATION MARINE CORPS

BOOK 1: RECRUIT

Colonel Jonathan P. Brazee
USMC (Ret)

Copyright © 2014 Jonathan Brazee

Semper Fi Press

A Semper Fi Press Book

Copyright © 2014 by Jonathan Brazee

ISBN-13: 978-0692254233 (Semper Fi Press)

Printed in the United States of America

All rights reserved. No part of this book may be used or reproduced by any means, graphic, electronic, or mechanical, including photocopying, recording, taping or by any information storage retrieval system without the written permission of the publisher except in the case of brief quotations embodied in critical articles and reviews.

This is a work of fiction. All of the characters, names, incidents, organizations, and dialogue in this novel are either the products of the author's imagination or are used fictitiously.

Acknowledgements:

I want to thank all those who took the time to pre-read this book, catching my mistakes in both content and typing. A special shout out goes to my comrades at VFW Post 9951 in Bangkok for their help and to the Royal Marines at the Once A Marine website for teaching me about British Royal Marine traditions and slang. And most of all, thanks to my editor, Anne Gentilucci for making me a better writer. All remaining typos and inaccuracies are solely my fault.

Original Cover Art by Almaz Sharipov

ATACAMA

Sergeant John Nbele barely glanced at his heads-up display as he climbed the huge rise of tailings leading to the open-pit mine. Small green triangles being projected onto his visor represented each of the men in the squad, and all were moving in the squad V formation, two fire teams out front, one trailing between them.

This was the sergeant's fifth campaign, but his first as a squad leader. He'd risen up through the ranks quickly, with two meritorious promotions, the last one a battlefield promotion for valor on Case's World.[1] He knew he was on the fast track, and this operation would cement his reputation as not only a fierce fighter, but also as a leader of Marines.

He didn't really expect this campaign to amount to much. Atacama was sparsely populated, and the miners didn't have a military as such, only a small police-slash-guard force (the type of guards Marines and Legionnaires called Jimmylegs) that was formed to protect the mines. They had no heavy weapons. John had bet a bottle of Jack—the real stuff from Earth, not the fake shit that most people drank—with Royal Teristry, a sergeant in Bravo Company, that the Jimmylegs would bolt at the sight of the platoon's Marines in the assault.

His suit subtly shifted to remain vertical as he started up the tailings. Wearing a suit was pretty easy. Most recruits could walk, run, and jump within 30 minutes of being introduced to them. Still, there were a few tricks to them. Sergeant Nbele's body instinctively

---

[1] Case's World: A Class 2 planet in Sector 14. Two corporate proxies started a war for control of the entire planet, causing the Federation to send in the Marines to quell the fighting before turning the mission over to the FCDC

wanted to lean into the hill as he climbed, and he had to relax and let the suit take over.

The suit was the 980 kg mechanical monster each of his Marines wore, the PICS, or Personal Integrated Combat Units. With its sandwiched Ceramic Array and LTC (Lutetium Tungsten Carbide) armor, it was impervious to all small arms and most larger weapons. While the Corp's PICS were not the modern Rigaudeau-3s that the Legion and some world militias had, or even the Brotherhood's Saul line of combat armor, it was more than enough proof for the poorly-armed miners. Naval intelligence had assured the Marine command of that.

"Bentley, close it up," he sent to the PFC in First Fire Team.

Corporal Kim should have caught his lagging Marine. He, as the squad leader shouldn't have to be getting after individual Marines. He'd have to have a one-on-one with Kim when all this was over. He stared directly at Bentley's triangular avatar, blinking his eyes once long and hard to initiate a full data dump. The Marine's data filled his visor. Heart rate, respiration, suit dynamics, all were within normal range. Bentley's nerves were fine; he had just lost focus.

That was a bad precedent. While this mission should be a cakewalk, losing focus on a more dangerous battlefield was a recipe for disaster. Nbele's battlefield promotion on Case's World was a result of his squad leader on that mission "losing focus." Three Marines had been KIA,[2] and Nbele had had to jump into the breach to save the rest.

He blinked away Bentley, then brought up Kim.

"Corporal Kim, monitor your Marines. I don't need to be keeping Bentley in line," he said on the direct person-to-person comms.

"Aye-aye, Sergeant," was the reply.

Sergeant Nbele's Second Squad was the point of main effort. He and his 12 Marines were the heavy squad, the ones with PICS. First Squad had taken a blocking position at a crossroads on the other side of the mine, some 15 kms out. Third was providing

---

[2] KIA: Killed in Action

security for the platoon headquarters back at the LZ.[3] Normally, 13 Marines, even suited, would be too few to be operating like this, but no one expected much, if any, resistance. Third Platoon had taken its objective, the mine headquarters at the planetary capital, over an hour ago without a fight.

His leading fire teams crested the tailings, ready to descend into the pit. He switched to monitor Corporal Kim's view, which showed up to the right of his visor. There were the same pieces of heavy equipment in the pit as he had seen on the satellite photo, but it was still good to get confirmation. There wasn't any sign of miners.

As always, the projected display was somewhat transparent so he could still see the real world through the image. He wanted a better view, so he picked up his pace from inside the V formation. His suit's servos adjusted. While it didn't take any more effort from him, the motion of the suit swung into a higher tempo as he went up the rest of the incline. Cresting the hill, he could see down into the pit, and he closed Kim's feed.

The pit was huge, maybe 1,500 meters across and 400 meters deep. Unlike the open-pit mines he'd seen elsewhere, this one had several smaller sub-mine heads, holes leading deeper into the ground as they followed veins. From the plans they had downloaded, he knew those mine shafts went on for kilometers underground.

He held up the squad as he linked to the eye-in-the-sky. The drone circled somewhere out of sight, but the feed was clear. There was no sign of any movement in the pit. It was possible that the miners had bugged out, but a leader who wanted to live a long and prosperous life didn't assume anything. He checked all his data feeds, but everything was quiet. He considered sending out one of the two dragonflies housed in his sleeve to get a close-up look, but the threat was pretty low, and he wanted to save them in case he might need them later.

"Zipper-six, this is Zipper-two. There is no indication of any enemy activity. We are commencing our descent into the mine,

---

[3] LZ: Landing Zone

over," he sent to his platoon commander, careful, as always to keep the Houseman slums out of his voice when on the radio.

"Roger that, Two. Keep your heads down. Six, out."

Sergeant Nbele gave the command, and the squad started moving down into the mine pit. Their march discipline remained tight with good dispersion as they descended. Unless the mine was abandoned, there had to be eyes on them now, and the more professional the Marines looked, the more intimidating and the less likely that any Jimmylegs would want to tangle with them. Loyalty to an employer could only go so far.

He glanced to his left for a visual on Kim's team. The icons projected onto his visor gave him an exact picture of their movement, but human nature sometimes took over, and he wanted to see them with his eyes. He could see three of the four Marines as they made their way through the rocks and dirt of the pit slope.

He blinked at Kim's icon to bring him up on a direct comms when with a flash, his visor's electronics went blank, and his suit came to a sudden halt. His PICS had failed, something that had never happened to him before. He thumbed the emergency reset, but nothing changed. He tried it again, but with the same result. Of all the times for this to happen, it had to happen now, on his first assault as a squad leader! He cursed CWO2 Slyth, the company ordnance officer, the man in charge of keeping the suits operational.

His Marines were well-trained. They would continue the mission, but he would be out of it. Corporal Castallano would have to take over the assault. It was only then that he looked out at Kim's fire team. While the projections on his visor were gone, he could still see through it. The three Marines in sight had also stopped, one in mid-stride.

Sergeant Nbele's heart sank. This wasn't a simple malfunction. Something had taken down all the PICS, not that he could imagine what could possibly accomplish that. But he couldn't ignore the evidence before his eyes. He kept hitting the reset, hoping against hope that it would finally work, but his suit remained a quiet prison. He started calculating. Third Squad was 15 km away, and with the lone company Stork, they could get there in a couple of minutes. But he didn't know where that transport was. It

4

might take 30 minutes or more to get it to Third's position, then another five to embark, reach the mine, and debark.

Sergeant Nbele felt his frustration threaten to take over. He took five deep breaths to calm himself. They would just have to wait there for however long it took for rescue. It wasn't as if the miners had any heavy weapons with which to attack them. With the power of the suits out, the kickbacks, the tiny jets that went off when a projectile hit the skin of a suit, thereby slowing down the projectile, wouldn't work, but the inherent protection of the sandwiched armor would still be effective.

Something stirred in his peripheral vision. He leaned forward, pushing his face closer to the clear visor, trying to see to the right. At the edge of his field of vision, several men came out of one of the mine shafts, hugging the rock walls. One took out what looked to be nothing more than a folded umbrella. Sergeant Nbele had no idea what it was until the miner pointed it at the sky, and with a flash, a rocket-like missile took off. The men ducked back into the shaft. Whatever that rocket was, it was certainly homemade, and if its target was the eye-in-the-sky, that drone had countermeasures.

His cheek was pressed against the visor as he tried to watch. A few moments later, the miners hesitantly came out again. They were searching the sky. They were a long way off, but with his electronics dead and zoom non-functioning, it seemed as if they were arguing on what to do.

More men came out, several pointing to where the Marines were. One man had the controls of an industrial mule which towed a piece of equipment out of one of the mine entrances, and with that in trace, he started guiding the mule up the slope, following the other men as they approached the Marines.

Sergeant Nbele kept hitting his reset, but still nothing changed. His suit was dead. He wasn't sure what the miners could have done. The suits were hardened against EMP[4] attacks, so as

---

[4] EMP: Electromagnetic Pulse. A type of weapon designed to scramble or destroy electronics by emitting a pulse electromagnetic energy.

long as they were intact, the suits should work. Obviously, however, the miners had managed to disable them somehow.

Halfway up the slope, several miners grouped together. Arms were pointed, then three men split off to move toward Corporal Kim's team. Two, including the guy controlling the mule, came forward toward Sergeant Nbele, and another three started to the squad leader's right, most likely heading to Second Fire Team. They were out of his field of vision within moments.

As the mule trundled forward, its six tires having no problem purchasing the rough ground, the sergeant's heart sank as he suddenly recognized what it was towing. It was a powerful industrial drill. As a boy in the Houseman slums, the young John had dreamed of working in road construction on the planet, where crews were blasting tunnels in the mountain ranges. One of their pieces of equipment was this type of drill. Sergeant Nbele wasn't sure if the hardened LTC bit could penetrate the LTC in his suit's armor, but he knew he didn't want to find out.

With all power gone from his suit, the first blast actually rocked him. A cloud of dust rose up from where Corporal Kim's team was frozen. Sergeant Nbele stared as explosion after explosion sent more plumes upwards.

"Get some!" he shouted as he realized the explosions were supporting artillery from his unit.

The incoming rounds started walking across the slope toward him. He glanced back to see the two miners who had been approaching him run pell-mell back down the slope to save themselves.

"Fuckin' A, I owe you bastards," he said in awe as round after round landed. "Screw Teristry, that Jack is comin' to you guys!"

Shrapnel pinged as it hit his suit. It didn't do any harm, as the arty Marines firing the shells would have known it wouldn't. But against unarmored miners, it would be devastating. Sergeant Nbele looked back over to the left. The three Marines he could see were still standing, but at least one of the miners was down, a bloody mess heaped in the dirt. He couldn't see the other two miners, but they had to be down as well.

It looked like the two men who had been approaching him had made it to safety, but the drill seemed to have taken a direct hit as the rounds were walked from his left to right. He wanted to shout out with joy each time a round landed. Too soon, though, the rounds stopped.

The platoon only had one tube, the old but venerable M229. It fired a 155 mm shell that packed a powerful punch. Some shells were anti-personnel, such as what had just been used, some were anti-armor, some were EMP and other pulse-type rounds. The gun was a great piece of gear, but even with advances in shell-casing technology, the rounds were still heavy and took up space. A mere Marine squad could only carry so much. They weren't some planet-bound militia that could stockpile huge stores of rounds ready for use. They had to carry in whatever they thought they might need.

Sergeant Nbele thought the platoon HQ had most likely expended all their anti-personnel rounds in that fire for effect. The question was if the miners knew that as well. Nbele hoped that the threat of more rounds would keep them in their hidey-holes until the rest of the platoon could come and get the squad out of this mess. Then the miners would find out what it meant to face the Marines.

Motion back at the entrance to the mine shaft caught his eye. The miners had to know that time was limited before reinforcements could arrive. If they were going to do something about his squad, they would have to act fast.

Four men darted out, and by bounding back and forth, hitting the deck before bouncing back up for another burst of 15 meters, they made their way up to the mule in front of Sergeant Nbele. Once there, they stood up and stared at it.

Typical civilians, he thought as he saw that. *All that dodgin' and bobbin' to get up the slope, then they stand around gawkin'. I wish to God I'd left a sniper up behind us.*

The mule looked worse for wear. He could see that several of the tires were blown. He hoped the drill had been messed up, too. All four men turned as one to look directly at him. They were only about 30 meters away, and Sergeant Nbele could see them arguing, several times pointing to the ground between them and him.

One guy got on the control and started the mule up again. It lurched forward, then the drive shaft of one wheel started to spin while pieces of the tire flew off. Two of the men got behind the mule and pushed. It lurched forward again, this time going maybe five meters before getting stuck once more. Once more, the men got behind, and with brute force, got it moving again.

Whatever Sergeant Nbele had hoped about the mule and its cargo, it looked like the miners would make it up to him. If they did, he had to rely on his armor to keep him safe until help could arrive. No matter how many scenarios he went over in his mind, nothing he could think of would make any difference. He had no secret powers, no way to fight back. He didn't even have some way to jury-rig a suicide blast that would take them out with him like what happened in the Hollybolly war flicks.

Within a surprisingly short time, the miners were right in front of him. One of them, an older guy with a two-day's stubble covering his face, stood on the mule to stare inside Sergeant Nbele's visor. The guy looked like anyone. Dark complected with a narrow face, the only thing notable about him was his icy-grey eyes. Even with the eyes, though, Nbele would never have given the man a second glance if he passed him walking down the street. He seemed so, well *normal*. The man looked to be studying him as well. After a few moments, he shrugged and got back off the mule.

As the men struggled to horse around the drill, Sergeant Nbele had a sudden urge to take a piss. With his suit powerless, though, he didn't know if the catchment gel would work, and he would be damned if he was going to piss down his legs with the miners out there. He couldn't see the drill bit anymore, but when it clanked against this armor, he almost let his bladder go.

He heard the muffled whine as the drill was turned on. His suit dampened most of the outside sounds, but as the drill bit started to try and force a way into his suit, the screeching reverberated loudly enough to make him wince. Sergeant Nbele felt the vibrations, and his suit tilted slightly back before the drill skittered to the side and lost contact.

His armor had held!

They wrestled the drill back, and set the bit directly on his front carapace. Once again, as the bit made contact, the sound filled the inside of the suit. But just as before, the suit deflected the drill, sending it off to the side. This seemed to put a pause to things as the men stopped and started discussing the issue.

"Fuck you too, you freakin' slugs," he said quietly to himself. "Just keep a'tryin', and before you know it, the lieutenant's goin' to get here, and pow, fuck you up but good! So, you keep talkin' and jabberin' like that, you stupid negats."

The men obviously came to a decision. Two of them got on the mule and put their hands on his chest carapace. Both seemed to be avoiding looking into the visor to see him. They looked back at the mule operator, and the vehicle gave a lurch. He heard it hit him low on the legs as it rocked him. It wasn't enough to tip him over though. But it backed up and lurched forward again, the men pushing as it hit him. The mule couldn't back up much or the two guys on top would fall, but even a foot or so gave it room to gain some momentum. On the third push, Sergeant Nbele thought he was going to fall over, but the suit's mass kept it upright. It took four more tries before that magic center of balance was surpassed. He teetered for a moment before falling over backward.

Without the motion suppressors working, Sergeant Nbele had the breath knocked out of him as he fell, something digging heavily into his back. The suits were pretty comfortable to wear normally, but without power, they were only so much junk.

On his back, he could only see the sky. He scanned what he could, waiting to see the Stork come into view with the rest of the platoon onboard. What he did see was the same guy who had looked at him before. The man leaned over to look into the visor. They stared at each other for a moment before the man crossed himself, bringing his fingers his lips as he finished the cross. Then he nodded and stepped back out of view.

When the drilling started again, the noise filled his ears. It kept going, though, not skittering off his armor. They must have gotten him wedged, or maybe the drill itself wedged. They still would have to penetrate his armor, though. It might be over 50 years old, but it was pretty formidable.

The sounds of the drilling changed pitch, getting lower. A sense of panic filled the squad leader. That meant the drill bit had gained purchase. The sound reverberated everywhere, but he tried to locate from where it emanated. With the vibrations that he could now feel, it seemed to be from about his waist, maybe where the chest carapace met the pelvic shield. The newest Legionaire suits were seamless, but the old Marine suits were not. Could the drill bit have gained some sort of purchase there?

The vibration started getting stronger, and the sounds of the bit slowed down even more.

"Break you mother!" he shouted at the unseen LTC bit.

Looking down into the small gap between the skin of his suit and his chest, he had a momentary glimpse of a spinning metallic shaft before it plunged into his groin. He was overcome by an intense flash of agony before his world went dark.

****

Private Ryck Lysander wiped the sweat from his brow as he caught his breath. He'd just brought up the platoon's entire load of the M887 anti-personal rounds for the M229. He was not a trained artillery Marine, and as the newest of newbies, just reporting in two days prior to embarkation, he hadn't been assigned to a squad yet and was instead the platoon runner, which meant doing whatever the platoon sergeant wanted him to do. In this case, it was to hump arty shells.

When Second Squad had somehow disappeared from the net, a sense of alarm, if not panic, had swept the platoon headquarters. The eye-in-the-sky had shown the Marines suddenly stopping cold before some miners had appeared in the pit, and the drone was knocked offline. Lieutenant Prowse and Staff Sergeant England had a heated discussion for a few moments as they reported back up to the company and went over their options. The platoon commander ordered Sergeant Dixon, the arty team leader, to saturate the open pit with anti-personnel fire. Without eyes on target and no comms, there wasn't any way to know how effective the support had been. The lieutenant had been burning up the comm lines with the company commander, demanding the Navy get eyes on the objective and the Stork pilot to get the transport back.

"Get your gear, boot. We're going in with the lieutenant," Doc Silestre told him.

The platoon corpsman calmly checked the charge on his M99.[5] Ryck hurriedly checked his, too. He hadn't fired his weapon, so it was still at 100%, enough to fire close to 1,000 rounds of the hypervelocity darts.

"What are we going to be doing?" he asked.

"Go get our guys, you dumbshit," the doc told him.

Ryck wanted to clarify that he meant what their orders would be and what he was supposed to do, but he bit his tongue. He tried to look alert as the lieutenant and platoon sergeant made last-minute plans. This wasn't going to be some well-planned op but more of an immediate-action drill. The problem was that Ryck hadn't been with the unit long enough to rehearse any of the drills back on the Dirtball, and aboard the *Adelaide*, there hadn't been much room for any sort of physical training.

Within moments, the platoon headquarters and Third Squad were forming up just as the Stork came floating over the LZ, its turbofans rotating to the vertical so the big transport could land. Staff Sergeant England already had the Marines moving before the Stork touched down, jumping up on the ramp while it was still a half a meter in the air. Ryck followed the rest of the Marines up into the belly of the bird.

"Boot, you stick with me like glue. I want you on my ass," Staff Sergeant England's voice came over his earbud, the triple tones preceding the voice message indicating that they were on a direct person-to-person circuit.

Ryck started to acknowledge when the double tone of an open-platoon circuit cut him off. The lieutenant started giving out his order as the Stork rose smoothly into the air. He spoke calmly, but Ryck could sense the underlying tension in his voice, even over

---

[5] M99: The basic personal weapon of the Marines. It is a lightweight carbine that fires hypervelocity 4 mm darts via magnetic rings that pull the darts down the barrel.

the M919 small unit communication modules. They didn't know what had frozen Second Squad or knocked out the drone, so the Stork would come in low and drop them below the lip of the mine before bolting off to pick up Third Squad. Two fire teams of Third, along with Staff Sergeant England and the squad leader, Sergeant Piccalo-Tensing, designated Element A, would move up and over the western side of the pit and get to the Marines below them. The remaining fire team and the rest of the platoon headquarters, Element B, would provide cover from the eastern side of the pit, then move down once Element A had consolidated its position. This was a very basic plan, much like what Ryck had conducted in his almost 10 months at recruit training and then another three months at IUT[6] at Camp Otrakovskiy. He knew there wasn't much time for anything else, but still, he expected something a little more . . . well, he didn't know what he expected, but it wasn't this.

Ryck still didn't know what he was supposed to do, but the platoon sergeant had told him to stay on his ass, so that was what Ryck was going to follow. He checked his M99 once more out of nervous habit before looking up at the other Marines. No one showed any signs of the butterflies that threatened to take over his own stomach. He wasn't sure if he was scared or excited, and he really didn't make an effort to figure out which it was. This was what he'd been trained to do. This was why he'd left Prophesy.

He tried to lean the M99 on his thigh, but it slid off his trousers, his "skins," which were slightly stiffened with the inserted STF armor protection, or "bones," and he almost dropped it, barely catching it with one gloved hand. Despite the imminent combat he faced, his mind snapped back to boot where dropping a weapon was a cardinal sin. He gave a sigh of relief that he hadn't dropped it as he secured his weapon.

And that was all the time he had. With less than two klicks to the mine, the Stork had them there quickly. It flew in with the gentle approach that still amazed Ryck. Something so big shouldn't fly as smooth as a maglev.

---

[6] IUT: Infantry Unit Training

The big bird flared, then the back ramp was lowered, and the Marines poured out. Ryck followed the staff sergeant, trying to orient himself. Within moments, the Stork took off, leaving the two elements alone to make their way up to the lip of the mine. Ryck tried to keep aware of his surroundings while still watching the ground in front of him in order to stay on his feet.

As they reached the lip of the mine, Staff Sergeant England motioned them down. He edged a small fiber-eye over the lip to see what was visible while they waited for the lieutenant to start the supporting fire.

"We've got three, I repeat three combatants at my 10 o'clock, 550 meters from our present position, standing next to our friendlies. The friendlies look to be down, over" the staff sergeant sent over the net to the lieutenant.

Two beeps then indicated that he had switched to the element circuit, followed by "Listen up. Do not, I repeat, do not stop to assist any of the downed Marines. We need to get to the mine entrance and inside, so get through the kill zone quickly. The lieutenant and Doc will see to Second Squad. Got it? I want each of you to acknowledge. No stopping, over."

Each Marine responded that he understood. No stopping.

Ryck checked his M99 once more. He hadn't fired yet, so nothing would have changed, but still, he had to check. He couldn't see where the other element was, so he hugged the dirt, listening to his heart pounding. If Second Squad, suited up in their PICS had been taken out, what could they do with only their skins and bones?

Lieutenant Prowse finally had Element B in position, and on order, the element opened fire. Element A immediately pushed over the lip and into the mine. Ryck had a glimpse of a miner off to his front left turning to flee, only to be cut down from the Marines' fire. Ryck hadn't even tried to fire himself. That was Element B's job, and he was having enough trouble following Staff Sergeant England as they raced pell-mell down the slope. It wasn't really pell-mell, though. Their jerky movements were reasoned. From an assaulted position's perspective, the rush was intended to make it difficult to bring the Marines under fire with any degree of effectiveness, and the Marines practiced this kind of movement until it was second nature to them. Ryck hadn't had any actual experience doing it yet, though, so he just focused on keeping up with the staff sergeant.

Trying to watch his element leader, look for the enemy, and observe his step, proved too much for him. He stumbled and fell, rolling over several times before he could get back to his feet. His bones protected him from too much damage to anything other than his pride. He focused a little more on his footing, relying on Element B behind him to take out any threat.

Ryck felt *extremely* exposed as they rushed to the bottom of the pit and the openings into the mine itself. He felt that he would be hit at any moment. The sight of a downed Marine, his PICS torn open, did not help. They rushed forward to their objective. There were two other doors, both larger to accommodate trucks, but the lieutenant had chosen the smaller of the three entrances, one only about two meters wide.

Just before reaching bottom, a blast erupted in front of Ryck. Smoke billowed up, and a body was thrown in the air. It came back down to land in a heap. Without hesitation, two other Marines closed in on the body, grabbed it, and pulled it forward.

Within moments, all the Marines reached the mined rock wall at the bottom into which the openings were cut. The Marines spread out on either side of their target door. Ryck slammed his back up against the rock, looking over to his right where the injured Marine was on his ass, leaning up against the rock wall as well. It was Corporal Singh. The bones provided excellent ballistic protection, but they did little to provide structural support. Singh's left leg was gruesomely twisted, the front of the foot facing back, the knee twisted at a 90-degree angle to the side. The mine blast had also damaged his skin's nanos. The small sensors and syntho-chromatophores in the fabric of his utilities, his skins, had obviously been knocked out of whack. His blouse had already shifted the color and pattern to match the rock against which he leaned, but the trou had turned to black. His non-stop stream of cursing actually calmed Ryck. If the corporal could keep that up, then he would be OK once the Navy docs got a hold of him.

Ryck subconsciously felt his own skins for the armor in them. It was hard to believe that what looked like stiff, heavy paper, the "bones," could give any support when slid into the pockets of his skins. They were pliable and permitted movement when they were in the skins, but when hit by a projectile, the molecular structure instantly crystallized to provide a casing that was proof against most small arms projectiles. Like all recruits, Ryck had watched a DI back at Camp Charles get shot right in the chest at close range with no injury, but seeing a demonstration of that and trusting his own armor to work as well was a huge jump in confidence.

He tore his eyes off the injured corporal to look back to where Lance Corporal Smith was placing the small breaching charge against the solid metal door of the entrance. Although weighing less than a kilo, it nonetheless packed a huge punch. If anyone was waiting on the other side of the door for the Marines, the blast would either take them out or render them incapable of offering any resistance.

"Fire in the hole!" Smitty yelled out before jumping back to hug the wall.

The breaching charge was very directional and could be dialed to various degrees of dispersion, but even with 10 meters between him and the door, Ryck moved away another step, pushing back up against the rock.

The resultant explosion was huge, much larger than the breaching charge alone would have made. Not only was the door breached, but also some of the rock jamb was blown off, sending rubble out into the mine pit.

"Those fracheads booby-trapped the son-of-a-bitch," Smitty shouted out. "They about got my ass."

By booby-trapping the door, the miners had ensured no one could have survived the resultant explosion on the inside. Staff Sergeant England realized that and was already in motion, rushing the blown entrance. Ryck hurried to catch up as they ducked inside the dust-filled room. Ryck cautiously crept forward about five meters and knelt across from the staff sergeant, M99 pointing down the passage leading deeper inside the mine. He couldn't see much, but he had practiced the action enough times in training even if he hadn't practiced it with these specific Marines.

Just inside the door was a holding room of some sort. What once had probably been a desk was now kindling. Ryck was kneeling in a short passage that led out of the room. As the dust settled, he could see the passage led to a T. Ryck knew that miners could be lying in wait right around the corner.

He focused on the edge of the T, barely listening to Staff Sergeant England's message to the lieutenant that they had breached the entrance. The element held its position, not moving deeper until the lieutenant could bring Element B down the slope. Ryck's team would have to move then as it would be too crowded for both elements in the room. The lieutenant came into the room, discussed it with the staff sergeant, then decided that Element A would clear the passage to the left, where the mine plans indicated the main spaces lay, while Element B would secure the entrance and clear the passage to the right.

Staff Sergeant England relayed the plan to the element. With Singh down, Pallas took over that fire team. The element was down to nine Marines in total, which didn't seem like much, but in a narrow corridor, though, it was crowded. They performed a bounding overwatch, one team rushing forward before kneeling and covering the front, then the other team getting up, moving past the covering team before it, too, kneeled and provided cover. The staff sergeant and Ryck kept attaching themselves to the back of whichever team was moving forward. Several times they had to stop and clear rooms that had been cut into the rock, but there was no sign of any of the miners.

The electricity was still running, so the corridor was well-lit. If the power went out, they would have to rely on their NVDs.[7] Deep inside a mine, though, there would be no ambient light for the NVDs to magnify, though, so they would have to turn on their infrared torches as well, and that never provided as good a field of vision as ambient light provided.

Ryck had been both excited and nervous as they entered the mine. Now, as odd as it seemed to him, he was getting almost bored as they got up, rushed, and got down again. There was no

---

[7] NVD: Night vision device

opposition, and Ryck wondered if the miners had fled. The mine was hot, and while his skins were wicking away his sweat, a little air conditioning would have been welcomed.

When the roof of the corridor collapsed ahead of him, it took him a moment to realize what had happened. One moment, he was following Staff Sergeant England and Pallas' team, the next, the roof fell in front of him, the team, the squad leader, and the staff sergeant disappearing as rocks fell at his feet. He started to turn around to Corporal Büyük and his team when something impacted on his side above his waist. He looked where he felt the impact. The STF bone insert there had crystallized and was only now beginning to soften. Then it hit him. He'd been shot!

In the corridor, there were only two directions in which he could go: forward or back. With the rubble on the floor, he could crouch and hope it offered some cover. But that would only delay the inevitable choice of what to do next. So that left attack or retreat.

Ryck didn't know how many miners were in front of him. He also forgot that just behind him, Corporal Büyük and three other Marines were only a few meters away. He just reverted to the mindset of over a year of training. He didn't think of danger, he didn't think of much. With a mindless yell, he rushed forward, bounding over the rubble on the deck and the four Marines trapped there.

He was vaguely aware of Büyük's team following him, but he had zeroed in on what was in front of him. About 15 meters ahead, another corridor branched off, and at that intersection, part of a person was barely visible, holding an old chemical rifle pointed back at him. The lights had been turned off at the intersection, but the flashes from the muzzle told Ryck he was being taken under fire. Just below his left collarbone, he felt the impact again of another round, the stiffening of the bone insert absorbing the impact. Another four centimeters higher, and the round would have hit his unprotected neck. Primitive weapon or not, a lead slug would really ruin his day.

Ryck sent a burst of fire back, aiming at the weapon itself. The darts moved at extremely high speeds, and when they hit, they generally created dust as the small needles pulverized metal, wood, or flesh. Ryck could see that he hit the old rifle, at least, and it fell to the deck. He couldn't tell if he had hit the person wielding it.

Ryck never stopped. He rushed forward, reaching the intersection in seconds. Without pausing, he turned into the other corridor. In front of him, he could make out two men. One was on the ground, his left arm bleeding. The second was kneeling, one arm around the other's back, as if to help him up. Ryck's undivided attention was caught by what was in the other miner's hand. From countless flicks, he recognized the Peacemaker in the man's hand. The old handgun looked enormous as he swung it up to point at Ryck.

The Peacemaker was a sonic disrupter. It had that certain historical panache that some weapons seem to capture among the public. That panache was lost on Ryck, though. Even with his body armor, that weapon would be deadly. The bones would stop and reflect the blast, at least where they covered, but with his exposed face, his head would be turned into so much mush. The weapon had a very limited range, and took a lot of energy, but this close to the miner, Ryck wouldn't stand a chance.

Without thinking, Ryck fired his M99 on full auto, stitching from low and left to high and right, exactly as he was taught at recruit training. Multiple rounds hit both men, and they immediately collapsed. Ryck stared at them, his intense adrenaline boost turning to numb amazement. He'd just killed two men—two living, breathing men.

Corporal Büyük rushed up behind him, staring around at the two men who seemed to collapse like slowly deflating balloons. They were already gone, but their bodies both continued to settle around each other.

The M99 darts didn't leave too many visible signs of damage. They were small, only a few millimeters across. What they were, though, was very, very fast, and not much could stop their progress. When they hit soft flesh, the vanes that kept them running true flipped out, becoming four small blades that slice through muscle and blood vessels.

From the front, the two men—boys might be more accurate—looked like they had fallen asleep in each other's arms. Blood was seeping out through several entrance wounds, but their miner's overalls were still whole, and in the shadowy light, the dark blood was not extremely noticeable.

"Damn, boot. Nice shooting," the corporal said to him.

Ryck felt both elated and a little nauseous at the same time. He was elated that he was still alive, that he had won this small battle of life and death. He had vindicated all those months of training. But these two men were not just electrons in the latest game. These were two people, and he had killed them. The first one, the one with the bloody arm, looked barely into his teens. He could have been a schoolboy back on Prophesy.

"Jenkins, you and the boot stay here and secure this intersection. Hu and Aesop, back to Pallas' team and let's see to them."

Without a word, Lance Corporal Jenkins flopped down on the deck, pulling one of the dead miners closer to provide a tiny bit of cover and act as a rifle rest. Ryck was a little more hesitant as he mimicked the more experienced Marine, gingerly placing his own M99 on the shoulder of the younger miner. The boy's sightless eyes stared back at him.

More to escape that gaze than anything else, Ryck made a quick glance back to where, much to his surprise, the buried Marines were being helped out from under the rubble. They were covered in dust, and one of them, who Ryck couldn't make out, was limping and had to be helped to the side of the corridor where he could sit, but no one looked seriously hurt.

"Um, boot, what say you look down there, you know, where the targets are?" Jenkins asked with a sarcastic tone.

Ryck wheeled his head around to look back down the corridor. He studiously kept his eyes elevated to escape the accusing, if dead, gaze of his rifle rest. He was quite relieved when Third Squad arrived on the scene and made a passage of lines to clear farther down the mine, and he was pulled back to provide security. He'd done what he'd been trained to do, and he felt no regrets. In all truth, he felt elated.

Boot or not, he was no longer a recruit. He was a blooded Marine.

PROPHESY
Thirteen months earlier . . .

Chapter 1

Ryck knelt next to the field of GKA Wheat, picking up some of the dirt and letting it tumble through his fingers to the ground. A good portion of it simply blew away as dust. United Ag had GM'd the GKA strain specifically for Prophesy, optimized for the planet's soil mix and lack of water. "Lack of water" did not mean "no" water, though, but since the bankruptcy and closing of the Prophesy Communal Development Corporation, PCDC, the water had ceased to flow in the irrigation canals with not enough rainfall to fill the reservoirs.

Ryck hadn't been born yet when his father had made the investment to become a shareholder in PCDC, moving the family from Ellison to Prophesy for a fresh start. Ryck didn't know anything about Ellison other than the fact that his parents and older brother had made a home there in a small apartment. He couldn't imagine living like that, in a small apartment in a huge building. The open plains of Prophesy were all he had known while growing up. Life had been tough on the newly terraformed world, but for Ryck, life was good. He reveled in the freedom to run around on his own without constant parental supervision. Together with Lysa, his twin, they had the full run of not only their own property, but also that of the entire community, something they could never have had on Ellison. The urban goliath of that planet was not conducive to children running around free and unsupervised. He was vaguely aware of his father's struggles to get crops in, but that didn't affect his early childhood of school and play.

Things changed when Ryck was ten, though, when PCDC went belly up. The planet was not completely terraformed, and without PCDC pulling up the water locked deep within the rocks, the reservoirs dried up, and the little moisture already released in the air was not enough to sustain a normal agricultural cycle.

PCDC had been a subsidiary of the universal giant, Excel Holdings, Ltd. When PCDC folded, not only was Ryck's father's stock worthless, but also through some legal machinations, he owed Excel for the remainder of his initial settlement buy-in. With the then value of the crops being grown at the time, that meant Excel would get 2/3 of the revenue for the wheat for the next 25 Earth years, which corresponded to 27 crop cycles on Prophesy.

That did not take into account that with PCDC gone, the planet's ecosystem itself tried to swing back to its natural equilibrium, and that meant a dry, dusty landscape. Crop yields plummeted, and it became clear that with interest on the debt, the family could never hope to pay it off.

Ryck's father tried, though. He scraped together some cash, and along with Mr. Choo on the next plot, tried to dig their own shared well. Over 200 dry meters later, they had reached the limit of the capabilities of the small drilling company they had hired, and they had no money to bring in a company with a bigger rig.

Ryck watched his father transform from the irreverent, fun-loving man he had known into someone breaking his back and spirit in an attempt merely to survive. Myke, his older brother, dropped out of school to help, but with less and less rain, even the GKA Wheat suffered, providing smaller and smaller yields.

The tipping point was when Ryck's mother caught the Dust. Ryck was fifteen at the time and still in school. He and Lysa had come home from school that fateful day when Myke met them at the door. He took both of them in his arms, saying nothing. Fear had swept through Ryck. He didn't know what was wrong, just that it was something big.

"Mom's got the Dust," he told them.

Ryck had just stared at his older brother, speechless. "The Dust" was the name given to the virus that struck the settlers each year. Not many people contracted it, but for those who did, 80%

died within hours, coughing out their lungs. Ryck and Lysa quietly followed Myke to the community clinic.

Their mother lay on the hospital bed, her face sallow. Their father sat by her side, holding her hand. Every few minutes, she would erupt into a coughing fit. The first time she did that after they got there, Ryck jumped up and ran to her, grabbing her other hand. Behind him, he could hear Lysa quietly sobbing.

The virus that caused the Dust had been identified, but without PCDC's funding, the research to figure out an effective treatment had been abandoned. With new worlds opening up, there were so many new diseases that the big pharmaceuticals focused on those diseases where they could help the most people—and make the most profit. On Prophesy, the medical technicians could treat the symptoms and ease the suffering, but that was all. Survival was up to the individual. Some made it, some did not. Ryck's mother was one of those who did not. With her family around her, she had one last coughing attack before she died, gasping for one final breath before letting go.

With Ryck's mother gone, his father sunk even further into depression. He still tried to farm, but it had become obvious that he was never going to be able to dig himself out of debt. Ryck offered to quit school to help out, but his father refused the offer.

A year after his mother's death, almost to the day, Ryck's father was driving the family Deere when it overturned into the gully that lined the western edge of the property. He was ejected from the cab and killed as he tumbled down the rocks.

Myke had erupted when TerraLife refused to pay the insurance policy, claiming "suspicious" circumstances of his father's death and citing their dad's treatment for depression as evidence of suicide. Myke fought the decision, but to no avail. Privately, Ryck thought the insurance company might have been correct. His father had been extremely withdrawn before the accident, and the insurance payout would have given the farm five or six more years of operating expenses. Most importantly, it would erase the debt to Excel. Ryck and Lysa were born on Prophesy, so legally, they could not owe a settlement buy-in. Myke had been a minor at the time, so he could not be assessed the fee, either. While the three of them still owed operating debts for seeds and fuel that came with the property, personal debts could not be assessed on surviving children.

Myke lasted one more year on the family farm. Ryck and Lysa had come home from school, excited about their upcoming high school graduation ceremony, to find Myke gone. A note with the single word "Sorry" was left on the kitchen table. Three weeks later, diploma in hand, Ryck turned from student to farmer.

For two years, he struggled. The first year, despite not knowing what he was doing but with the help from Mr. Choo, he'd managed to barely keep afloat. This year, though, the wheat crop had almost totally failed. Only the monk melons growing in a small patch near the house had come in well, but even if he sold them himself at the market, the revenue would not come close to what he needed for the next crop's planting. With his credit maxed out to get the Deere back up and running, he didn't think the co-op would be lending him anything.

He dropped the remaining dirt from his hand and glanced up at the sun. Its unrelenting rays had burnt out every last drop of moisture from the soil. As a kid, he had loved the bright sunshine. Now, the sun had become his enemy, at least to his mind.

Well, that's that, he thought to himself. *It's done.*

He slowly stood up, and without a backward glance, walked up the gentle slope and to the home compound. It already looked deserted. The old coop in which his mother had tried to raise chickens was leaning precariously to the right, waiting for the next strong wind to knock it over. Ruined parts for the Deere had been discarded near the shed, good only for scrap. Only the house itself looked like it hadn't been abandoned. The bright pink curtains that were visible through the open kitchen window were about the only splash of color in the washed-out scene.

Ryck kicked off his shoes as he came in the front door. It was only late afternoon, earlier than when he usually quit work. Lysa wouldn't be back for quite some time yet. He decided that maybe a good meal was in order. Opening up the cabinet, he took out the last two bottles of Recife Pinot Noir. This was all that was left of the case his father had brought from Ellison. He busied himself in the kitchen, more to take his mind off things than anything else as he cut the onions, carrots, garlic, and Hank's Beef. Hank's Beef was not really good for bourguignon. The texture was too soft, and it didn't hold up well to slow cooking. Ryck would rather be using Sunshine or even Healthy Choice, but all he had was Hank's. As a kid, he thought there really was a person named Hank who raised actual cows. He'd been oddly disappointed to learn that "Hank" was a corporation, and the "ranch" was a soy and peanut-processing factory in the capital.

He browned the beef, taking care not to let it break apart, then put it in the slow cooker. In the same pan, he browned the veggies before adding them to the beef. When his mom had made bourguignon, she had also used lardons, which she had Mr. Compton make for her. Compton was long gone, after having given up his farm, but Ryck liked to think that his own version without the pork was just fine.

He opened one bottle of wine. Lysa would be upset at his lack of manners, but she wasn't there, so he tilted the bottle up and took a long swallow. Ryck wasn't overly fond of most off-world products, but wine was different. They had a synthetic local "wine" available, but to Ryck, it could just as easily have been purple-colored vodka, good for getting drunk, but not much else. The real stuff, though, well, he could get used to having a glass of that with each meal.

With a sigh, he emptied the bottle into the slow cooker, closed the lid, and turned it on low. He'd make noodles later, something that tasted so much better when made by hand. Bourguignon was Lysa's favorite meal, so hopefully, that would ease the blow.

It was almost seven hours later, the aroma of the meal filling the home, when the front door opened. Ryck was sitting in his father's easy chair, back toward the door when his sister entered. He tried to ignore her, but her skintight blue jumpsuit had tiny luminescent micro-LEDs embedded in the fabric that lit in strategic areas as the fabric stretched and pulled. She was a flashing advertisement of her womanly curves. She didn't like to talk when she was in her working clothes, though, so he didn't say a word as she walked past him and into her room.

"Something sure smells good," she remarked as she came back out about five minutes later. "Special occasion?"

"Anytime you come home is a special occasion," he said.

"Ah, no wonder you're still single, with lines like that," she told him as she settled in their mom's chair, her legs drawn up under her.

She had come in the home dressed in high-tech sluttiness. Now she sat in baggy cotton pants and an oversized t-shirt, all trace of make-up on her face gone. She looked younger than their 19 years.

He'd opened the second bottle of wine about two hours before to let it breathe. Getting up, he poured her a glass and took one for himself.

"The Recife? This is a special occasion. And I smell bourguignon. What gives?"

"Eat first, then talk," he said.

Normally, they ate in front of their parents' chairs watching the vid. Today, though, the formal table seemed more appropriate. They ate their meal mostly in silence, only talking to pass the food to each other. Lysa knew something big was up, and Ryck was trying to marshal his thoughts. Finally, though, dinner was over and the table cleared.

"OK, little brother, what's up?" she asked as she pushed his chair around and sat side-saddle on his lap, her arms around his neck.

Lysa had been born first, twelve minutes before Ryck, and she had lorded that over him as children. Now "little brother" had just become part of his name, so to speak.

"The wheat crop's failed," he simply said. "Nothing to harvest."

"I know. I've been watching. Maybe the next crop will come in."

"It's just this. I don't think we can get credit for seeds. We're still maxed out from the Deere repairs from, what, three years ago?" he asked.

"You know I can probably swing the seeds. We won't need that money for another month or so, and I've got several friends who'll be happy to help."

Ryck knew what kind of "friends" she meant. He never pried into what she was doing, but it was obvious. He had kept quiet both because it was her choice, and frankly, they needed the money she brought in.

"It's just that, I mean, uh, I don't know. I mean, I don't know if we should plant again. Who knows if next year'll be better? I mean, ah, grub. I don't want you to be working like you do just to support us."

There, he'd said it. It was out in the open.

Lysa leaned back, then slowly got up and pulled out one of the dining chairs and sat down. She seemed to be considering what to say next.

"You have a problem with what I do? With how I support us?" she quietly asked.

"No, no, you've got me wrong. I am so grateful for you. For what you've done. It's just that I don't think it's worth it. Not your work, but the farm. I don't think we can ever make a living here."

"So, what're you saying?" she asked, her voice sounding only slightly mollified.

"What I'm saying is," he started, pausing to take a deep breath, "is that I don't want to farm anymore. I'm done with it."

Telling her that was a huge weight off of his shoulders. What had been an internal debate was now out there for his sister to hear.

She was quiet for a full minute while Ryck waited to hear her response. If she disagreed, he wasn't quite sure what he'd do.

Finally, she asked, "So, what would we do with the farm?"

"Oh, you can have it. I can sign everything over to you."

She gave a chuckle. "You think I want it? With the debts, the work? Do I look like a farm girl to you?" She raised two hands to frame her face. "Do I want this lovely skin wind and sunburnt? Not on your life, little brother, not on your life. Let's see if Old Man Choo wants it. He might pay enough to cover our debts."

Ryck was shocked. This was their home. They had grown up together in it. And Lysa was ready to toss it, just like that. Of course, he was ready to leave, but he hadn't thought Lysa would be willing, too.

"So, what are you going to do? Find work in Williamson?" she asked him.

"I'm going to the capital, yeah, but not to work there. I'm thinking of the Legion."

"The Legion? You sure?"

"Kinda sure. I don't think I can work inside, cooped up in an office or a factory. And what skills do I have? I can't even farm, and that's my job," he told her with a smile on his face.

"Oh, wow! My little brother's going to be a soldier-boy? That blows my mind."

"Well, I'm not 100% sure, but I want to go down and learn more. They might not even take me," he told her.

"Not take you? A good, strapping farmboy like you? Of course, they'll take you."

"Well, we'll see. But what about you? If we sell to Mr. Choo, what are you going to do?"

She hesitated. Ryck knew his twin, and he knew she was wondering what she could and could not tell him. He leaned forward and took her right hand in both of his.

"If I get into the Legion, I'll be off-world. We'll need to keep in contact. I can't do that if you don't tell me where you are," he said.

"Oh, grub. Well, I've got a friend, and he, well, he says he wants to marry me."

"A friend?" he asked.

He knew what kind of men her "friends" were.

"Oh, don't get too grubbing sanctimonious on me now. Yes, Barret, my 'friend,' asked me over four months ago. He's been keeping food on our table since then, so he's your 'friend,' too, there, big boy. You've seen him. He was the guy who took me home last week when you were trying to fix the power junction."

Ryck tried to think back. A fairly new Lexus had skimmed into the yard in a cloud of dust. He had purposely not watched directly, but in his peripheral vision, an older man had gotten out and come around to open the passenger door. Lysa had gotten out of the car, kissed the man on the cheek, then hurried into the home. Ryck had wanted the man off their property, but the guy had just stood there for a minute or so, watching Lysa, before getting back in the Lexus and driving off.

"That guy? But he's . . ."

"Old? Unattractive? Is that what you were going to say?"

"No, I mean . . ."

"Can it, Ryck. I know you, and I know what you were going to say. But let me say this first. Yeah, he's older. And yeah, he isn't the most handsome guy around. But he has a good heart. He treats me like a lady, not like those other grubbing bungmen. He treats me with respect. And yeah, I know you saw his car, so yeah, he's got money. He can give me the life I want. We both watched mom and dad scrabble in the dust of this grubbing farm, we watched it kill them. We watched the dust drive away Myke. I don't want that. I want a nice life, where I can live comfortably, where my kids, your future nieces and nephews, little brother, can live a normal life. I wouldn't marry any grubbing asshole just because he has money, but Barret, he's a good man, and I think I love him."

Ryck was taken aback. He had no idea. He generally tried not to think of Lysa's job. He knew that she made drinks in a coyote bar, and sometimes strangers paid her to sit and have those drinks with them. Whether she did more than join the other bartenders every hour for a choreographed dance on top of the bar or share drinks with the customers was something he didn't know, nor did he want to know. She'd invited him to the bar more than once to check out the fun, but he'd refused. Regardless of the fact that he really didn't know what went on there, however, he resented all the men and women whom she encountered on the job. It was a huge 180 for him to try and grasp that the men and women might not all be the perverted, despicable garbage ogling the bartenders and wait staff that he had made them out to be in his mind. But he trusted his twin. If she said this Barret guy was a good man, well, that was that. It was going to take a while for it to really sink in, but if that was what Lysa wanted, that was what he wanted, too.

"OK, I believe you. But, I don't get it. If he asked you four months ago, why are you still here with me?"

Lysa broke out in laughter before answering, "Oh, little brother, you really are an innocent. How could I leave you here, working the farm alone? You wouldn't have lasted a month without me. But now, if you really are going to enlist . . ."

". . . you are free to go on with your life without having to take care of me," he finished her sentence for her.

He got up, walked over to her, and this time, he sat in her lap. He lay his head down on her shoulder while she reached up to pat it.

"No matter what, we need to keep in touch," he murmured into her shoulder. "I'll be damned if I'm going to let you raise my nieces and nephews without me getting to know them."

"And spoil them, I know," she added.

"We're family, you and me. You might be getting married, but we're still blood. 'Why?' Because there's no . . ."

". . . 'I' in the Lysander family," she completed the family motto, one their father had drilled into their heads. It was a philosophy so ingrained in him that he'd even kept the "i's" out of each of his children's first names.

For the first time in months, maybe years, Ryck felt at peace sitting on his sister's lap. He didn't know what his future would bring, what their futures would bring, but he was anxious to find out.

"Oof, little brother. You're not so little anymore. How about getting your fat butt off of me and pour me another glass of that Recife. No use keeping it around, right?"

Ryck got up, poured them both another glass.

"To our futures," he said in a toast. "Whatever may come, and may it be wonderful, we will always be family."

Chapter 2

The maglev whispered to a stop at Jacob Station. The maglev was an exception to the planet's infrastructure problems. It still worked perfectly despite the collapse of PCDC.

Ryck had stayed on the farm for another week, helping Lysa set up the auction of it, then selling the bulk of their personal possessions. They'd raised enough to get out of debt for the repairs and supplies to run the farm after Myke had left and even have a bit left over. They hadn't sold everything, though. They'd kept some family heirlooms. Lysa had taken some into Barret's home, and Ryck had rented a small storage locker for his things, paying for a year's rent out of his share of the sales proceeds.

Barret had turned out to be a nice, if too-eager-to-please guy. Ryck was surprised to find out that he actually liked the man. He obviously adored Lysa, and that was good enough for Ryck. Ryck and Lysa had made their goodbyes after handing over the deed to the property to Mr. Choo, who'd placed the top bid on the place. Ryck had figured Lysa would take him to the station, but it was Barret who had driven him. During the ride, Barret had haltingly explained that he loved Lysa, that he would take care of her, and asked if Ryck would give them his blessing. It felt strange that a forty-year-old man was asking a 19-year-old one for a blessing, but it made Ryck feel appreciation for the man's heart. They even had an awkward hug at the station as Ryck boarded the maglev.

The maglev ride had been smooth, and Ryck had fallen asleep during the three hours it took to arrive in Williamson. Jacob Station, as the main station for both of the western maglev lines, was packed with people moving to and fro, all locked into their own thoughts and purposes. Five young men, maybe a little older than Ryck, squatted against a wall, simply watching the people walk by. They seemed out of the flow of humanity, and their languid insolence grated on Ryck's nerves. He refused to catch any of their eyes as he hurried past to catch a tram to Corporate Center.

The tram was not as well-kept as the maglev, and it was crammed full. Ryck couldn't get a seat, and his country boy mindset was wary of the dangers of city life. He swung his backpack around to his front and wrapped his arms around it. He knew better than to take much with him, but other than what he'd put in storage, this was the entirety of his worldly possessions. He was sure that given the chance, someone would slit his pack and slide all his belongings out.

The tram finally pulled into Corporate Center. The name of the station had stuck despite PCDC pulling off the planet. The Federation had installed an interim governing body when PCDC folded. "Interim" had lasted eight years (so far) as the Federation tried to find a corporate backer to take over.

Ryck went up the escalator and into the sun-lit square. He'd made an appointment with the Legion recruiter for 2:30, and he had plenty of time before that, but he was anxious to get going, so he went into the Federation Building, passing through the security scan and following the directions he'd received at the information desk for the recruiting stations. The Navy Liaison Office was the first one he passed in the corridor. The Navy held the prestige in the Federation. With no official standing army, the Navy formed the bulk of the armed forces of the Federation. They were deeply involved in politics, and the current Federation chairman, like a number of his predecessors, had been a Navy admiral. The main office was all glass and metal with smartly-dressed sailors rushing about their business. There were about five separate offices lining the corridor with the recruitment station at the end. A number of blue chairs were in the small reception area of the office, each one filled with a young man or woman.

Ryck had considered the Navy, of course. It was a sure way to move up in the world, but the thought of being encased in a ship for his enlistment seemed a little claustrophobic. He realized that most Navy jobs did not entail being in space, but he didn't want some sort of desk job. He wanted to get out and see some action. He'd considered the almost mythical SEALs, but his research revealed that only 3% of those who volunteered made it through the training, and if he washed out, he would have had no say in where the Navy would stick him next or what job he would have.

No, the Legion would be a better choice. The Legion was only semi-official, not a true branch of the Federation government. It was still technically sponsored by France, one of the last independent nations of old Earth, but everyone realized the Federation still helped support it. While it could be hired out by planetary governments or corporations for missions, the Federation was not above using it for missions that it could not send the Navy or Marines on due to legal issues.

Ryck made his way down to the Legion offices. There were four other guys sitting in the line of chairs in the hallway in front of the recruiting office. Ryck reported into the legionnaire sitting at the reception desk and was told to take a seat. Where he waited. And waited. At 3:00, he went back up to the legionnaire.

"Sorry, but we're running behind," the soldier told him. "You'll just have to take a seat and wait."

"I shoulda told ya," the guy next to him said as Ryck sat back down. "I be waitin' since lunchtime. Somtin's goin' on in dere, and we just be coolin' our heels out here."

Ryck had already noted the black trousers and dark blue shirt, the indication that his seat companion was probably a Torritite, but the accent was a dead giveaway.

"Ryck Lysander," he told the guy, holding out his hand. "My appointment was at 2:30."

"Joshua Hope-of-Life," the guy replied, taking Ryck's hand in a surprisingly strong grip.

"So, you're joining the Legion?" Ryck asked, a question evident in his voice.

The Torritites were a fundamentalist religious sect. There weren't any Torritite communities up near Ryck, but he knew there were several to the south of Williamson. They generally kept to themselves in big combined families, running their farms as communal property. It seemed odd to see a Torty there signing up for the military.

"Don' ask. I know what you question. You Gentiles think we Brethren all be peace-lovin' do-gooders. We do believe in what the Good Book says about lovin' your neighbor, but that only goes so far. I be named for Joshua, and he was a soldier most 'standing. He took down Jericho's walls, after all."

Ryck leaned back. He hadn't wanted to piss the guy off. He'd just been curious.

"I didn't mean anything. I just was surprised. I thought you guys kept to yourself and all," he stammered out.

Joshua raised his eyes and mouthed something silently before turning back to Ryck. "Take my pardon, Ryck. No offense takin' or givin'. It's just here, in Williamson, with every soul lookin' and gawkin' at me, like they know me, well, forgive me for assumin' anything about you."

"Don't worry about it," Ryck said. "I was just curious. I thought you couldn't fight or hit people back."

"Well, we turn the other cheek, true, but that's only afore we light the other guy up," he said with a laugh. "Truly, though, we always have men in the military, especially afta Sygylla. Sometimes in the militia, but some of us, we go Navy, Marines, or Legion. We even got an admiral now with the squids."

"No grubbing shit?" Ryck asked. "Oh sorry, I didn't mean to curse like that."

"Yeah, no grubbing mother grubber shit," Joshua said with a laugh. "We be religious and all, but don't worry none about cursin'. We don' take the Lord's name in vain, but everythin' else be fair game."

Ryck realized he liked Joshua. He'd never had contact with a Torty before, and except for his way of speaking and his clothes, he could be anyone else Ryck had ever known. Before too long, even the clothing difference would be gone when they were wearing the Legion kepi and 42's.

They sat together, getting to know about each other as they waited for their interview. Their daily lives were really not that much different beyond their family organization. With Ryck, it had been their small five-member family, then eventually just Lysa and him. Joshua, though, lived in an extended family with nine mothers, twelve fathers, and thirty-six siblings. Ryck couldn't imagine living like that, but as far as the rest: the farming, the schooling, the sports, the entertainment, the girl-chasing, they were surprisingly the same.

"Ryck Lysander, what the hell are you doing here, aside from the obvious, I mean," a voice called out.

Ryck looked up to see Proctor Miller standing there. Proctor was from the next settlement to the north of his. They attended different schools, but had competed against each other in lineball, b-ball, and they'd even wrestled each other. They couldn't really be called good friends, but they were at least friendly competitors.

Ryck jumped up to shake Proctor's hand.

"Good to see you! I'm here just enlisting. How about you? You here for the Legion, too?"

"Legion? No way. I've already been accepted into the Marines. I'm just here to get my ticket to report in. The Marine's are where it's at, there, Ryck. Not the fancy-ass Legion. Oh, no offense intended," he added, as two of the others waiting overheard him and started to get up.

"Really, Ryck. Why do you want to join the Legion? They're mercenaries," he asked in a subdued voice.

"We all be mercenaries, Marines, Navy, or Legion. Only the militias be true home fighters," Joshua said, standing up beside Ryck.

"Oh, Proctor, this is Joshua Hope-is- . . . Joshua, what's your last name again?"

"Hope-of-Life," Joshua said, holding out his hand to Proctor.

"Good to meet you," Proctor said. "And there's a lot of truth to what you just said. But the militias and the planetary armies never leave their home planet, never go off-world. I want to see our galaxy. I want to go places. I'm not cut out to be a sailor. That leaves the Legion and the Marines, and at least the Marines don't get hired out as mercenaries. The Marines fight for a cause."

"And you don' think the Fed uses the Marines for its own purposes? Things not for altruistic causes?" Joshua asked.

"Of course, I know that," Proctor conceded. "But not as much as the Legion is used by whoever has the bigger bank account."

"But I keep hearing about how the Marines have to take second-hand equipment. Even some armies are better armed, and the Legion had all the newest gear," Ryck said.

"True, but those armies don't have the power of the Navy behind them, and when are we ever going to fight the Legion? Besides, any Marine can kick any kepi-wearing froggie if it came to that.

"Easy does it, fellow. You're not even a legionnaire, yet, and I'm just trash-talking," he said to one of the other waiting guys who had actually stood up upon overhearing Proctor's boast. "We love the Legion, and you guys are all superhuman soldiers," he added.

"Just not as tough as Marines," he whispered to Ryck and Joshua as the guy sat back down.

"Look, I'm going down to get my ticket out of here. Why don't you two come down with me? It won't hurt just to get some information, right? Then you can come back down here if you still want to get in line for your kepi," Proctor said.

"I don't know," Ryck said. "I've got an appointment, and what if they call my name while I'm gone?"

"Hey, what time be your appointment?" Joshua asked the guy who was the one who had started to take offense at Proctor's earlier words.

"Eleven," the guy said, obviously still not completely mollified by Proctor's apologies.

"See, they aren't going to get to you for a long time. Come on down with me," Proctor said.

"I . . . well, I think the Legion gives more opportunities. I can appreciate what you're saying, but . . ." Ryck said before Joshua interrupted.

"I'll do it. Lead on."

Ryck turned to stare at Joshua.

"You're joining the Marines? What about the Legion?" Ryck asked.

He'd only just met Joshua, but the thought of going to Camerone for recruit training with Joshua sounded a whole lot better than going without anyone he knew.

"Not to join. But to get information be the smart thing to do. I considered the Marines, but my brother be a legionnaire, so I chose the Legion. Our good friend here," he said, indicating the guy with the eleven o'clock appointment, "still waits, so we have time. I be tired of sittin' here, so a walk will let me get off my grubbin' ass and stretch my legs."

"Well, just to get more information?" Ryck asked.

"Just info," Proctor assured him.

"I guess it wouldn't hurt. Maybe we can hit the snack bar and get something to eat, too," Ryck told them.

Ryck and Joshua followed Proctor farther down the hallway while Proctor told them about his orders, about his departure in three days, about how his girlfriend had come with him and they were shacking up in the Holiday Inn until he left. Proctor hadn't even gotten warmed up when they reached the Marine recruiting station.

Where the Navy office was opulent in a technically-advanced setting and the Legion's office was understated, but classy, the Marine Corps recruiting station was Spartan. There was a plastocrete desk serving for reception, and on a poster on the wall behind it was an image of a steely-eyed young man in the Marine Dress Blues staring at whoever would be standing in front of the desk. His chest was adorned in ribbons. Unlike at the Navy and Legion recruiting offices, there was no one waiting. In fact, there was no one in the front office at all.

Proctor started to reach over the front reception desk when a door opened, and a Marine and a young man walked out. The Marine was in a khaki shirt and blue trousers, a red stripe running down each leg. His left arm was shorter than normal and covered in the blue bio-wrap that indicated his arm was in the process of being regenerated. Ryck couldn't help but wonder what happened to his original arm.

"That is what we can offer you. After that, it would be in your hands. We aren't going to coddle you, but we will give you the opportunity to maximize your capabilities. That we can promise you," the Marine was saying.

"You've got my number. If you have any further questions, I'm here for you," he continued, shaking the young man's hands.

"Mr. Miller. You're here for your ticket," the Marine said as the young guy left the office. "Let me get that."

He pulled out his PA and hit a few keys. "Open your PA and give it to me," he told Proctor.

Proctor complied, and the Marine tapped his PA on Proctor's.

"OK, you've got it. Be there three hours prior. Take only the items on the list I gave you. Nothing else," he told Proctor before taking his hand and shaking it. "And are these your friends coming to see you off? A couple nights on the town before we own your soul?"

If the Marine thought it odd that a Torritite would be hanging out with "Gentiles," he never let that show.

"No, Staff Sergeant Wassari, these are my friends, Ryck and Joshua. I just rescued them from in front of the Legion recruiting station, and I thought that since they have to wait anyway, they might as well come down and talk to you, you know, only for information, of course."

"The Legion? Good unit. Good men. They're not Marines, of course, but if that's what you want to achieve in your life, then I'm sure you'll do well. But as Mr. Miller says, it doesn't hurt to find out about the Corps and how we differ from the rest. Why don't you step back into my lair and have a seat?" he asked.

Said the spider to the fly, Ryck thought.

"I'll wait for you here," Proctor said, taking a seat. "Maybe we can get dinner together after you're all done for the day."

Ryck followed Joshua into the Marine's office.

Forty-five minutes later, new Marine Corps recruits Ryck Lysander and Joshua Hope-of-Life walked back out to a smiling Proctor.

TARAWA: RECRUIT TRAINING

Chapter 3

The ship landed in the middle of the night on Tarawa.[8] The recruits debarked the *Sally Ling* when most of the passengers were either in the casino or in their staterooms asleep. The other passengers probably had no idea that more than 300 recruits had shared the voyage from Vegas. They'd been confined to their billets on F Deck since coming on board. The recruits had been quietly herded out of a cargo hatch, so as not to disturb the paying passengers' night.

It was still hot when they walked down the ramp despite the late hour. Ryck strained to make out anything about where he would be spending the next 42 weeks. It was just a standard spaceport, though, and as it didn't have the glamour and non-stop advertising of Vegas' main spaceport, it was not much different from the one back on Prophesy. There were a few murmurs coming from the recruits, but most of them walked in silence.

That silence lasted until they passed through the door over which hung the innocuous sign with "RECEIVING" printed on it. Several civilians directed them to a processing center with five desks in the front. Each recruit gave his name and was scanned. Told to move in by their handlers, they were led outside where buses waited. Ryck got on board, saving seats for Joshua and Proctor.

"That wasn't too bad," Proctor said as he got on and took the seat.

---

[8] Tarawa: Originally named Hollison, the planet was renamed when it became the prime training base and headquarters for the Federation Marines.

"Yeah, I thought it would be tougher. I know the training itself will be harder, but I guess it isn't as bad as what we read on the net," Ryck said.

The buses hissed as they lifted off the ground, and the drivers eased the rigs forward. The three recruits were in the second-to-last bus, and as they moved through the streets of Gibraltar, they tried to catch a view of the city's infamous nightlife. Either that nightlife was somewhere else in the city, or the extent of it was something else that had been exaggerated on the net.

It was after midnight, but excitement kept most of them awake as the buses picked up speed outside the city. Recruits talked in quiet voices as they discussed what was ahead of them. An hour later, the lights of Camp Charles broke the darkness. Everyone on board shut up as the buses slowed down in front of the gates. Two Marines in their dress blues were manning it, and they motioned the buses to enter. Ryck pushed his face up against the window to be able to see the arch over the gate, *Per Terra et Mare*[9] written in gold-colored metal tubing.

The buses pulled into a courtyard and stopped. Their civilian guide stood up in front of the bus, turning to face them.

"OK, this is it. Welcome to Camp Charles. I need all of you to file off the bus, then cross in front and to the area to our left."

"What do we do then?" a voice asked toward the rear of the bus.

"Oh, someone will tell you what to do. Don't worry about that," the man said with a chuckle. "And good luck," he added as they started to file off.

Ryck, Joshua, and Proctor stuck together as they moved past the bus and into a square with buildings closing in on three sides. Three hundred-plus recruits milled about, wondering what was next. Two doors in one of the buildings opened, sending light out into the square.

"Come on, you spineless worms, get your sorry asses on the yellow footprints!" a voice yelled out.

---

[9] *Per Terra et Mare*: "By Land and Sea." The motto of the Spanish *Infantería de Marina,* the oldest extant Marine Corps at the time of the formation of the Federation Marine Corps

Ryck couldn't see who was yelling, and he couldn't see any yellow footprints, but he pushed ahead with the herd. He'd read about the infamous yellow footprints before leaving Prophesy and expected them, but reading about something and experiencing it were two different things. Despite himself, he could feel his heart rate soar.

"Come on," he told Joshua. "Push. We don't want to be the last ones there."

"Move it, move it!" the voice screamed. "I can't believe what I'm seeing here! I refuse to see what pieces of shit think they can be Marines!"

Other voices chimed in, coming from the sides. Ryck glanced around and caught sight of a drill instructor closing in from behind. Like a minnow trying to escape a pike, he darted forward, pushing other recruits aside, not wanting to let the drill instructor get close. He'd lost Joshua and Proctor, but he saw the yellow footprints on the floor and got on top of the first free one he reached.

The DIs continued to scream, their orders only interrupted by their observations of the worth of this batch of recruits; that worth wasn't much. In position on his claimed footprints, he could see the DI in front of him. The man was red in the face and seemed to be in the throes of an epileptic fit. He was screaming out his displeasure, and Ryck was in awe of the man's mastery of expressing his distaste. Ryck let his eyes drift down to the DI's arms. He couldn't remember if the stripes on the sleeves of his uniform meant the DI was a sergeant or corporal.

"You eyeballing me, you piece of slime?" the DI shouted at Ryck.

The shorter DI rushed forward, bending down slightly, then crooking his neck to look right up Ryck's nostrils, it seemed to him.

"You don't rate eyeballing me, farm boy. You keep your eyeballs locked to the front, got it?"

"Yes, sir!" Ryck shouted, looking straight ahead.

"'Sir?' 'Sir?' Do I look like a fucking officer? I work for a living. It's 'Aye-aye sergeant,' or 'aye-aye drill instructor.' Don't ever call me sir."

"Yes, sir, sergeant!" Ryck stammered out.

"'Sir?' What the hell did I just tell you? Can't you follow a simple order?" the DI screamed.

"Uh, aye-aye, sergeant!" he managed to get out.

"Oh, my loving Mary! I asked you a question! You answer yes or no. Not 'aye-aye.' If I tell you to do something, then it's 'aye-aye.' My three-year-old niece can manage that!"

Ryck had to think a moment before offering, "Yes, sergeant."

He wasn't sure he was correct, but the DI had moved on to torment someone else. Ryck let out a sigh of relief.

How did he know I was a farm boy? he wondered. *Do I look like one?*

The next few hours were a blur. A roll call was made, and Ryck remembered to respond with the "Here, drill instructor" as directed. Quite a few other recruits couldn't manage even that, and they paid the price with pushups. They were broken into groups, then herded to the barber, where their heads were shaved, to the sickbay, as Ryck learned the medical facility was called, for an analysis, and to uniform issue. Ryck had a complete physical two days before leaving Prophesy, so he wondered why another physical was necessary. Did they think they'd gotten some disqualifying condition while en route?

Uniform issue was done within moments. They were lined up and handed a bundle of clothing, then told to march into an adjoining room to change. The uniforms were plain brown trousers and a shirt, a belt, boots, and a helmet. There hadn't seemed to be any rhyme or reason to the issuance, and there didn't look to be any nano-sizing that would adjust the uniforms to each recruit, but the uniforms seemed to fit. The old clothes that they had been wearing were put into plastic bags, sealed, and then taken away.

Dawn was already breaking four hours later when they were marched into a cafeteria. They went through the receiving line to get their breakfast. Ryck caught a glimpse of Joshua, but they'd all been warned to keep their eyes to the front, so he couldn't risk trying to catch his attention. He just sat down and shoveled in the food. It was tasteless, but he didn't care. It was energy, and he'd had a feeling he was going to need as much energy as he could over the course of the day.

Twenty minutes later, they were herded into an auditorium where they sat and waited.

"What do you think is next?" the recruit to his left whispered.

Ryck ignored the question. He wasn't going to give the DIs any reason to target him.

After another ten minutes or so, a voice rang out with "Attention on deck!"

Ryck jumped to his feet, eyes to the front as everyone stood up. With his peripheral vision, he saw eight Marines making their way down the center aisle and up on the stage. One Marine moved to center stage with another to his left. Another Marine took a position behind him, with a Marine to his left as well. A final four Marines marched to stand at attention in back of them.

"At ease, recruits," the one who had taken center stage said. "Take your seats. I am Captain Petrov, company commander for Delta Company, 1st Recruit Training Battalion," he continued after the auditorium settled down. "To my left is First Sergeant Tyliman, the company chief drill instructor. Behind me is the series commander and series senior drill instructor, and behind them are the four senior drill instructors for the recruit platoons that make up the Follow Series. Each of you has been assigned to a training platoon. The number below the name on your chest is the number of your platoon. Get used to it. That platoon will be your home and family for the next 42 weeks."

Despite himself, Ryck glanced down at the white tag on his chest. Below the "Lysander, R." was the number "1044."

"All of you have volunteered to become a Federation Marine. Many of you will not make it through recruit training. Some will wash out, some will quit. A few of you will probably die during training."

That made Ryck take notice. He knew that Marines faced danger in battle, but in recruit training?

"One thing I need to make absolutely clear," the captain went on, "is that we are not here to make you Marines. We are only here to give you the opportunity to earn the title of Marine. Whether you earn that title or not is up to you. We will not coddle you, we will not lead you by the hand. All we will do is show you the way. It will be up to you to make the journey and grab the prize at the end.

"We have recruits from 53 planets here in the class, coming from 81 separate governing bodies. Some of your governments have been at odds with each other. All that stops here. The only tie you have now is to your squad, to your platoon, to the Corps. When you are sworn in, you are cutting the ties to the past.

"Four other platoons in the Lead Series were formed yesterday. In a few minutes, you will formally join them, and your training will officially begin. I won't wish you good luck. We don't want Marines who were lucky to make it through training. We want Marines who fought for the title, who kicked and clawed past all the bad luck thrown their way to succeed."

The captain paused to scan the auditorium. Ryck couldn't tell if he looked disappointed or please with the gathered recruits.

"First Sergeant, bring the recruits to attention," he told the Marine to his left.

That Marine stepped forward before bellowing out, "Company, atten-hut!" and then "Raise your right hand and repeat after Captain Petrov," once everyone was standing.

"I, state your name," the captain started, to be followed by an uneven chorus from the recruits,

> . . .*do solemnly swear, to support and defend Articles of Council of the United Federation of Nations, against all enemies, foreign and domestic; that I will bear true faith and allegiance to the same and above all others; and that I will obey the orders of the Chairman of the United Federation and the orders of the officers appointed over me, according to the Uniform Code of Military Justice. So help me God.*

"You are now officially recruits in the United Federation Marine Corps," the company commander said.

He did an about-face and said to the six Marines now in front of him, "Series commander, take charge of your series and carry out the remainder of the training schedule."

He did another about-face, and without a word, marched off the stage and down the center aisle, followed by his first sergeant. Ryck risked a glance, then jerked his head back forward as four sets of drill instructors marched down the aisles to the front of the auditorium.

Recruit training had begun.

Chapter 4

No Initial huffed alongside Ryck, his mouth open as he gasped for air. Up ahead, just outside the Liberty gate, Ryck could see Drill Instructor Despri waiting for them.

"Come on, No Initial, another 500 meters, and we're done," he got out between his own breathing. "Cold water, aircon; think of it."

Moreau just nodded, too winded to speak. "No Initial" Moreau was a big guy, almost two meters tall, and a solid 120 kg. He looked the part, but he'd struggled during the heavy PT[10] the recruits had been put through the first four days of training, particularly during the runs. This run had "only" been six kilometers, two loops between the gate and The Lost Lady, a rock formation south of the camp wall, but it was with a 35 kg ruck full of sand. The training rucks weren't like the nice commercial rucks available to any civilian. This was basically a synthetic fiber sack with two thin straps that dug into the recruits' shoulders as they ran.

Moreau was from Tai 'pao, and like most of the residents there, he had only one name. That didn't fit the Marine standard, so his name tag read "Moreau, N.I.." The "N.I." quickly turned into "No Initial."

Ryck didn't know if No Initial was going to make it. Platoon 1044 had already lost five recruits: one was whisked away less than an hour after they'd been sworn in for reasons that still fueled the rumor mill four days later. The other four recruits had simply quit. No one knew what had become of them. Technically, most recruits could not just give up their obligations once sworn in, but as the DIs kept drilling into their heads, the Marine Corps did not want anyone less than the best in its ranks. The Navy might snag a few

---

[10] PT: Physical Training

depending on the reasons a recruit quit, his capabilities, and his enlistment contract, but the general consensus was that most who quit during training would just be sent home.

If No Initial was having so many problems with the PT now, Ryck wondered how he would cope when the tempo was increased. One of the required events during the Crucible just before graduation was a 25 km run with 50 kg on their backs. If you couldn't keep up or quit, it was either get out or get recycled.

The PT was kicking Ryck's ass, too, but he managed to struggle through it. It was kicking everyone's ass except for Clary Won and Born Brilliant. Clary was just a stud, but Born Brilliant seemed to escape to some other plane and breeze through when the going got rough.

"Tighten it up, ladies," Drill Instructor Lorenz said as he ran beside the loose formation. He was carrying the same ruck as the recruits, and it looked like it was loaded with twice as much sand as any of them had. "Look good coming in."

Ryck hated him at the moment. How could he look so good, so at ease, when most of them were dying?

Ryck knew the heavy PT was part of the indoctrination, but still, why the rucks? As Marines, they would be in PICS battle suits, or at least with exoskeleton assists embedded into their uniforms. When would they have to carry loads like this without assistance, with only their God-given bodies? He tried to put that thought out of his mind. His was not to reason why, after all.

Moreau started to fall back.

"Grab my ruck," Ryck told him, hoping against hope that Moreau wouldn't hear the offer or wouldn't take it.

The sudden pull against him threw that hope out the window. He sighed and leaned into the run, pulling No Initial along. It was only 300 meters, then 200, then 100. The platoon started to slow down, over 75 pairs of feet preparing to come to a halt at the gate. Drill Instructor Despiri watch them approach, then motioned his arm around, pointing back out along the trail.

"Not together," he said in his usual clipped manner. "Again."

The moans were not suppressed as Drill Instructor Lorenz swung the platoon around and back on the trail to The Lost Lady.

"Do it right the first time, ladies, and we won't have to go at it again," he told them.

Ryck wasn't sure how 75 men could make the run and stay in formation. There were others besides No Initial who were struggling, some straggling behind. As far as Ryck was concerned, let those guys run another loop. Let the ones who kept up stop and rest. At least No Initial had let go of him as they had approached the gate.

He tried to adjust the ruck on his back to a more comfortable position, but that was hopeless. Three more kilometers, and they'd better all be in formation when they got back, or someone might be facing a blanket party.

Chapter 5

Ryck slid into the seat, grateful to be off his feet. This was their first history class, and one of the few training events in which there were no DIs. Drill Instructor Lorenz, looking refreshed and as if he hadn't just been with them on the nine-kilometer ruck run, had marched the platoon to the classroom, then left after each rank had filed in.

The platoon already had a number of classes in subjects such as rank structure, military etiquette, Marine Corps organization, and the UCMJ.[11] Some of the other platoons had already started history classes, but with only one instructor, classes had to be juggled. They were scheduled for 20 hours in just this single classroom before graduation. Ryck wasn't sure just why recruits needed that much time, but any time without the DIs was welcomed.

Dr. Berber stood at the front of the classroom, watching each file of recruits march in and take a seat. When the last recruit sat down, he started right in.

"When was the first Marine Corps formed?" he asked without any attempt at an introduction.

Not that an introduction was really needed. Everyone knew about Dr. Berber. He'd been a Marine, but he was a fixture at Camp Charles and had been teaching there for over 40 years. He was a lean, almost skeletal figure, and he spoke with a sharp staccato.

Several hands shot up. Ryck kept his face neutral, hiding the distaste he had for the springbutts. Recruit training was not a place to put yourself in the limelight where you could draw attention to yourself.

---

[11] UCMJ: The Uniform Code of Military Justice. These are the rules and regulations governing servicemen and women in the Federation armed forces.

"You," Dr. Berber said, pointing a long arm at Doggie Jenkins.

"Doggie" was an appropriate name for a guy who kept seeking approval. Ryck could almost imagine a tail under his trou, wagging in excitement.

"The *Infantería de Marina,* established on February 27, 1537, by Charles the First, for whom this camp was named," Doggie recited.

"Wrong!" shouted Dr. Berber.

That caught Ryck's attention. Doggie was not any sort of history buff. What he'd just said was right out of our Marine Corps Handbook, the printed book that recruits were required to carry at all times. The book was filled with all sorts of Marine Corps knowledge, not the least being the origins of the Corps.

"The *Infantería de Marina* was the oldest extant Marine Corps when the Federation Marine Corps was formed. But there were many different naval infantry, or marine units formed before that. During the Chinese Warring States of 481-221 BC, soldiers armed with dagger-halberds were put on ships to ward off boarders. The ancient Greeks used hoplites as naval infantry. Mighty Imperial Rome, though, in the year 68 AD, might have been the first government to form specific marine units, the First and Second Adiutrix. The point I am making is two-fold. The first is listen to the question, not just in history, but in life. I asked one thing, and our volunteer there, Mr. Jenkins," he said after peering at Doggie's nametag, "answered what he thought I asked instead of what I asked. Doing that in combat could have drastic consequences. The second point is that from the time of navies, there had to be soldiers to protect them. These soldiers of the seas are your direct forebears. We didn't need Chuck the First to suddenly come up with the idea. All he did was put into a decree what was already a proven need. That need has not changed from the time of war galleys to our newest Prion Class carrier today.

"I hope you will take advantage of not only listening, but also learning from this class. Yes, I know that you miss your drill instructors," he said to the laughter breaking out in the classroom, "and you need them to tell you how to fart," as even louder laughter broke out. "But this is your heritage. This is what makes you what you are. I'm not going to be ratting out any of you if you fall asleep, but I hope you have the pride and discipline to listen and learn."

The "falling asleep" comment hit home. Ryck had it in the back of his mind to do just that if he could get away with it. But Dr. Berber's comment and appeal to their own sense of discipline instilled something more in him. He was going to be a Marine, and he should know its history, what would soon be his history.

"Settle back and relax. I will let you know," Dr. Berber said, stomping his foot in an exaggerated manner, "what you will have to know for the test. What you think the Corps doesn't test everything here at Camp Charles?" he said to the groans that had come at the word "test." "The Corps tests everything, so get used to it. Anyway, I'll let you know what will be tested," he said, once again making the exaggerated stomp. "But what I want you to absorb is the makings of the Marines and how our own culture has been developed. We work closely with the Navy, but we are different animals.

"Over our twenty classes together, we will examine the birth of dedicated naval infantry units, of the proliferation and periodic demise of marine units, of the 43 national and three planetary Marine Corps that were combined to form the Federation Marines, and of our own Federation Marine Corps' history, our greatest battles and heroes. Much of this will directly affect you, from why we celebrate both February 27 and November 10 as our Marine Corps birthdays, why NCOs wear the red stripe on their blues, and why a drummer in the Marine band wears a leopard skin over his uniform.

"Today, we will go over the foundation of how naval infantry was developed."

A vid of some sort of war galley appeared over his arena.

"I won't be foot-stomping anything during this class. There won't be anything on the test from today, so just listen and let it sink in.

"The first recorded naval battle was the Battle of the Delta, between the Egyptians under Ramses III and a group known as the Sea Peoples. In this battle, which took place around 1175 BC, the ships were used as platforms from which archers could fire toward shore-based troops, so in a way, the naval infantry preceded the use of a navy ship as a weapon in and of itself. Ships continued to be more of floating transports, and it wasn't until the rise of the Greeks and Phoenicians around 1000 BC that the war galley was developed. This is what is called a *triaconter*, or 'thirty-oared ship.' Not only could it transport troops, but also it could attack and destroy other ships, quite often through ramming" he said, pointing to the image above his desk arena. Another image of a galley appeared, and the first one turned to face it before oars started it forward toward the new ship.

Ryck leaned forward in his seat. He had a feeling that the 20 hours he was scheduled to be in class with the good doctor were going to be interesting.

Chapter 6

Recruit Squad Leader Ryck Lysander took a few steps to his left and yelled, "Hodges, get your grubbing team up in position!"

This was the first training evolution in his new recruit billet, and he was bound and determined to keep it all the way through graduation. He didn't need Hodges to get him fired before he'd even had a chance to show the DIs what he was capable of.

They were outside the camp walls, in TA103, "Training Area 103," a good-sized expanse of open ground. It wasn't as clear as a parade deck, but it was as close to being clear as any other training area. There were a few gentle rises and one gully, but a DI could pretty much view the entire area. Ryck couldn't afford to focus on any of the other squads in sight, though. He had to watch his four fire teams as they walked through the various formations they'd just learned.

As he'd wondered before, he wasn't sure why they were walking around, their M99s in hand, but nothing else. No comms, no armor, nothing. Ryck knew they'd never be without their comms, and trying to control four fire teams by shouting was not the most efficient way of getting the job done. Why not just give them a club and animal skins, and let them grunt out their commands?

Not that the M99s they carried were anything more than clubs, and not very effective clubs at that. Ryck had been thrilled when he'd been issued his, but that thrill faded when he realized the weapon was a liability to a recruit. Not only did it have the bright pink safety tie that kept the chamber from closing, showing the world that he wasn't trusted yet to have a live weapon, but also even dropping it, much less getting separated from it, resulted in a punishment that was better blocked out of the mind. One recruit DOR'd[12] right in the middle of his pushups he'd been assigned for dropping his. The DIs had been in his face, screaming, and the guy just stopped. Leaving his weapon on the deck, he'd just stood up, then walked back toward the barracks.

"Are you DOR'ing?" the top hat had screamed.

"Yep," had been the reply.

As if a switch had been thrown, the DIs quit their tirade. Drill Instructor Lorenz picked up the recruit's M99 and slung it on his back as the other DIs turned their attention back to the rest of the platoon.

Ryck had already forgotten the recruit's name. He was only one of six recruits who were gone.

"Damn it Hodges, get your team up!" he shouted again, running a few steps toward him until he stumbled over a rock and almost went to his knees.

He risked a glance back to the bleachers where they had been given their lesson. Not only were his DIs there watching, but also the series commander and senior were there as well, all observing the training. Ryck hoped no one had noticed him stumbling.

Recruit Hodges slowly moved his fire team up in position. The DI field instructor had told them that formations like this had been the mainstay of military operations since warfare began, but Ryck thought that had no bearing on modern warfare. Marines were not going to be trudging into battle in nice little squad V's, Wedges, or Echelons. Even the most ill-equipped enemy would be able to hold off a company of Marines if this was all they did. They might just as well line up in three ranks and conduct volley fire at the enemy.

They finally made it to the yellow flag that indicated they had to shift to the next formation. This changing formations was called "Battle Drill." Ryck looked down at his instruction sheet.

"OK, listen up! We're going to a Squad V," he shouted, holding up both arms at an angle above his head.

At least the fire teams didn't have to change formations at the same time, something for which Ryck was grateful. That would

---

[12] DOR: Drop on Request. This is the formal term for a recruit quitting recruit training.

be a royal clusterfuck. He shifted to his own position as he watched the fire teams slowly make the change.

"Hodges! Where are you supposed to be in a Squad V? To the right of the formation! No, to your other right! You see Fourth Fire Team there? You really think you both are going to march together like that?" Ryck shouted as he sprinted toward his wayward team.

Observers be damned, Ryck was going to grab that grubbing idiot by the collar and drag him into position if he had to.

Chapter 7

Ryck strapped on his armor. Not the body armor they would be
issued at the end of Phase 2, but plastic armor, gloves, and a helmet
that looked like some old-time football gear. This was pugil stick
training, what some said was the highlight of Phase 1.

Ryck wouldn't call it the highlight, himself. What was next?
Jousting? Sword fighting? He thought that in today's Marine
Corps, the weapons were just slightly more advanced than smacking
each other with padded sticks. It didn't matter what Ryck thought,
though. For the Drill Instructors, this was life and death.
Competition between squads, platoons, and companies was the very
lifeblood of the DIs. Each unit had to do better than the rest, and
the DIs held their recruits' victories over each other. The pugil stick
tournament was the first major competition within the company,
and all the DIs were anxious for an early victory.

They'd been introduced to the sticks in the morning session.
There was actually some technique involved, but from the
undercurrent being discussed, the actual bouts were more like two
recruits simply trying to bash out each other's brains.

Now, after chow and after a class on first aid, which Ryck
thought was appropriate just prior to the tourney, it was time to
have at it. It was First Squad against Second, and Third against
Fourth. The final platoon winners would go up against the other
platoon champ in a death match at the end of Phase 1.

Ryck figured he would be matched against Raj Simperson,
the Third Squad leader, but the DIs chose No Initial as his first
opponent. Ryck's first reaction was *why me?* No Initial was huge,
but then as he thought about it, Ryck figured this would be a way for
him to shine. Ryck already knew that No Initial didn't have stamina
and that he was slow. All Ryck would have to do would be to dance

around, darting in and out, landing what blows he could until the big guy from Craxion 4 tired.

With his gear on and checked by Drill Instructor Lorenz, Ryck joined the rest of the squad around the huge sawdust-filled circle just to the east of the obstacle course. The circle was only used for pugil stick training. A recruit would think this was sacred ground. Woe and behold any recruit who happened to try and walk across it. That had happened to Hodges when he was told to go back to the start of the obstacle course back on T4, or "Training Day 4," and what happened to him was something Ryck never wanted to see again. He thought Hodges was going to DOR right there, but somehow, the guy had stuck through his "motivational training."

First Squad and Second were going at it. Some bouts were quick, some took time. Du Boc, a smaller recruit from Harmony, and Graeme Styles, a heavy-worlder from Rio Tinto, had an epic battle, with all the recruits and drill instructors cheering. Du was quicker than the stockier Graeme, and he kept up a tremendous flurry of blows that the heavy-worlder absorbed as he tracked down his lighter opponent. Heavy-worlder or not, though, Du was getting through, staggering Graeme twice. Finally, as Du darted in for another shot, Graeme connected, almost sending Du down. Somehow, Du stayed up as Graeme waded in. Several blows hit Du from each side, yet he would just not give up. His helmet was knocked askew, blinding him. Graeme lunged forward to take advantage of it, but Du lashed out with a wild roundhouse swing, going yard. Somehow, he connected against Graeme's head, and the Rio Tinto recruit almost went down.

The rest of the recruits, even those in Third and Fourth Squads, were going crazy. Just to his right, the Second Squad "coach," Drill Instructor Mendez, was in full apoplectic fit mode, screaming as it looked that Du might pull it out.

The recruits wore big, bulky gloves while fighting, and these gloves fit through the padding on the sticks to allow a combatant to get a firm grip. It was considered a coward's loss to drop a pugil stick, akin to a Spartan coming home without his shield, so the gloves and handhold made it easier to hang on, almost locking the hand in place. This didn't make the gloves very useful for anything else though, and when Du removed one hand to try and twist his helmet back so he could see again, he couldn't get a good grasp on it.

When Graeme's next blow hit him, it smashed through Du's hand and lifted the taller, but lighter recruit up right off his feet to crash down in the sawdust. Lying flat on his back, Du weakly lifted his left hand, which had somehow still retained its grip on his pugil stick. This was no coward's loss.

Graeme strode forward, and for a moment, Ryck thought the guy was still in attack mode. When the bloodlust was up, anything could happen, and more than once, DIs had to wade in to separate fighters. Graeme was a heavy-worlder, too, and while Ryck had never really known one, he knew their reputation as undisciplined brawlers. He was surprised, then, when Graeme merely bent over to help Du to his feet. Graeme even held up Du's arm in the victor pose. The senior moved into the ring and held up both of their arms. Winning was drilled into each recruit's head, but it seemed that even in losing, Du had gained the DIs' respect.

Despite himself, Ryck could feel his own competitive blood boil. This might be antiquated, it might be useless, but Ryck was getting psyched. He wondered what his chances were to emerge as the platoon champ. He was already a squad leader, but that was assigned to him. Platoon pugil stick champ would be earned.

When First and Second completed the first round, the winners were all taken to the side where they would await the winners between Third and Fourth. Due to drops, the squads were not even, so two recruits from First had joined Third for their first bout. If they won though, it would still be a First Squad win.

Drill Instructor Lorenz gathered them all around before they started their bouts.

"I can give you an 'oorah' speech, but frankly, if it isn't in you, then I'm not going implant it into your heart with a 30-second speech. This, recruits, is up to you. No one else. Yeah, I want you to win, because I'd love to stick it in Drill Instructor Temperance," he said, holding one hand up as if it was on back of the neck of someone, then taking his right and driving it up as if thrusting a knife, then twisting it back and forth. "If you lose, you're going to wish you hadn't, I promise you. But that's not why you want to win.

You should need to win because you're the baddest, meanest motherfuckers around, and you want the world to know it."

He looked around at the 18 of the recruits in turn, catching each one of them eye-to eye, before saying, "OK, bring it in. On three. One, two three!"

"Fourth Squad, 1044! We bring it!" they shouted almost in unison.

Then it was time. Despite himself, Ryck forgot about his previously-held notion that pugil stick bouts were a waste of time. He jumped up and down, shaking out his arms, feeling the aggressor in him surface. He was going to kick some grubbing ass! He didn't lose that when the first two recruits in Fourth Squad fell quick victim to their Third Squad opponents. He was going to break that trend.

"So, what are you going to do, Recruit Lysander?" Drill Instructor Lorenz asked him as he gave Ryck's equipment one last check.

"He ain't nothing but a grub, Drill Instructor. He can't even run. He's got no heart, I'm gonna dash in and hit him, then I'm gonna . . ."

"Don't give me all the details, recruit. Just tell me what you're going to do."

"Uh . . . oh, I'm going to destroy him! Oorah!" Ryck shouted.

"OK, go do it."

Ryck stepped into the ring and approached the center. He and No Initial got there at the same time. The TDI running the bouts started going over the rules once more.

I don't need no grubbing rules, Ryck thought, tuning out the Green Shirt. *No rules in war!*

He looked at No Initial. Ryck knew the recruit was stronger than he was, but Ryck also knew he owed Ryck. Without Ryck helping him, he would have fallen out of a number of runs. So Ryck knew No Initial wouldn't go after him too hard. And that was his Achilles' Heel.

Ryck has considered putting on his warface, the expression of determination and mayhem that most of the recruits had tried to cultivate. But he thought it better to lull No Initial by not seeming too aggressive. Instead, he smiled and gave a shrug. Just two friends who would do enough to appease the DIs, but not enough to really hurt each other. No Initial smiled back. He was copacetic with it.

The Green Shirt was done and stepped back. He raised the whistle to his lips.

Ryck tried to look relaxed. At the whistle, he was going to spring before No Initial could react and knock the big guy on his ass for a quick win. He almost felt sorry for him. They had just agreed to an unspoken arrangement to take it easy, and Ryck was going to break that to win. But Ryck was tired of carrying No Initial around, both literally and figuratively. Better he learned his lesson here at the Depot then in combat.

The whistle sounded, and Ryck lunged. He had his pugil stick swinging in an uppercut, ready to connect with No Initial's chin. He barely saw No Initial's own stick swinging, then he saw nothing at all.

Chapter 8

"Doggie, check for the DIs," Hamilton Ceres, the recruit squad leader for First said. Hamilton had gathered Doggie and the other three squad leaders, the platoon guide, the whiskey locker recruit, and the scribe for an impromptu meeting. Doggie was the "house mouse," the recruit tasked with cleaning the DIs' office, so if he checked and a DI was still there, it should rouse no suspicion.

The seven of them, the entirety of the recruit leadership in the platoon, waited silently in the head until Doggie came back with news that the DIs were gone. They could get down to business. Ryck already had a good idea about what Hamilton wanted to tell them. Earlier in the day, Seth MacPruit, a recruit in First, had told Hamilton to fuck off, reminding the squad leader that Hamilton was a recruit just like the rest of them, and that he had no real authority over him. Technically, that was true. The recruit squad leaders were only acting squad leaders. All authority was in the hands of the DIs. If Hamilton was having a problem with Seth, then he could go to the DI and report the other recruit, but that would show a lack of leadership capability, and Hamilton could be stripped of his position right then and there.

Seth knew that. Seth also knew that Hamilton couldn't force him to comply with any order. Seth was a Combined Martial Arts phenom, actually having fought in the Ultimate Warrior Tournament, winning his weight class at the planetary level before bowing out. He proclaimed this loudly and often from their first training day, and many of the other recruits, Ryck included, thought he was spewing so much BS. But in the Marine Corps Martial Art class four days before, he'd taken on the instructor, a MCMA black belt, and handily beat him. Seth was the real deal.

Seth was also an asshole. Now that the others knew what he was capable of in a fight, he'd become even more arrogant and unruly. Telling Hamilton to fuck off was the final straw.

"So, I know you all know why I've called you here. The question is what do we do about it," Hamilton told the group, keeping his voice low.

The DIs might not be in their office, but they had a habit of turning up anywhere at any time. This meeting, after lights out, was against the rules, and recruits who broke the rules almost always wished they hadn't after they'd been caught.

"Not much of a choice, as I see it," John McGruder said without much emotion. "We can't let anyone flaunt our authority."

"I hear you, Mac, but we really don't have any authority," Shaymall Cammille, the platoon guide said.

The guide was the top recruit billet, naturally assigned to the recruit who the DIs thought was the strongest. That opinion affected the rest of the recruits, and he was unconsciously considered the first among equals by the others.

"Bullshit, Shay-man. The Senior gave me this position, and that's all the perking authority I fucking need. Ham, you need to call this perking arsehole out. Now," Mac said.

Hamilton visibly blanched before stammering out, "I can do it, I mean I can call him out, but shit on me, you saw him with that DI. He flattened the guy. A MCMA black belt! I'd only last an ant's heartbeat."

Mac rolled his eyes, but Ryck answered for him, "Not just you, Hamilton. You call him out, but all of us take care of him. You bring him in here, and we'll be waiting."

The thought had obviously never occurred to Hamilton, and he seemed to think it over for a moment before asking, "But what does that say about me? That I can't handle my own problems? And is it fair, eight against one?"

"Stick it, Ham," Mac told him. "All's fair in perking love and war. We love that arsehole as a fellow Marine recruit, as a platoon mate, but this is war when he thinks he's too perking special to follow the rules. And when he tells you to fuck off, he's telling all of us to fuck off. So, all of us need to give him a little 'extra instruction' on following orders. A beasting he's asking for, and a beasting we'll give him."

"You mean a 'beating?'" Ham asked, obviously confused.

"What? No. Don't you speak Standard? This is a 'beating,'" he said, mimicking the pounding on a drum. "This is a 'beasting'" he added, pounding one fist into his opposite open palm.

Hamilton took in Mac's meaning before looking at each of the others in turn.

"Do you all agree with that?"

Each one of them nodded, even if Doggie's nod was late and without enthusiasm.

"And none of you think I'm wimping out?" Hamilton asked.

Each head shook in a "no."

"OK, then. So, I guess it's now or never. Let me go get him and bring him back here," he said as he left the showers and made his way into the darkened squadbay.

The seven recruits moved closer to the entrance to the showers so they wouldn't be seen when Hamilton and Seth walked up.

"Shit, shit, shit . . ." Doggie whispered to himself, fear evident in his voice to those who overheard him.

Ryck sympathized, but he was not going to voice that. Even with eight of them, Seth was a grubbing monster, and there could be some serious ass-kicking going on—not all of it on Seth. He swung his arms back and forth, trying to get ready, only stopping when he heard murmuring as the two recruits approached.

"I gotta give you props. I never thought you had the balls to call me out. It ain't gonna make any difference 'cause I'm still gonna to take you apart, but I gotta respect your effort," Seth said as they walked into the showers.

He stopped dead as the seven recruits waiting moved to surround him. Hamilton stepped back to join the circle of recruits.

"Hey, what's this bullshit? It's jus' me an' fuckhead here. This is between me an' him," Seth protested.

"Well, you see, Mac-Pisshead, it's like this. When a chav like you goes and disrespects one of us, you disrespect all of us. So, we all need to sort of, you know, show you the error of your ways."

Seth stood there looking at them, hands on his hips.

"What a bunch of fucking marigolds. My great-granny's got more balls than you, an' she's been dead for two years," he said with a sneer on his face. "I guess I'll have to show you the fucking error of *your* ways. You don't mess with me! Which one of you pussies is first?" he asked, rising up on the balls of his feet, fists raised.

Mac rushed him, head down, arms outstretched. Seth's foot caught him on the chin, folding him in a heap on the tile deck. Seth somehow kept his foot going, bringing it to his right, connecting with the side of Du Boc's neck, sending him to his knees. At that moment, Ryck's fist connected with the back of Seth's neck, right below the skull. Seth staggered forward, clearly stunned, and Shaymall's fist came up in a picture perfect-uppercut, catching Seth on the chin. He went down hard, head bouncing off the tile. Despite Seth being down and out, several more punches and kicks were thrown at his unresponsive body, the last by Du after the recruit squad leader got back up to his feet.

Ryck's heart was pounding. It had all happened so quickly. His fist hurt, but the adrenaline kept most of the pain at bay. He had to concentrate on calming down. Taking care of Seth was only half of the equation. Now they had to get back into their racks before there was a bed check.

Shaymall was checking on Mac, who was just coming to. Ryck joined him as they pulled Mac into a sitting position.

"Mother-fuck! What train hit me?" he asked groggily. "What about Mac-Pisshead?" he asked, trying to see around the two other recruits.

"Lesson learned," Shaymall said. "He was too busy with you, so we got him."

"Copacetic! Figured that would work. That perking arsehole knew I was the harry von bad one, right? Knew he had to take me out first, right?" Mac said, his words only slightly slurred.

"You were right, Mac," Shaymall answered. "Think you can get up? We need to get back in our racks."

"Oh, sure, man," Mac responded.

With a little help, the two of them got Mac out of the showers and up into his rack before going back and helping carry the limp body of Seth to his rack, an upper bunk. They had to push him up, stepping on the rack below to get him in. Ryck stepped on Seth's bunkmate in the process, but that recruit never said a word.

The seven of them got Seth up and under his sheets, then scattered for their own racks. Ryck had just gotten in and pulled up his sheets when the front hatch opened. A flashlight pierced the darkness and swept over the sleeping, or at least prone, recruits.

"All quiet, fire watch?" the unseen DI asked the recruit standing at the fire watch podium at the front of the squadbay.

Recruit Dixby Zeller, who had observed everything except for what actually occurred in the showers, said, "All quiet, Drill Instructor!"

"OK, carry on," the voice reached out to them.

The next morning, despite two recruits with very visible bruises, the DIs seemed not to notice that anything had happened during the night.

Chapter 9

"Fucking A, Calderón, get it right! Look at the grubbing diagram, for J's sake!" Ryck said as he looked over Recruit Jorge Calderón's junk-on-the-bunk.

This was the last scheduled function in Phase 1 of recruit training, and Ryck wanted to make sure it was done right. Recruits from the other platoons had started calling 1044 the "booger platoon," and Drill Instructor Phantawisangtong, the platoon "heavy hat," was on the warpath. Du had already lost his billet as squad leader, and his replacement, Scotland Blythe, lasted less than two hours before he was relieved.

Phase 1 had been boring—it had been a bitch, but a boring bitch. It had been PT, close order drill, more PT, basic tactical formations, history classes, more PT, inspections, martial arts training, swimming, pugil stick bouts, more PT, and still more PT. Ryck hated it. He hated doing things he'd never do once he was actually in the Corps. He hated the stupid pink safety tie that rendered his weapon inoperable, and he really hated the "pink baby" catcalls they got from the more advanced recruits. The history classes turned out to be pretty interesting, but Ryck wanted to fire his M99, he wanted to maneuver in a PICS. This inspection was so the DIs could check their gear for their trip to the range in the morning, their first training event of Phase 2. No more pink babies!

Calderón was a gumball. Every squad seemingly had a Calderón, one place where the Hollybolly tropes were reflected in real military life. Calderón wasn't the only one, Ryck thought, as he glanced around at the rest of the squad. Just like in every boot camp flick and vid, they had the screwup, the rich kid trying to make good on his own, the poor kid from Nova Esperança's favelas without a future, the heavy-worlder with a gentle soul. Hell, Ryck himself was a living trope, the farmboy seeking fame and fortune off planet

He turned his attention back to Calderón. Frankly, Ryck was surprised that he'd made it to T24. Twenty-four days of difficult training, and this royal fuck-up couldn't do anything right. Ryck was sure he spent 80% of his squad leader time with the guy, and that was a burden. Ryck might be a recruit squad leader, but the key word was "recruit." He still had to hit every training objective for himself just like everyone else. Sometimes, he resented being held accountable for the others, but still, he liked the ego boost. He was bound and determined to keep his billet all the way to graduation, something almost never achieved.

Calderón placed his Goodell at the top right of his rack. The molecular blade was supposed to go on the top left side, not the right.

"Damn it! Can't you fucking read? I've about had it with you," Ryck told the other recruit. "I've got to get my own gear laid out, and we've got less than ten minutes to get it done, so you're on your own. King Tong's going to fry your ass if you screw it up."

At the mention of the nickname the platoon had given the heavy hat, Calderón looked up in alarm as if the drill instructor was already there. Ryck just turned away, not willing to waste another precious second on that lost cause.

He hurried to get his own gear laid out and had just finished when the fire watch called the squadbay to attention and the entire DI team marched in. Ryck jumped to the foot of his rack and came to the position of attention, hoping everyone was inspection-ready. He'd checked the others, of course, and they had been making good progress—all except Calderón, that was.

I hope the sorry sack of shit fucks up, he thought. *And then Despiri or Tong'll see the guy just can't cut it and recommend him for a retention hearing.*

The DIs started their inspection at the other end of the barracks. Ryck could hear low murmurs as they spoke to the recruits being inspected. Once, there was a huge crash coming from Second Squad's area as gear was thrown on the floor. King Tong was going at it but good, and Ryck pitied whoever was at the receiving end of that tirade.

It took a while as the sounds of inspections got closer and closer, but finally, Senior Drill Instructor Despiri moved in front of Ryck.

"Recruit Lysander ready for inspection, Senior Drill Instructor Despiri!" he told the DI.

Ryck wasn't sure if he should be relieved or worried that he'd drawn Despri. The drill instructor didn't scream and shout as much as the others, but he was very demanding, and his eyes missed nothing. Ryck made an about-face and stood ready to respond to any questions the DI might ask during the inspection. He slightly broke his position to look out of the corner of his eyes at Despiri, trying to gauge the progress as the DI inspected his gear.

"Serial number?" Despiri asked.

"4795553744, Senior Drill Instructor" he responded immediately.

That was an easy one. He had his M99 memorized five minutes after being issued it.

Despiri picked up Ryck's powerpack from the rack, then turned it around to look at the back.

"Wrong. Again, serial number?"

Ryck was confused. DIs always asked for the weapon's serial number, not anything else. Ryck didn't have a clue as to the powerpack's serial number.

"I . . . uh . . .this recruit does not know his powerpack's serial number, Drill Instructor," he stammered out.

"Find out. And if a question or order is not clear, clarify it. You have five items with serial numbers on your rack. I could have been asking about any one of them," the DI said.

"Aye-aye, Senior Drill Instructor Despiri," Ryck said.

Despiri gave one more glance at the gear on the rack before turning to move on to Hodge's rack. Ryck let out a sigh of relief. Despite getting caught by the blindside, it seemed his gear was passable. He returned to his position of attention at the end of the rack, listening in as the DIs hit the rest of his squad. He caught some corrections, and Lipitski stumbled over the normal combat load of M505 grenades, but it seemed like it was going well—until King Tong, of all DIs, hit Calderón's rack. Ryck heard the recruit report ready for inspection, and not 15 seconds later, the eruption began. King Tong was in rare form, screaming at the top of his lungs. Ryck could hear gear being slammed on the deck.

Serves the shithead right, he thought, a small smile creeping onto his face despite him being at attention.

"Who's your squad leader?" King Tong shouted, despite knowing the answer, and Ryck blanched for a moment. He knew he would be questioned, but all he had to do was be straightforward and recite the facts. The prime fact was that Calderón was not suited to be a Marine.

Ryck heard a murmur in response, then "Recruit Lysander, front and center!" from the DI.

Ryck did a right face, then double-timed down the three racks to where King Tong waited.

Ryck didn't even have a chance to report in before King Tong went off, "What kind of sorry-ass preparation is this? Didn't Recruit *Calder-none* know we were having a junk-on-the-bunk? Didn't he think it was important that his gear be squared away before you piss-poor excuses go to the field?"

Drill Instructors were not supposed to alter any recruit's name, but no one ever complained. Suicide by DI was not something anyone wanted to experience.

"Yes, Drill Instructor Phantawisangtong," he said, slightly stumbling over the name.

All of the recruits practiced saying his name, afraid of messing it up, but the stress might have gotten to Ryck.

"Recruit Calderón was aware of the inspection. He was told to get his gear ready. This recruit attempted to assist Recruit Calderón, but it was hopeless. This recruit told him to get it done, and it was up to him to pass or fail."

"You told him to get it done. And he did not do as ordered, is that what you are saying?" King Tong asked.

"Yes, Drill Instructor!"

"Recruit Squad Leader Lysander, in your most expert opinion, does Recruit Calderón have what it takes to be a Marine?" King Tong asked.

This was it. The bottom line. Ryck had to respond truthfully.

"No, Drill Instructor, this recruit does not believe that Recruit Calderón has it in him to be a Marine. He is not Marine material."

There was silence in the squadbay. Ryck could almost feel the attention of 66 recruits and eight DIs on him.

"Recruit Squad Leader Lysander," Senior Drill Instructor Despiri's voice cut through to him. "Are you Recruit Calderón's squad leader?"

"Yes, Senior Drill Instructor!"

"Was it your task to get your squad ready for inspection?"

"Yes, Senior Drill Instructor!"

"If you are going into a fight, are you just going to tell your Marines to have their proper battle load, or are you going to check them?"

"Uh . . ." he started, unable to forego the using the "uh" sound, "No Senior Drill Instructor. This recruit would inspect each Marine."

This wasn't going as he expected.

"Yet during this inspection, you decided to let one of your charges sink or swim on his own?"

"Yes, Senior Drill Instructor," he responded, his heart falling.

"In battle, one unprepared Marine can get his unit killed. Here, one unprepared recruit means your squad has failed the inspection. Drill Instructor Phantawisangtong, at the conclusion of this inspection, take Third Squad out on a run to the Lost Lady, full rucks."

Ryck grimaced. The squad might be pissed at him, but they should be pissed at Calderón. He was the idiot who couldn't even prepare for a junk-on-the-bunk.

"Recruit Lysander, hand me your tab," Despiri said.

Ryck's heart fell. The tab was a small red piece of fabric that attached to his left collar. It was the only thing that visually identified him as a recruit squad leader. He slowly reached up and took it off, handing it to the senior when the DI walked up to him.

Despiri took it without a word, then turned toward King Tong. It wasn't the heavy hat, though, to whom the senior was facing.

"Recruit Squad Leader Calderón, you will have 10 minutes at the conclusion of this inspection to have your squad, in full kit, mustered on the parade deck. I suggest you make sure everyone is ready to go," he said, handing Calderón the tab.

Ryck's plan on keeping his billet until graduation was over, just like that.

Chapter 10

Ryck was excited. This was their first time in the RCET, the Realistic Combat Environment Trainer. He'd played in the vanilla civilian version of the game before back on Prophesy, but wearing a sim-helmet and "walking" around in his bedroom, fighting others online was a far cry from what he expected in the real deal. He'd watched a Discovery show on military training once, so he had an idea of what the RCET was like, and the show had just enhanced his expectations.

The civilian operator was a young guy, not much older than most of the recruits, but Ryck listened intently to the brief. The first evolution would be fire team formations. Nothing this afternoon would be graded, but that would change the next morning. Scores would be tallied for the fire team, squad, and platoon stages, and those scores would reflect on platoon standings. The highest scoring platoon would not only have a big boost to its total running score, but also it would receive a purple "battle streamer" to attach to the guidon through graduation. The RCET streamer and the red marksmanship streamer were the only two such streamers that could be earned by a platoon, and 1044 hadn't done so well at the range the week before. This was not only the platoon's last chance to earn a recruit streamer, but it should pull it out of being the consensus company booger platoon.

Finally, the operator was done with his brief. It was time to get going. Third and Fourth squads went to Arena B where several more civilians were handing out the armor inserts. Actual personal armor would not be issued until the start of Phase 3, but as RCET was to be conducted in full combat gear, training armor would be used. As they had discovered in Phase 1, the training armor was not only in bad shape, but the "one size fits most" philosophy meant that even if the inserts sort of fit a recruit, they never quite matched up with a recruit's body, especially at the joints. Although the recruits were all assured that their own armor would be tailor-made for each of them, the beat-up training armor inserts were a royal pain in the ass.

The battle helmets were almost as bad. They had been introduced to the helmets during Phase 1, so the recruits knew how to operate them, but these had seen years of use. There was no way to fit nor optimize them for each recruit, so most of the capabilities had simply been disconnected. Each first-person visual would be recorded and would be transmitted in real time to the monitors so the RCET personnel, the DIs, and the other recruits could observe what was happening. Monitors would also show the overall picture as well as what the electronic bad guys would be seeing as the recruits approached them. All of this would be recorded and used to analyze and critique each event.

Ryck had tried on three helmets before finding one that was close to fitting. Despite the antiseptic smell, he could imagine the sweat of hundreds, maybe thousands of recruits who had worn this particular helmet before him. The mere thought made his forehead itch where the brow-pad rested against it.

Geared up, Ryck was ready to go. He checked his weapon out of force of habit. At least, now that the platoon had finished Range Week, the recruits were trusted to handle their weapons and no longer needed the horrid pink safety ties.

When the Arena Chief finally gave the OK, Ryck eagerly stepped forward. As the First Fire Team rifleman, he was the first to get inspected. Pink tie or not, one of the operators gave his weapon a safety check, as professionally as any DI. First, he cleared the weapon. They'd been off the range for four days, and this was probably the 10th time his M99 had been cleared to make sure there were no rounds in the chamber. As the darts were inserted in self-contained magazines, and as none of the recruits had access to any ammo lockers, Ryck wasn't sure when and where he was supposed to have found a magazine and gotten a round loaded since the last time his weapon had been checked. After clearing the M99, the operator initiated the SFA. The Simulated Firing Attachment would calculate a dart trajectory and transmit that to the RCET computer where it would be inserted into the simulation enabling the RCET brain to be the high judge and jury as to what would be happening if this was an actual combat mission with Ryck firing real rounds at a real enemy.

Ryck received the OK, and he stepped through the hatch into the Arena.

Copacetic! was all he could think. *No, this was beyond copacetic, this was, grubbing "fantasmagorical," as the Earth recruits say.*

With his little commercial sim-helmet back at home, the game was pretty awesome. But now, being in the Arena rendered playing at home as the black-and-white version.

He was not observing the game, he was *in* it. Intellectually, he knew he was in a huge room, 700 meters long and 200 meters wide, adjoining another just like it with a wall that could be removed, making a single 400-meter wide space. The room was empty except for the equipment needed to run it.

Ryck knew that from the brief and from what he had seen on the vids, but now, his senses rejected that explanation. At the moment, Ryck was in a partially wooded landscape, standing on dark brown dirt covered with brown leaf-fall. A breeze brushed up against him, and he could smell the dusky aroma of vegetation. He scanned the scene. Small birds flitted from branch to branch. Sunlight filtered through the trees. The detail was amazing.

He was aware of someone joining him. That would be Preston "Wagons" Ho, the team AR man.

"Oh, wow. Fantasmagorical!" Wagons said.

Ryck almost laughed out loud. He called that one right. Ryck didn't use all the slang used by recruits from other planets, but this time, the Earth phrase fit. Some words, such as "copacetic," which was the catchphrase of Captain Titan in the *Swordbinder* series, were more universally popular. Other words, such as "fantasmagorical," or even Ryck's own use of "grubbing," were more regional.

Within a few more minutes, Hodges and Calderón had joined them. Calderón had lasted as squad leader for less than 24 hours before being fired. Hodges, of all people, was now the fire team leader. Hodges still seemed lost at times, but he had raised a few eyebrows on the range. The guy could shoot.

Ryck and Wagons had already discussed their situation. With the two weaker recruits in the team, it would be up to them to pull the team through, even if Hodges was the team leader.

The four of them quickly moved into a wedge. Ryck had the point, Hodges was behind him and to his right, Calderón was even with Hodges and to Ryck's left, while Wagons was in trace of Ryck and behind the other two. Their first mission would be a simple movement to contact.

"Fire team, you may begin," a voice told them over their comms.

Ryck didn't wait for Hodges; he simply stepped off, senses on high alert.

He scanned the area in front of him, trying to see any movement, any tripwires, any sign of danger. He knew that this could be a simple movement, just to let them get used to the simulation, but somehow, he doubted it. There would be bad guys out there.

He had been intensely aware that what he was seeing would be on a monitor outside, but he quickly forgot about that. He had immersed himself in the scenario.

What is that? he asked himself.

He held up one fist, the ancient hand-and-arm signal to stop, and edged over to look at the ground in front of him. Something had caught his eye. It was a stick, but it looked out of place. Carefully, he pulled back the grass from around it, the front of his mind reveling in the tactile feel of the grass despite the back of his mind knowing there was nothing actually there.

"What is it, Lysander?" Hodges asked.

"Maybe a booby trap, over," Ryck responded.

Ryck examined it from every angle possible, wishing his helmet had full capabilities so he could do one of the several scans an operational helmet could make. Finally, he decided it was just a stick.

He started moving the team forward again. The terrain seemed to rise as if they were walking up a hill. Once again, Ryck knew the room was level, but his senses warred with that knowledge. He wondered at the technology that made all of this possible. This was head and shoulders above what he'd ever experienced in any game before.

Focus! he reminded himself. *Think about how amazing this is after the exercise!*

They continued forward, tension building. If they were going to be hit, it would have to be soon. Simple logistics told them that with seven fire teams—four from Fourth Squad and only three now from Third Squad—and the number of runs each team was scheduled for the day, each go-through could only take up so much time.

Ryck just happened to be looking right at a jumble of logs ahead when the enemy soldier rose and fired. Instinctively, Ryck pulled the trigger, lifting his M99 from low and left to high and right, stitching a line across his target. This was a technique taught during the last two days of Range Week, after initial qualification, and Ryck was surprised that it worked just as well in this scenario as on an open rifle range. The enemy disappeared, whether hit or merely taking cover, Ryck would find out during the debrief.

He half-waited for Hodges to shout out an order, and when nothing was forthcoming, he did what Wagons and he had decided earlier. Charge the bastards. They had practiced this during Immediate Action Drills, so Wagons and he thought that would be a good excuse if reacting without orders was considered a no-no.

He saw movement to his front left, so he went right at it, weapon blazing. A line of fire reached back out to him. The helmets didn't have many of the capabilities of an actual combat helmet, but due to the nature of the training, the ballistic indictor was enabled. A trace appeared on the visor showing the trajectory of the incoming rounds. The trace started from Ryck's right, then began to sweep toward him. Ryck dove to the deck untouched. He tried to peer ahead and see who had fired at him. He had a general idea about from where the rounds had come, but he couldn't see anything. An explosion sounded to the front, and dirt and debris fell around him. Ryck could actually feel the clods hit his body.

By now, Hodges was yammering over the comms, asking for an update. He sounded excited, but not in a good way. There was a hint of panic to his voice. At the fire team level, the recruits could communicate directly with each other. The fire team comms circuit was open between the four of them.

"We've got at least three hostiles to my eleven o'clock. I'm gonna shift to the right, so cover me," Ryck transmitted.

"Roger that," Wagons' voice came over the circuit. "Give me a count, then move."

"Roger. I am moving in three . . . two . . . one!"

At "one," Ryck jumped to his feet and darted to his 2 o'clock—and his helmet siren went off.

"Mother grubber!" he shouted as he stopped and dutifully got back down on the ground. He was "dead" and so could not participate in any more action—not that he could even if he wanted to. Getting killed also disabled his SFA, keeping him from firing any more simulated rounds.

He'd been looking forward when he'd been hit, and he'd seen no trace coming at him. Still sitting, he looked back. Hodges was behind him, looking guilty.

That fucking idiot shot me! Ryck thought. *I'm gonna kick his grubbing ass!*

The rest of the engagement didn't take long. Wagons lasted the longest at another two minutes. Once he went down, the simulation faded. They were sitting in an empty space. The trees, dirt, smells, enemy: all were gone.

Ryck had been killed, and by friendly fire, of all things. The fire team had gotten wiped out. But damn it all, it had been a perking blast! He couldn't wait for their next turn in the breach.

"Fire team, return to the front hatch," came over the helmet comms.

Looking back, an innocuous red "EXIT" sign showed them the way.

Chapter 11

Ryck watched the server plop the shit-on-a-shingle on his plate. He actually liked the gloppy mess, but he had to wonder just how many millions of soldiers had been fed it over the centuries. He was pretty sure Roman legionnaires had fueled their marches into Gaul with it. Hadn't Dr. Berber said they'd been fed some sort of gruel? Wasn't gruel kind of like shit-on-a-shingle?

He moved on down the line, grabbing a panderfruit. The Roman's hadn't eaten those, though. The hybrid fruit had only been introduced about ten years before. Their ability to withstand rough handling and their long shelf life had made them an instant hit with industrial food service. They were pretty damn delicious, too. Ryck had never actually tried one before getting to Camp Charles, and now he was hooked on them.

He squirted some ketchup and polly sauce on his breakfast, a combination that some of the other recruits thought was vile, grabbed a cup of coffee, and looked around for a seat. Platoon 1045 had preceded them in the chow line, and he saw Joshua had taken a seat at the far end of his platoon area. He waved Ryck over.

There were no rules about where a recruit sat to eat, but common practice was to eat with the others in the unit. Joshua had seen Ryck and had taken a seat at the edge of 1045's grouping. The empty seats next to him were being taken up by 1044 recruits, so Ryck could sit there and still catch up with Joshua. They'd only known each other for a few days back home before shipping and then while en route, but still, it was good to see someone from home. Without time the opportunity to socialize, even if Joshua was only in the next squadbay, he might as well have been on another planet most of the time.

"Take a load off, brother-boy," Joshua said as Ryck walked over. "Oh, man, what you doin' to that grubbing food, there?" he added, pointing at the ketchup-and-polly-sauce mix.

"What you grubbing doing to that grubbing food?" one of the recruits next to Joshua mimicked.

"You grubbing mother grubber, grub off," another said, drawing a laugh from those around Joshua.

"Not only is he from the booger platoon, but he's one of Josh's homeys," chimed in a third recruit. "Are you another farmer boy? Josh here's a right solid recruit, even if he talks like shit. And he still can't tell us what 'grubbing' means."

"Well, please allow me the opportunity to introduce you to my planetary compatriot, Mr. Ryck Lysander. To respond to your inquiry, affirmative, Mr. Lysander was an agricultural engineer at his former abode. Currently, in the present time continuum, he occupies the position of Marine Corps recruit," Joshua said with an affected accent, one hand raised, little finger extended. "Even if he be from the booger platoon," he added, back to his Torritite accent.

Ryck extended his middle finger before picking up his fork. "Good to see you, too. And great to meet all of you grubbing freaks," he added to the others.

Recruit culture had a decided aggressive nature with smack-talk rampant. He didn't take the planetary comments seriously. Heck, he had given out worse. The "booger platoon" comment cut though, not that he was going to let anyone know that. More of 1044's recruits took their seats, but this was a chance to talk to Joshua.

"You heard about Proctor, right?" Ryck asked.

"Yeah, DOR'd. That shocked me, I be sayin'. Did you talk to him?" Joshua asked.

"Only for a minute. I was platoon runner for the day and had to take some papers to the company office. He was out on the bench, waiting," Ryck told him.

The "bench" was right outside the company office hatch. Any recruits leaving training, whether being dropped or by DOR, sat on the bench while awaiting their series and company commander interviews. Occasionally, a recruit being dropped could convince the officers to overrule the DIs and give a recruit another chance, but normally, once they had plopped their butt on the bench, it was the start of an inextirpable exit process. The other recruits considered it bad juju to catch the eye of anyone on the bench, so they were usually studiously ignored.

"I asked him what happened, and he said it was just too tough. I didn't have much time to ask anything else, and, you know . . ."

"Yeah, I know. You didn't want any of that bad karma rubbing off. He was on a 556 contract, right? So, he's goin' to be a squid now?" Joshua asked.

"Yeah. Remember, he already got his enlistment bonus, so he has to serve for three years in the Navy," Ryck confirmed.

Most of the recruits were on a normal 550 contract. This enlistment contract technically provided only for the opportunity to serve. If a recruit DOR'd or was dropped, then no harm, no foul. The recruit usually just went home. The 556 contract was only offered to highly-qualified recruits, and it came with certain guarantees along with an enlistment bonus. If a recruit was dropped, he might or might not be required to "pay back" his bonus with service in the Navy. It depended on just why he was being dropped. If a 556 baby DOR'd though, it was usually to be shipped off for three year's service as a sailor.

"He got us to switch to the Corps, but he be DOR'in' himself. That be messed up. That *is* messed up," he said, correcting himself.

On Prophesy, the Torritites seemed to take pride in their differences, including their manner of speaking, almost keeping those differences as badges of distinction. At Camp Charles, though, there was a significant gravitation to the center, that being Earth Standard. At least Joshua's accent and speech really weren't that much different. Many of the recruits came from planets with another primary language, but they also spoke Standard as did 99% of humanity. Some recruits had more difficulty. There was K'Ato Pluz from First Squad, for example. The DIs rode him unmercifully for his almost incomprehensible speech. The rest of the squad had to drill him on cleaning up his Standard.

"So, what else is goin' on with you?" Joshua asked. "1044 goin' to stay booger platoon?"

"Oh, man, don't even think it," Ryck said. "King Tong's going batshit crazy. He says he's never had a booger platoon, and we're not going to be the first. I swear, if I have to 'visit' The Lost Lady one more time, I'm just going to lose it."

"You know our heavy hat, Sorensen, right? Even he thinks Phana-whatever-tong be certified looney," Joshua said. "1042's supposed to be messin' up, too. You think you can catch them?"

"I don't know. We've got platoon RCET tomorrow. That's a graded event. I think we're doing OK, but who the hell knows?"

"Well, good luck on that," Joshua said as the first of the recruits in his platoon started standing to get rid of their trays. "What about your sister? She OK?" he asked before shoveling in the last of his eggs.

"Check it out," Ryck said, pulling out his PDA and opening the gallery and selecting a photo.

"She got married? And look at her! If my dear mama wouldn't die of a heart attack, if you had told me she was this hot, I would have come an' grabbed her!"

"In your grubbing dreams," Ryck told him. "She got married Friday night. That's what she said, at least, but maybe it was really in the morning. I think she's trying to adjust date and time since I'm over here on Tarawa. So, she either meant Friday night in Williamson, Friday night here at Camp Charles, or Friday night Universal Greenwich."

"1045, get it moving," Joshua's platoon guide shouted.

"It seems as if my esteemed leader desires our presence post haste in order to stave off the incipient vitriol of our drill instructors, so while I would love to offer discourse on your sibling's matrimony, I must take leave, monsieur," Joshua said as he stood up and offered a sweeping Three Musketeers bow. "Adieu!"

Ryck laughed out loud before responding, "You're still a grubbing land-worm, even if you can manage to sound like a pantywaist."

"You wound me, comrade," Joshua said, still in character, as he walked off.

Jonathan P. Brazee

"What's with him?" Hodges asked from the other side of Ryck. "Why's he talking like that?"

"Oh, you know. He's with 1045, and they are all messed in the head there," Ryck said before focusing back on his shit-on-a-shingle.

Chapter 12

Ryck liked RCET, but he absolutely loved Camp Lympstone, where the field training was conducted. During Phases 1 and 2, the platoon DIs were God and Satan combined with full and constant control over the recruits. At Lympstone, the DIs were still ever-present, but the TDIs[13] took over more of the recruits' time. The TDIs were not pushovers, though. They would still explode with the best of the DIs, and they would still assign "motivational training," but the focus was more on teaching recruits the skills they needed to function as combat Marines.

Camp Charles was no Hilton resort, but it was plush when compared to Lympstone. Recruits slept in small two-man tents called "bivvies," bathed in field showers, and ate combat rations twice a day. It was rough, uncomfortable, and Spartan—and Ryck couldn't get enough.

As with the Legion, a Marine's origin was meaningless. What mattered was being a Marine. However, tradition had it that the senior TDI at Lympstone came from the UK back on Earth or from Mollytot, Liverpool, or Barclays, the three UK-settled worlds. Master Sergeant Cletton Smith was no exception to this tradition. He was a short, very dark-skinned SNCO,[14] whose eyes seemed to miss nothing. The officer in charge was Major Simms, who unlike most of the officers at Camp Charles, did not observe from afar but actively got involved with the recruits. Training Drill Instructor Smith scared Ryck, as he scared most recruits, but Ryck knew his place with him. It was disconcerting, though, when running during PT to have Major Simms show up, jogging beside a recruit, casually asking how things were going.

---

[13] TDI: Training Drill Instructor
[14] SNCO: Staff Non-commissioned Officer

83

Part of the Lympstone experience was the use of an entirely new vocabulary. Chow was no longer chow, for example, but "scran," and the one hot scran each day was served in a "galley," not a mess hall. The first few days at Charles had been bad enough, learning to use, for example, "head" instead of toilet, "deck" instead of floor, and "hatch" instead of door. At Lympstone, they took it even further, and messing up was sure to result in push-ups—or "press-ups," that is. The TDI who took it most to heart was not even from a British background. The bull-necked Training Drill Instructor Jorge Jarumba was from Rio Tinto. The Tintoites still spoke Spanish as their primary language, yet the TDI was the most fervent keeper of the tradition.

"You ready?" Recruit Fire Team Leader Lysander asked Wagons.

Ryck had been promoted back to fire team leader two more times—which meant he'd been fired from the position, too. The platoon as a whole was down to 52 recruits. Ben Sutcliff had broken a leg on the obstacle course and been recycled, but the rest had been either drops or DORs. The recruits were now organized into three squads of either three or four fire teams each. Somehow, beyond all of Ryck's expectations, his fire team, with Wagons, Hodges, and Calderón was intact. Hodges was even showing signs of developing into an asset.

"I was born ready," Wagons replied. "Let's kick some ass, OK?"

'That's fine, except we're only facing hulks and targets out there. No incoming," Ryck said.

"Plenty of incoming, there, recruit," Wagons told him.

"You know what I mean. No rounds from an aggressor. The 'incoming' is our supporting arms," Ryck said.

Today's training evolution was to be the first of many combined arms exercises. The recruits had practiced every movement up to a company level. They had done it under simulated fire, with enemy "hits" recorded, assessing simulated casualties. They had moved against each other in mini-war games. What they had not yet done was move in conjunction with Navy and Marine Corps space, air, artillery, and armor assets. The day before, they had sat in the stands at Range 109 while the artillery had lit up the range. It had been an amazing sight, and the concussions could be felt shaking their very bones. It had been both impressive and frightening. For the day's evolution they would have to maneuver in conjunction with not only that level of destruction, but also the presence of a tank.

"Five mikes!" Shaymall shouted out. "Squad leaders, get at them."

Ryck glanced up as the squad's current leader, Harris Thompson, made a quick check of First Fire Team. With the new skins issued on the last day of Phase 2, there wasn't as much to check. There was the omnipresent weapons safety check and a quick check of the required battle gear, but their personal Marine armor had proven to be pretty much as advertised. The body armor consisted of two levels. The first was the "skins." The trousers and blouse looked and felt like normal civvies aside from the cammo patterns. The fabric, though, was interwoven with nano-fibers which offered some ballistic and fire protection, monitored physical readings, and chameleoned to the surroundings. The chameleon function was disabled during boot and was set on a dull yellow for all recruits and then changing to other colors for different training functions, but this was the actual working uniform each recruit would take with him into the fleet.

The second level was the added armor. Each Marine had a custom-fitted set of armor inserts, the "bones." The inserts weren't actually inserted into the skins, though. The bones, which weighed only 5 kg in total, came in 22 pieces, not counting the gloves. Each piece was pushed up against the appropriate body part, and it immediately lampreyed onto the fabric, drawing both power and the appropriate camouflage pattern from it.

During the first week of Phase 1, each recruit had been required to get his bones on within 30 seconds. Ryck's first attempt was over one-and-a-half minutes, and he thought 30 seconds was impossible. It really hadn't taken too many more attempts, though, to reach the required speed. By now, it had already become second nature.

Harris was shouting at them to get in the bleachers, so Ryck and the other three trooped over and filed in to take their seats. One good thing about Lympstone was that they basically took their "squadbay" with them. Their bivvies were lined up 20 meters behind the bleachers for Range 109, the Combined Firing Range. Their one hot would be packed out to them, so they had no nice galley at which to sit, but they were not humping back and forth each day while at the range.

Captain Jericho welcomed them to the range and the day's evolution. At Charles, the officers did formal inspections and handled interviews for drops or anything else that came up, and they sometimes observed training, but at Lympstone, they were more involved. Each and every safety brief was conducted by an officer. Captain Jericho had done many of their briefs, so he was a familiar face. He had the frame prosthetic that hid his regen for both legs. Rumor had it that this was his fourth regen: two as an enlisted Marine, two as an officer. Regens were rejected after too many attempts, and Ryck didn't know just how many times that was. If Captain Jericho deployed again and lost another arm or leg, could his body handle one more regen? Would he actually go through life with a prosthetic? That was a sobering thought.

The safety speech was pretty much the same as for every other training evolution: listen to the TDIs, pay attention to everything, keep the weapon on safe until ready to fire, make sure to identify a target before firing, and so on. The platoon had been doing pretty well in this area, at least. Ben-ben had been their only casualty, and he would be back in a follow-on training company. Platoon 1042 had two recruits seriously hurt, and one of them wasn't likely to ever fully recover. The worst case was in 1043, though. A recruit had suddenly dropped dead during a simple training run back on T4. They'd only gone a klick or so when bam, he was gone. He was rushed to sickbay within minutes, but the docs couldn't bring him back.

Captain Jericho finally finished, and Gunny de Gruit took over. The gunny was the TDI in charge of combined arms training, and he went over the first evolution for the umpteenth time.

We know, we know, Ryck thought, careful to keep an expression of rapt attention on his face, though. Let's get this thing going!

It really was a simple evolution. Each squad would move on line up the range, firing at targets as they popped up. Supporting fires would precede them, walking them up to the objective, which was a trenchline about a klick away. Once they reached the trenchline, the exercise would cease, and they would march back in a column to the starting line.

There were two platoons doing the exercise, and 1044 would go second, so Ryck settled in for a long wait for his squad's turn. The first squad to go was lined up, their armor shifting to the red of live-fire training. For this evolution, the recruit squad leader didn't give any orders. A TDI took over that, standing in the center of the squad line, and two other TDIs followed on either flank. Their skins and bones were adjusted to the bright green of their usual identifying colors, making them stand out against the recruits.

Training Drill Instructor de Gruit gave the OK, and the squad hesitantly stepped off. Within moments, the impacts of the 60mm mortars were visible, 100 meters downrange. The mortars' ECR[15] could be adjusted from 10-60 meters. When the recruits had been introduced to the rounds, boxes had been set up on the range, and a TDI casually sauntered to within about 15 meters from the closest of the boxes. He turned to look back at the expectant recruits as the mortars were fired. Three rounds landed spot-on in the middle of the assembled boxes, and they were totally destroyed. The TDI was untouched, and he just as casually sauntered back to the bleachers. The recruits were taught that the mortars sent out a blanket of poly-matrix darts with the darts disintegrating to dust at a set range, but it was a relief to see this actually work in a real-life demonstration.

Despite knowing this, several of the recruits in 1045's First Squad faltered as the mortars landed. Ryck could sympathize with them—he'd even flinched sitting in the stands another 50 meters

---

[15] ECR: Effective Casualty Radius. This is the radius at which a projected 50% of those within the radius would suffer from the round's impact and detonation.

back, but he knew they deserved the hell the TDIs dropped on them. One lesson drilled into them over and over was that with combined arms, it was vital to keep in formation. Even when individual infantry positions could be monitored by the arty or mortar sections, a mortar round took some time to impact, and moving out of an expected formation could be dangerous.

In combat, things tended to be more fluid, but in training, it was safety, safety, safety. The envelope would be pushed, especially in Phase 5, so the staff worked to minimize casualties in the earlier phases. Too many dead recruits wouldn't make the bigwigs back in the Federation Council happy.

To the side of the range, a big M1 Davis had been sitting idle. It was in defilade, so the recruits could not really see much of the tank, but when it opened up with its 75 mm hypervelocity rail gun, the excitement level perceptibly rose in the bleachers. The firing report was rather subdued, more of a crack as the round exceeded Mach 5, but the explosion as the round impacted on a truck hulk was awe-inspiring. This was the first time any of the recruits had actually witness a tank firing.

"That's what I want to do," Wagons whispered beside him. "Armor is where it's at."

Quite a few of the recruits wanted to go armor, but they would have to prove themselves as infantry first. Those with the aptitude would be siphoned off, just as with other branches. With armor, though, there were size limitations. Larger Marines just need not apply.

The Davis fired only once, then the 81 and 120mm mortars and the 105 and 155 howitzers opened up while Marine air came streaking in, all while the squad moved forward. Several times, targets popped up, and the recruits opened fire. Their reports sounded like little pop guns in the midst of all the bigger explosions.

Finally, the recruits reached their objective. Flashing range lights indicated a cold range, and the squad was marched back. The recruits took their positions in the stands. Ryck could see they were pretty amped, but he couldn't just wander over to them and ask them how it had been.

The range staff and TDIs were going over the monitors, and it took them a good five minutes before the next squad was given the order to get in position. When the squad started moving, it was pretty much a repeat. They got on line, there were lots of explosions, and they reached the objective.

When the third squad made their run, the Davis' impact had faded. It had only been assigned one target, an old truck of some sort, and after hitting it twice, it was pretty much scrap. The hypervelocity round didn't have much to hit, and impacting on the ground was not half as spectacular as when the round hit a vehicle.

Fourth platoon's last squad offered something different in the routine, though, and not in a good way. They were about 500 meters downrange when the range lights flashed, sending the range cold. Ryck couldn't see what had happened. He was too far away for a direct view, and he was not in position to see the monitors, but one of the greenshirts came back escorting a recruit. They reached the stands, and one of Fourth Platoon's DIs, not the Lympstone TDIs, took over, leading the ashen-faced recruit off the range and back to the bivvie. Ryck didn't really know the recruit, but he knew he wouldn't want to be in his shoes, whatever he had done.

The TDI marched back out to the where the squad was still in a line. The whirling red lights changed to a steady green, and the loudspeakers announced a hot range.

Finally, it was 1044's turn. First Squad was ready, with Second on deck. When First stepped off, Third Squad left the bleachers to get its check. Ryck felt the excitement building as the TDI inspected each Marine, even tugging on every piece of bone. They were pretty foolproof, as far as Ryck could see, and he thought the degree of inspection was overkill. But it impressed upon him the fact that this really was a dangerous situation. If the TDIs were that cautious, maybe he should be, too.

Ryck was ready to go, but there was still quite a bit of standing around and waiting. First had to finish, which it eventually did, and Second had to take off. Third Squad moved into position, and they could finally see downrange again. They watched Second maneuver down the range, eventually reaching the objective before coming back. It had been a long day, but it was finally Third Squad's turn in the breach.

The TDIs accompanying the recruit squads had been alternating between two teams. Third Squad had Training Drill Instructor Hyunh as the squad leader and TDIs Papagana and Rose to assist him.

"Pay attention to me at all times," Hyunh told them once more. "You've seen everyone else go through. Now it's your turn, so let's get it done."

The lights turned to green, and Hyunh gave the "Move out" order.

With one step, Ryck was over the white line that was the boundary for the range. It was only half a meter, but it was a different world. One step back, and he was simply at Lympstone. One step forward, and he was in a live impact area, one in which death was falling from the sky.

"Keep it even," Hyunh intoned over the comms. "First team, you're lagging."

Ryck was aware of Training Drill Instructor Papagana moving First Team forward, but he was concentrating on his own movement. He focused on keeping his position, but still looking forward, expecting the impact of the 60's. Even though he was anticipating it, he jumped when the rounds landed. The explosions had to be closer than they were for the other squads! But nothing reached them.

"Keep moving," TDI Hyunh went on, his voice sounding calm and collected.

There was a crack as the tank round went zipping by to their right, but the 60's had grabbed their attention more. With the Davis round, there was a plume of dirt ahead at impact, and that was about it.

"First Team, you are still lagging. Get on line." Training Drill Instructor Hyunh said, his voice sounding a little harsher over the comms.

Ryck risked a quick glance to his left where First Team was moving. They had curved back a bit, and the green shirt with them was physically pushing someone—Tad, it looked like—to get him back in line with the rest. Making a quick glance to the right, he could see that Second Team was even with his own Third Team.

When the first of the 81s and the howitzer rounds impacted, Ryck could feel the concussion hitting his chest. His lungs actually compressed from the pressure waves. Clods of dirt followed the smoke into the air to come raining back down, a few clods reaching their line.

"Last warning, First Team. Get online or I'm going to shut this down," TDI Hyunh said.

Ryck wondered if he was chewing out the other TDI, the one with First. Of course, that would never be on the open circuit.

"Oh, fuck! Too far!" Ryck heard, not over the circuit, but through the air as Hyunh started running to the left, coming right behind him. Then, on the open circuit, "Get back, that's too far forward. Cease fire, cease fire! All hands freeze!"

Ryck stopped in his tracks. Training Drill Instructor Hyunh had shut down the range, and he was running to the left to pull back First Team. Ryck expected an explosion of shouting, whether that was to the TDI who was with First or to the recruits, he wasn't sure.

The explosion he did see was not what he expected. Even though a cease-fire had been called, there had been rounds in the air, and now they were impacting. The first couple were well ahead of them, as they had been so far. The third, though, was short, and it landed just in front of Mike Yount, who had stopped and was looking back at the TDI. Mike was violently blown forward, something that etched itself in Ryck's mind before the blast reached him as well. Ryck was knocked down, and he felt the impact of the shrapnel or darts from the big round pepper him.

Stunned, Ryck lay on the ground, vaguely aware of shouting through his ringing ears. He was sure he'd been killed. Hands grabbed him, turning him over.

"You OK?" one of the TDIs asked him.

Ryck looked at his left front, where he'd been hit. He didn't see anything major. He flexed his left arm. It worked.

"You're OK," the TDI told him before dashing off to someone else.

Ryck was surprised. Looking closer at his bones, he could see a few faint marks. The armor had saved him. He got to his feet, looking around to see if he could help. The range corpsman had already opened someone's armor and was working on him feverishly. From 20 meters away, the bright red blood stood out like a neon sign. Training Drill Instructor Rose stood over the corpsman, helmet off. It was only then that Ryck took in the bright green armor. It was Hyunh.

Ryck took a faltering step forward when King Tong rushed by, shouting, "Get back to the bleachers, Lysander."

Ryck took one more look around, wanting to help. It looked like there were five prone bodies, all of whom had people around them. Several recruits were slowly moving back. A TDI was rounding up all the rest of the recruits, those who were not injured, and sending them back in a column. Ryck turned to join them. The walk back to the bleachers seemed to take forever. Halfway back, a field ambulance blew past them, bringing more corpsmen to the scene. Finally, Ryck got back and was told to sit. Yet another corpsman checked him out, giving him the OK. Ryck was relieved, but as he looked back downrange, and the Stork that had landed to casevac those hurt, he realized that there, but for the Grace of God, could have been him.

The platoon had lost its first members.

Chapter 13

"Squad leaders, perform your EVA[16] checks" King Tong shouted out.

Ryck locked his weapon in the leg holster, a simple magnetic lock that kept the M99 out of the way while EVA, but readily available. The weapon could actually fire in the vacuum of open space, but there wouldn't be any soft targets at which to fire.

This was Ryck's third time as recruit squad leader. At T288, there were only seven days left until graduation, and Ryck was determined to keep the billet until the end. Of course, two of the remaining days were The Crucible, the final test of a recruit's mettle and worthiness to become a Marine. Ryck could easily lose the billet during that non-stop hell.

He snapped back to the job at hand. This was the final practical app for Phase Four, space training. The first part of the training phase had been conducted back at Camp Charles, in classrooms and mock-ups. For such a modern setting, the mock-ups had been surprisingly basic. There was a hulk of a section of a cargo ship on its side in the dirt, then a simple model of an airlock. The recruits "cycled" through the airlock, then "flew" through the space to the hulk to perform forced entry procedures. It had been a bit surreal, seemingly floating through "space" in the bright sunlight, then "floating weightlessly" through the hulk's corridors to rescue the ship's crew (four hopelessly degraded dummies). All of that has been done in the skins and bones as the EVA suits were too valuable to use on the ground at Camp Charles. Each recruit had practiced getting in and out of an EVA, of course, and operating the suits' systems, but that was with one of the three suits at the space training classroom.

---

[16] EVA: Extra-vehicular Activity

This final exercise was with the real thing, though. Marines would not be issued their own EVA suit unless they were assigned to a ship, so this was once more a bit of trying to make do with what was available. Recruit Dharma, a heavy-worlder in 1043, couldn't even get a suit within the safety parameters, so he wasn't going to participate. The suits would not be perfect fits, of course, but unlike the training events back on Tarawa's surface, a poorly fitting suit had more severe ramifications, and Dharma's shoulders were just too broad, and he was too short for any of the standard suits.

Ryck called up his four fire team leaders. When he'd first been a recruit squad leader, he'd had four fire teams then, too, but now, 1044's Fourth Squad had been merged with Third due to drops. Hodges and Wagons, from the old Fourth, were both fire team leaders, but the other two were No Initial and Raj from the old Third. Ryck was rather surprised that both Hodges and No Initial were still in the program, but he had to grudgingly give them their just due. Both had come along quite well, and if Ryck was to get fired again, he thought Hodges might actually get the nod as the new recruit squad leader.

"Have you completed the suit checks?' he asked them. All nodded back, so he continued, "Check each other, then I'll be doing my check in three."

Ryck knew that there would be no sabotage by the DIs on this evolution. The inherent danger was too great. But that made it all the more reason to have a thorough check before they went out. He was nervous, even if one of the DIs did re-inspect each recruit after he did his inspection.

There wasn't much room in the prep hold aboard the *Castor Wong*, the navy corvette assigned to the training. Ryck was forced too close to each recruit as he inspected them, but he just repeated the inspection checklist as a mantra, checking each and every step. The recruits had no live ammo, but he checked the dummies and blanks as if they were live. Each recruit looked good, although he had Carl Kingsman reseat his M99.

Usually, for this type of training evolution, it was only the TDIs who ran the show. This time, though, the platoon DIs, the series senior, and the series commander were there to assist as well.

Even Captain Petrov, the company commander, was there to observe. After Ryck conducted his inspection, no less than three others re-inspected the squad. King Tong was one of the inspectors, then one of the TDIs conducted another. Captain Terzey, the series commander, inspected them one final time.

The hold light went from red to amber. It was almost time. TDI Flores went over the procedure yet once more. Each squad would cycle out the lock, make the jump to the target ship, go through the forced entry (simulated, of course: the *Wilma Pritchard* was too valuable to actually blow holes in her), then conduct the movement to the bridge and rescue the hostages. There would be a safety officer at the *Wong's* airlock and another at the airlock on the *Pritchard.* A TDI would handle the debarkation of the *Wong*, another would run the jump, and yet one more would lead each squad during the assault phase.

Once the bridge was secured, the tactical phase would be over, and the squad would move to the forward airlock where they would cycle out, then take one of the EVA sleds back to the *Wong*. There were three types of sleds, and it would be basically first-come, first-served. Ryck wanted one of the single-man sleds, but with the graded part of the exercise completed, any sled should be a blast.

The *Castor Wong*, as a corvette, was not a huge vessel, so only one platoon was embarked at a time. The cycle for a platoon was about two-and-a-half hours, so while there was time to get everyone through in the course of the day, the schedule had to be kept. 1043 had already completed its training, and the other two platoons were still down at the spaceport waiting their turn.

Ryck wanted to get it over with. First Squad, though, was, as usual, first to go. At least with them gone, there was more room in the hold. The series senior took that opportunity to inspect the squad again. That made six total inspections.

The hold had ½ gravity, which made preparation and inspections easier than null grav. Even at ½ gravity, though, the suit was somewhat bulky, somewhat heavy, and quite uncomfortable. It would be better when they left the ship, Ryck knew. They had already spent one training day outside the *Wong*, tethered together, but enough to get the feel of weightlessness and maneuvering in it. But in the ship, the suit pulled down on the shoulders, hips, and knees. The fabric of the suit itself wasn't bad, and the helmet was surprisingly light, but the thruster pack and ammunition magazines pulled down and back. The suits could be worn in gravity, either on a planet or aboard a ship, but they were designed for weightlessness. On a planet though, at least the thruster pack could be dropped.

Second Squad, with its three fire teams, was next to go, and the hold became roomier still. He went to each fire team leader and went over the plan once again. This had to go without a hitch.

"You ready, Lysander?" King Tong asked as he came up.

"Yes, Drill Instructor Phantawisangtong, we're ready to kick some ass," Ryck replied.

"Don't worry too much about that. Just make sure no one does anything stupid," the DI told him.

The DIs were still DIs, and incentive training was still on the menu. But either the recruits were getting used to the harassment or the DIs were mellowing a bit. Even King Tong could act like an actual human being—at least at times.

The light finally changed to amber. They were up.

"Lock them up," the TDI told them.

Each recruit closed his face shield and pressurized his suit. Ryck could feel it puff out slightly as the air circulated. This created one more degree of insulation, but it also allowed sweat to be whisked away.

Before each recruit was allowed into the lock, one TDI and the safety officer conducted a final check of the integrity of each suit.

With 15 recruits, a TDI, two DIs, a navy operator, and a safety officer, the airlock was crowded. The inner lock closing had a degree of finality. Each recruit and Marine had to report by name to the Navy airlock operator that he was ready before the air was pumped out. The red airlock light turned to green, and the outer lock opened.

Outside the lock, four Marines in their bright green suits waited for them. Ryck recognized SDI Despiri through his face shield, but he couldn't make out the others. Thrusters were not to be initiated within the lock; each recruit stepped to the edge and pushed off with their legs. Still within the ship, gravity pulled them down. Looking out into to vastness of space, but still feeling a "down," Ryck had to steel himself to push off. His mind told him he was about to fall to his death. It wasn't until he cleared the lock and was in the weightlessness of open space that the vertigo disappeared.

"Form it up," a voice intoned over the comms.

The jump would be done with four teams in a column with Ryck behind the first one. Each group of red-suited recruits would be accompanied by a green-suited DI.

Ahead of them, about 300 meters away, was the *Wilma Pritchard*. Every recruit for the last 30 years, at least, had been aboard her. She was an old freighter that the Corps purchased for training. She stayed in a geosynchronous orbit, too fragile to make repeated landing and takeoffs. Each time she came in for her annual maintenance, people took bets on whether she would be deemed spaceworthy enough to take off again. Rumor had it that the Corps wanted to scrap her, but with anti-piracy as one of the Corps' primary missions, they had to keep her up and running. Aside from a few fast Gulfstreams for the brass to use to get around, she was the only real spaceship in the Marine's fleet. Many of the tactical aircraft could get into space of course, but not to travel across space to other solar systems.

With small jets of the thrusters, the recruits got into position. In front of Ryck, two recruits collided with each other, one spinning off a good 10 meters before he could stop himself and edge back. Without a real working display, Ryck couldn't tell who the two were, but he intended to have words with them when they got back.

Finally in place, the DI with First Fire Team signaled them with a simple arm signal to move out. Ryck followed in trace, careful to keep far enough back not to run into the team. He felt naked without having the tether that had kept them together and around the *Wong* the day before.

The thrusters had enough power to push Marines along at a healthy acceleration. There were rumors of lost Marines corpses traveling between the galaxies at close to the speed of light. Ryck doubted that there was enough fuel to accelerate to those speeds, but he didn't want to test that. Of course, being recruit training, the red training EVA suits had their thrusters modified to minimize their thrust. Any power, though, in weightlessness, had the mathematical capability to reach a high velocity. It would just take a recruit EVA suit much, much longer to reach such a speed.

Their point of entry on the *Wilma* was facing them. A green-suited DI was clearly visible in the bright, harsh light of Tarawa's sun. He seemed to grow larger as the recruits got closer.

The DI with First made the cutting motion at what was about half-way to the ship. They had been moving under low acceleration, but even with only 300 meters, they had to reverse that to slow down again. Ryck had no sensation, really, of motion, but when he followed suit and began to decelerate, he was "pushed forward" slightly against the front of his suit. It took a moment or two, but he could sense his approach was slowing. He gave the tiny jets on his heels a spurt, bringing him around, but he hoped he would stop just at the lock without having to use his legs to halt on the *Wilma's* skin.

Ryck had just come to a halt a meter or so from the ship when the open circuit blared with "Recruit Thomas, reverse your thrust. You are too hot!"

Grant Thomas was with Second Fire Team, one of the recruits originally with Third Squad. He was from Earth itself. Grant was one of the guys who was always just there, just part of the landscape. He didn't make waves for good or bad.

Ryck looked "up," or at least away from the *Wilma* and back toward the *Wong*. A recruit in red was coming at him, growing bigger as he approached. One of the DIs lunged forward, but the distance was too great and he missed the recruit. Ryck reached out to stop Grant, who was coming in way too fast. That wasn't the smartest thing to do in weightlessness. Grant hit Ryck, spinning him aside before the wayward recruit hit the side of the *Wilma*. He bounced off before being slammed back. A moment later, a DI reached him, manually turning off the thrusters at the feed valve.

In reality, Grant had probably been moving at less than a couple of kilometers an hour, certainly nothing extraordinary had he been down on Tarawa's surface. In space, though, that was too fast.

The comms crackled as the DIs and the safety officer asked for updates. After a quick check, the Di who had turned off the thrusters gave the OK, and the training was given the go-ahead. Grant was going to get his ass chewed but good, but open space was not the place for that.

The breaching chamber, or the "can opener," had been previously ferried over by 1042. At first glance, it looked like nothing more than a fat metal tube. What it had, though, was the capability to open up almost any ship that existed. Usually, it was put over the target ship's airlock, but it could force entry into the ship anywhere. Going through the airlock, though, would keep the target ship spaceworthy. Ship line owners, while they wanted pirated vessels recovered, wanted their ships to be able to still ply their routes without extensive time in the yards.

First Fire Team, led by No Initial, maneuvered the can opener over the airlock. The DIs drifted over to observe as it was put into position. Of course, there would be no breach of the *Wilma*. Once in final position, the breaching itself would be simulated with a TDI inside simply cycling through the *Wilma's* lock.

Ryck glanced back at the rest of the squad. The two remaining teams hung in space, ready to move forward and enter the ship. Something caught his eye, though, against the blackness of space. A small puff of vapor suddenly sprouted out from the waist of the recruit nearest to him. The puff started turning the recruit around. It was Grant. There was a breach in his suit. Small breaches from microdust were closed by the suit's internal repair nanos, but as Ryck watched, the breach opened wider, sending out more air.

The recruits were supposed to stay off the comms during the transit, keeping them clear for emergencies. Ryck figured this was an emergency. So did Grant.

"Help!" Grant screamed as he started spinning away.

His thrusters were far more powerful than the force of the escaping air, but he evidently didn't think of that. He was panicking as he was losing his oxygen. He actually still had air being fed into the suit faster than it was being expelled, but if the spreading rip got too big, he would have a catastrophic suit failure.

"Emergency, emergency!" Ryck shouted, not knowing what else to say.

Grant was slowly spinning now, moving away from the others. Ryck was the closest to him, so he turned himself around and blasted forward, colliding with Grant in a classic tackle. He wrapped his arms around Grant's waist, plastering his chest against the rip in Grant's suit. He pulled as tightly as he could. He had to get Grant inside a ship. The *Wilma* was not ready, and looking around Grant's waist, he could see that the *Wong's* forward airlock was not closed as it awaited the arrival of the previous squad on the sleds.

"Recruit Lysander to the captain of the *Wong*, keep your forward airlock open. I am returning with Recruit Thomas!" he shouted into his mic.

He ignored the blast of comms chatter as he tried to align the two of them on the *Wong*, then gave his thruster a blast.

He felt the thrust build up before it cut off. Had his thruster failed?

"Lysander, do not engage your thruster. Do you understand? Keep your hold on Thomas, but do not engage your thruster," King Tong's voice broke through the voices as his speaker switched to a direct circuit.

It was only then that Ryck became aware of three green-suited figures around him. He felt hands on him as the DIs took in the situation, probably discussing things on another circuit. Ryck had been cut off the open circuit. He just sat there, arms clamped around Grant, who had stopped moving. Ryck hoped he was OK.

Finally, King Tong's voice came back to him. "Recruit Lysander, listen carefully. We are going to tow you back to the Wong. No matter what happens, you keep squeezing Recruit Thomas just like you are doing. We've told him to be completely still. You do not let go until we tell you to. You got that?"

"Yes, drill instructor. I've got it."

With his face pressed up against Grant's waist, Ryck couldn't see much, but he felt his suit adjust as hands grabbed him. Within moments, he started to move. He squeezed harder on Grant, not wanting to lose his grip. At one point, Grant started to squirm, but he stopped suddenly. Ryck hoped that was because someone told him to stop and not that he had passed out—or worse.

It seemed like forever to him, but it was probably closer to two minutes before the DIs reversed thrust at the last moment, slamming them headfirst into the Wong's open airlock. The gravity hit them, and they fell to the deck. Ryck almost lost his grip.

The outer door closed behind them, and the air started rushing in. Sound from something outside his suit once again returned to Ryck.

"OK, Lysander, you can let go," a voice, a real voice, not over the comms, said as hands reached down to pull apart his arms.

Ryck let go and sat back, looking to where he had seen the breach in Grant's suit. It was larger than he had thought, a good 30 cms across. The suits were not supposed to fail like that, but these were old, ill-fitting suits. Hitting the side of the *Wilma* as hard as Grant had done must have started the failure, something beyond the old suit's nanos' ability to repair.

It took a few more moments for the air to cycle completely through and the inner door to open. Several Marines and a corpsman rushed in. Grant's helmet had already been popped, and he sat there, eyes wide in contained panic. He was breathing heavily.

Ryck popped his own helmet. He felt relief that Grant was OK. Up until that moment, adrenalin had been coursing through him. Now, it left his body, and he started trembling.

"So, Recruit Lysander, you were all set to order the captain of the *Wong* to keep the airlock open, then take your buddy back to the ship all by your lonesome? With me and the other DIs there at the scene?' King Tong asked, standing over him.

Ryck felt his heart fall. Had he screwed up again? Of course, the DIs were more capable of handling the situation than he was.

"I . . . uh, I guess I wasn't thinking. I just saw him and reacted," he stammered out, getting to his feet.

"That you did. Sometimes, though, reaction is the best action. You saw an emergency, then did something about it. Trying to take him back on your lonesome might have been a little much, but you did manage to limit the breach on Thomas' suit. If it had grown into a catastrophic failure before the rest of us got there, who knows what would have happened?"

"I didn't screw up?"

King Tong laughed, then said, "No, you didn't screw up. Hugging another recruit was an odd way of saving his sorry ass, but it worked. Good job, Ryck. Good fucking job."

Relief swept over him. He was glad that Grant was OK, of course, but he felt a twinge of guilt that he was happier that he was still a recruit squad leader. He hadn't been fired.

Chapter 14

Ten more steps. That's all. Just ten more steps.

Ryck had been reciting that mantra for the last hour, trying to fool his tired body that the Crucible was almost over. It wasn't true, and he knew it wasn't true, but it was the only way he knew to keep going.

He'd been pretty excited when DIs had rushed into the squadbay, throwing gas grenades almost 40 hours before. This was the start of the Crucible, where each recruit would finally be forged into a Marine. This was the culmination of over 290 days on Tarawa. Ryck was confident that he could not only survive, but excel. Nothing could stop him.

The first six hours had been brutal, but not one recruit had dropped. They had the pass/fail 25 km ruck run, the obstacle course, and over an hour of "motivational" PT. They had done all of this before during training. The only difference was that this was with the entire company. It had actually felt invigorating being out there on the grinder, doing flutter kicks, push-ups, good morning darlings, and squat thrusts with close to 500 other recruits. The run was not as fun. Being toward the rear of the company for the first half of the run, they had mercilessly accordioned, slowing down almost to stop at times only to have to then sprint to catch up. At least after the half-way point, they had switched the order of march, and the lead series was in the rear. For something that had loomed over their heads, though, since T1, it was a relief to have it over, with not one 1044 recruit dropping out.

Immediately after the run came the "Road to Heaven." During the last week of training, the recruits were run through events taken from all the 46 extant corps that had been combined to form the Federation Marine Corps. The Road to Heaven came courtesy of the Republic of China Marine Corps. The recruits stripped down to their skivvies, then belly-crawled, rolled, and performed maneuvers to get down 50 meters of jumbled lava rock, all the time screaming "I fear no pain!" No one dropped, but the cuts on their bodies stung with sweat, something that would only get worse as the Crucible continued.

After that welcome-to-the-Crucible, they had broken back into platoons to go tactical. Storks had lifted them to the mountain training area on the other side of the valley where they were given a patrol mission. The patrol went up and down the almost impassible terrain. That was bad enough, but the cold was unrelenting. It was here that 1044 had their first drop. Garret Shin had sat down in the snow during a five-minute break and simply didn't get back up. He was whisked away by two of the DIs. No one knew if he DOR'd or was suffering from a cold-related injury. So close to the end, no one wanted to pry into it, the old superstition about knowing too much kicking in. The recruits studiously ignored what had taken place.

By morning, they had reached their objective. But no Storks would be taking them to their final destination. It was a 65 km march down the mountains and across the valley to Camp Prettyjohn and Mount Motherfucker. Camp Prettyjohn, named for a British Royal Marine hero, was a restricted base for special operations training. The recruits had never been taken there, but Mount Motherfucker was in full view of Camp Charles, hanging over them like their own version of hell. It wasn't so much its appearance, but rather its reputation. Rising up almost a thousand meters above the valley floor, it actually seemed innocuous, almost serene. But each recruit knew that he had to make it to the summit with his weapon and full kit. Ryck had often gazed at the mountain while at Charles, thinking he could run up it. But that was without being up for two days during the Crucible and after a 65 km hump to the base.

The hump itself had been a bitch. They had to move tactically, making two river crossings during the route. Several times, they had been ambushed by other DIs, getting gassed in the process. After the last ambush, three of the recruits had been "killed," forcing the rest to carry not only them, but their gear as well.

Ryck barely noticed as they entered Prettyjohn. He had often wondered what the snake-eaters did there, but as they passed through the gate, he was too tired to care. He knew he should be urging the recruits in the squad on, but with half of Duc's gear in his pack, Duc being one of the "dead" recruits, he had turned inward just to keep going.

At the base of Mount Motherfucker, he might as well have been looking up Mount Ascent back on Prophesy. The treeless mountain would have offered a stunning vista of the valley and Camp Charles 10 kilometers or so to the south, but that would be if they had time to sit and take in the view. The dirt path leading up was fairly even, but the operational word was "up." Ryck managed one "let's keep it tight" before he just leaned forward, trying to keep himself moving.

Tradition had it that there had been a "Mount Motherfucker" since the early Marines on Earth, something the brass liked so much that on the Federated Marines' first base on New Beginnings, they had searched for one there. This was going to be the United States Marines' contribution to the final week. When they had again moved to Tarawa, this current mountain was chosen to carry on the tradition. It had seemed more uplifting when they had first heard of the tradition. Humping up it, Ryck probably joined thousands and thousands of Marine recruits who had wished that this was one tradition that would have died before they ever got to boot camp.

At about 200 meters up, Duc quietly slipped out of the makeshift stretcher being carried by No Initial and Petir Borisovitch, letting John Emerson get on. John's feet were mangled with huge blisters, but at the last stop, he'd just jammed his bloody feet back into his boots, refusing to let the corpsman see them. The DIs had to have noticed the switch, but not one took issue with it.

Ryck was vaguely aware of another platoon marching up the mountain on an adjoining trail, but he was focused on his own mission. He had to will one foot being put in front of the other. When he bumped into the recruit in front of him, it took him a moment to realize that he wasn't moving.

Hodges was in front of him, bent over at the waist, hands on his knees. His weapon dangled, the butt in the dirt, but the sling still in his hands.

Ryck straightened up, catching his breath. They were moving up the trail in a column of twos, all pretense at tactical dispersion gone. To his right, Seth MacPruit was doggedly marching. A hand was attached to Seth's ruck—the recruit was pulling Ham Ceres, the very guy who had arranged for Seth's beasting in the showers not so long ago. Seth was still an asshole, but he had come around. If he could do that, then so could Ryck.

"Come on, Terry," he told Hodges. "Just a little more. Grab my ruck and let me pull you."

He moved past the recruit and felt the tug as Hodges grabbed the "dead man's strap" on the side of Ryck's ruck.

Ten more steps. That's all. Just ten more steps.

Then suddenly it really was only ten more steps. They crested a ridge, and there, lining the dirt path, were the company's DIs and officers. Behind them were a number of the TDIs. Ryck was confused for a moment, but as he passed Captain Petrov, the officer slapped him on the back with a "Good job, Marine."

It took a moment for that to sink in. "Marine?"

It wasn't a mistake, though. Each Marine on the top of the mountain greeted them, saying the same thing. They had made it. They were Marines!

Several corpsmen were up there as well, and they quickly took those who needed help from the arms of those who had carried them up the hill. 1043 was already there, along with 1039 from the lead platoon. Most of them were on their butts with their rucks off, but they shouted out their greetings. 1044 was not the first to finish, but it wasn't the last, either.

"Keep your heads up!" Ryck told the others as they moved to their staging area.

He wanted nothing more than to flop down on the ground, but he was going to keep it strong until the end. They reached the small 1044 sign that indicated their staging area, and Ryck managed to keep on his feet until each recruit—each *Marine*, that was—sat down. He checked them for water before he eased down himself. He didn't think he would ever get up again.

When 1045 marched up, he surprised himself, though. Led by their platoon guide, Joshua Hope-is-Life, he couldn't help himself. He jumped up and ran to embrace his friend.

"Hey, Marine," Ryck said, "you grubbing son-of-a-bitch. We made it!"

Chapter 15

Ryck held his eyes high as the colonel gave his speech. He'd never even seen the man before. He didn't really give him much thought. Boot camp consisted of his fellow recruits, the DIs, the TDIs, even some of the officers. Out of the corner of his eyes, he could just make out the colonel, up on the podium in his dress blues.

In front of him, though, was the contingent from Eltsworld. Not many family members had come to graduation, but at least fifty Eltsworlders had made the trip in a private ship, and they made quite an impression in their minton-robes and head coverings, the colors changing with each movement or shift of the breeze. They comprised the extended family of Dhakwan Nagi, "Duckman," from 1045. Since their arrival the day before, rumors had started swirling about Duckman, that he was some sort royal prince, out to prove his courage as a warrior before going back to take over the government.

Ryck would have loved for Lysa to come, but with a new baby, and more importantly, with the cost of a ticket, it just didn't make much sense. It didn't matter, though. What mattered was that he had made it. In two more days, he was shipping off to his first duty station, The Third Marine Division at Camp Kolesnikov on Alexander. He would have to attend the 12-week IUT, Initial Unit Training, there before getting to his unit, but it would be as a Marine, not as a recruit.

". . . and so, I am proud to be sending you to where your Marine Corps career will take you. I know you will make me proud, you will make the Corps proud, but more importantly, you will make yourself proud. From our forefathers, *Per Terra et Mare, Per Mare, Per Terram, Qua Patet Orbis, and Semper Fidelis*. And from the here and now, *Audaces Fortuna Iuvat*, Marines."

"Captain Petrov, you may dismiss your Marines," the colonel told the company commander.

The company commander saluted, did an about-face, then called forward the first sergeant and turned over the company to him. He took a step back, did an about-face, and marched off, the other officers following him as the seniors replaced them.

Ryck could feel the excitement build in him. He waited eagerly for the seniors to get the command. Staff Sergeant Despiri received the order, did an about-face, and stared at the new Marines for a moment.

"Platoon 1044, dismissed!" he barked out.

"Aye-aye!" they yelled out in chorus, taking one step back before performing an about-face.

The band kicked in as the platoon erupted into cheers. Ryck pounded the back of Shaymall, who as the platoon guide, sported the single stripe of a Private First Class on his sleeve.

"We did it!" he shouted as he was pulled off Shaymall and bear-hugged by No Initial. The next few minutes were a scrum of hugs, arm punches, and back-pounding. These were his brothers, the men with whom he'd accomplished the toughest challenge of this life. He couldn't have made it without them, and he knew they had needed him. Hodges, No Initial, Duc, Wagons, Ham, Mac, even MacPruit, they were all family. They were all going their separate ways, but this was a watershed moment that none would forget.

The platoons started breaking up, a few Marines going into the stands to greet family, others seeking friends in other platoons. Ryck started to wander over to 1045, but Joshua met him halfway. They gripped arms, Roman style, before pulling each other in for another bear hug.

"Congratulations, Marine," they said in unison.

"Well, you glad we went Marines instead of the Legion?" Ryck asked.

"Damn right, I am. You?"

"Nothing but the best, and fuck the rest," Ryck responded with a laugh. "When you taking off?"

"Tonight, 2200," Joshua told him.

"Wish I could go," Ryck said.

Joshua's parents had sent a ticket for him to go back home for graduation leave. Joshua would be spending two uncharged weeks back there before reporting to First Marine Division right back here on Tarawa. Ryck could have taken the same leave, but he really didn't have the money to spend on the ticket, and even if he went back to Prophesy, he didn't have a home there. He could stay with Lysa and her family, but with little Kylee there now, he didn't want to intrude.

"I'll be stopping by and seeing your sis and niece, bro. Tell them all what a bad-ass you are."

"Me a bad-ass? What about you?" Ryck asked, pointing at the PFC stripes Joshua had earned as the 1045 guide.

"Ah, I jus' fooled them but good. Act like you know what you be doing, and they all believe it. 'Sides, we all know what you did up there on the *Wong.*"

"Well, yeah, I guess."

They both stood there for a moment, not knowing what to say.

"Hey, Ryck! You coming?" Ham shouted out. Most of the platoon was going to go out in town to sample the infamous nightlife and probably get stinking drunk, and the new Marines were drifting back to the squad bay.

"Yeah, give me a sec, OK?"

"Well, I'll be seeing you. Keep in touch, brother," he told Joshua.

"Yeah, you too. Fair winds and following seas and all of that."

They shook hands, then turned to join their platoon mates.

Ryck picked up his pace. He was going to tie one on, and one of those bastards was going to buy him the first round!

THIRD MARINE DIVISION
EMBARKED ON THE FSS ADELAIDE

Chapter 16

"Ready to get off this motherfucker?" Sparta asked him.

"Right skippy, there, corporal. Let's diddi ho," Private First Class Ryck Lysander responded.

Ryck was still the platoon boot, but taking out two of the miners had given him a degree of credibility. He'd been tested and blooded. Once the insurrection had been put down (not that they were allowed to use the "I" word), the lieutenant had even put him in for a meritorious promotion to PFC. He would have made it anyway in another month and a half, but this gave him a leg up on most of the rest of his recruit class. More than the stripe, though, when it came time to assign him to a squad, Sergeant Piccalo-Tensing had fought for him. He joined Corporal Pallas' fire team, which was down a man with Corporal Singh casevac'd back to the Dirtball. It felt good to Ryck to belong to a unit instead of being just an add-on.

The platoon had taken a heavy hit. Four of the Marines in Second Squad had been opened up like a can of sardines by the miners and killed. Three Marines had been injured enough while clearing the mine to warrant being casevac'd. This was supposed to have been a cakewalk, but that was before someone at UTOM Industries, the company that performed maintenance of the PICS, had both interjected a trojan in the electronics, then sold the information on how to exploit that breach to the miners. A patch had already been installed on the suits, and NIS was supposedly hot on the trail of tracking down the traitor. The scuttlebutt was that the breach was a pretty simple one, but one that could not have been implanted in the Legion's Rigaudeau-3 suits. Underlying the fuck-up was the knowledge that the Marines had gotten off easy. They did not need the PICS to suppress a tax revolt on a piddly-ass mining planet like Atacama. If the suits had been neutralized while in combat with a real opponent, however, it might have been a disaster of epic proportions.

The issue with the suits, though, had kept the Marines on Atacama longer than usual while the vulnerability was investigated. By Federation charter, the Marines were not allowed to remain on a "peaceful" world while in a combat posture. In other words, they were not occupation nor police troops. They had a limited amount of time to consolidate, then leave the planet to the Federation Civil Development Corps.[17] The FCDC was there to "assist in the restoration of civil order and commerce," but they had an awful lot of military gear and men to use it all for a supposed bunch of engineers and economists. With the security breach, though, the Council had extended the timeline of the campaign for an extra 45 days.

With the bulk of the FCDC kept off the planet, the Marines had taken over most of the processing of the civilians. This was something the Marines didn't like to do, and they lacked the manpower to do it well. Certain FCDC teams were assigned to the Marines and even given Marine uniforms, so at least the interrogation of the leaders of the revolt was left to someone else. Ryck had watched four of these fake Marines march into the internment camp while he was on watch and drag off one of the women there. Ryck had no love lost for the miners, but he didn't want to think of what would happen to that woman. It was her own fault, wasn't it? Refusing to pay the taxes to the Federation, the same Federation that paid for the Navy, the Marines, and the FCDC to protect them? The Federation was the strongest power in the

---

[17] Federation Civil Development Corps: The FCDC is the federation's answer to a land Army. Heavily armed and outfitted, it is not technically a military which gives the Federation more leeway in its deployment.

known galaxy, but still, there were threats, both from the other non-aligned planets and groups as well as conflicts between planets within the Federation's sphere.

All of that was way above Ryck's pay grade. What he did know was that he hadn't joined the Corps to be a prison guard. The eight weeks he'd spent being just that had been more than enough. At least he wasn't the junior man in the platoon anymore, even if he was still the boot, although the reason for that was not what he would have wished. Two Marines in Third Fire Team, LCpls Verrit and Samuelson had been caught fucking one of the detainees. There was no indication that this was anything other than consensual, so there was no court convened for rape, but contact like that was strictly verboten, and both men had been busted to private and would serve 30 days in the brig after they returned to the Dirtball. Ryck had talked to Sams about it, and the big guy had smiled and said it was totally worth it, even with the brig time and getting busted.

Now, finally, it was time to leave. All their gear had already been embarked, and with the FCDC personnel on deck, they were free to leave for the trip back to the Dirtball. Rumor had it that they were getting a diversion to Vegas for three days liberty, but the brass refused to confirm that. Like most Marines, Ryck had been on Vegas on the way to Tarawa for boot, but he had never gotten out of the spaceport.

Ryck shouldered his ruck and filed after Sparta. He didn't look back as he entered the *Adelaide's* personnel hatch.

Chapter 17

"You are one sick mother," Sams said as he sat down, looking at Ryck's breakfast.

"Eat me," came Ryck's rote reply.

Food aboard the *Adelaide* was pretty damn good, even for a farmboy such as Ryck who was used to a degree of "real" food. Sure, his family had a home fabricator, and sure, they bought manufactured food, but being on a farm and surrounded by other farmers, Ryck had often eaten natural food, even meats. While some of the other Marines, mostly from the big industrialized worlds, blanched at the thought of eating animal flesh, to Ryck, it was a special treat. He thought those who said animal flesh was not "normal" were pretty weird, given that some of the bases for the fabricators came from pulverized insects, coal by-products, or other things best not imagined.

The Navy being the Navy, the *Adelaide* had one hellacious commercial fabricator. It shouldn't have made a difference as the bases were all the same and a fabricator followed set formulas, but the senior chief in charge of the mess could whip up some tasty chow, better than a grunt could expect. It was common knowledge that the officers got some natural foods in their mess, but Ryck didn't care. The crew's mess was plenty fine. Even the bacon he was eating tasted natural. Ryck knew that it was made from a mixture of some of the twelve bases that fed the fabricator, but when he ate it, it seemed like the real deal to him. Sams wasn't commenting on that, but with what Ryck had covered it.

As a young boy, bacon had been Ryck's favorite food—real bacon, not the fake bacon made by Sunshine or Healthy Choice. On each birthday, that was what he wanted. That and ice cream. Fab ice cream was pretty indistinguishable from hand-cranked ice-cream made from cow's cream, even if the luxury brands such as

Swiss Heaven or Ben and Jerry's tried to convince people otherwise. Their little home fabricator could do a pretty decent job on sweet sauces, too, such as chocolate and strawberry. Ryck, though, loved the raspberry sauce, and he lathered it over his ice cream. On his seventh birthday, he had jokingly said he was going to put the sauce on his bacon. All his family had laughed at that, telling him that was silly. Ryck had meant it as a joke, but their reaction raised a degree of stubbornness in him. They couldn't tell him he was silly. So, he insisted on it. His mother had given in, and with ten slices of sizzling bacon on his plate, had hesitantly dribbled the raspberry sauce on it.

"More," he had insisted.

His parents, Myke, and Lysa watched him as he defiantly raised a forkful of raspberry-covered bacon to his mouth and put it in his mouth. He had thought he would have to choke it down, doing it just to show his family that he was not some little kid, but to his surprise, he actually liked it. Now, aboard the Navy ship where fab bacon was offered at each breakfast and he could dial fab raspberry sauce from the dessert line anytime he wanted, this had become his daily ritual.

"Really, man, why do you always do that? That and your ketchup and polly sauce shit you put on stuff?" Sams persisted.

Ryck just raised his middle finger in response.

Life aboard the *Adelaide* was an odd confluence of relaxation, stimulation, and boredom. There really wasn't that much for Marines to do. They had cleaned and re-cleaned all their gear. They had taken care of some admin. The little "gym" on the ship was not much and large enough for only a handful of people at a time. On the plus side, the ship's entertainment system was immense, with what had to be every flick, song, book, and vid ever recorded. They couldn't communicate with the outside while in bubble space (unless a message torp was sent to pierce their bubble, and that was done only for extremely high-priority communications), so camming family or friends was out until they dropped back into real space, but still, there was more available to watch than anyone could view in their lifetime. The food was great, and there was plenty of rack time. It should have been a Marine's dream, but in reality, after a day or two, most Marines became antsy. They wanted to do something, not just be cargo.

Sams sat down and dug into his pancakes. He made exaggerated eating sounds, smacking his lips.

"Enjoy it now, Sams, 'cause you ain't getting any of that when your ass is locked up in the brig," T-Rex told him.

T-Rex was Lance Corporal Sylvester Harrington Smith Pulaski. He was an immensely strong Marine, with broad shoulders that had to give the armorers nervous breakdowns when it came to fitting him. He had essentially no neck and seemingly little short arms, hence the "T-Rex" nickname. He was also about the smartest Marine Ryck had met, with a broad knowledge on just about everything. He spoke as if he was barely educated, but that didn't fool anyone.

"Don't need food there. I'll have my memories of the lovely Miss Sorada to fulfill me," Sams said dramatically, his voice pitched higher than normal.

"Hope she was really worth it, when we all are out on the ville, getting some," T-Rex replied.

"Oh, she was, she was. Better than any D-town ho, that's for sure."

That brought a round of laughter. Ryck was glad he wasn't facing the same fate as Sams, but still, there was a degree of envy in him. Getting laid while on a mission had a certain swashbuckling flair, something to tell the other grandpaps as they sat around the retirement home years from now.

Ryck took another bite of his bacon, looking around at the other Marines. He'd been with the unit only a short time, but somehow, it seemed longer. He felt like he fit in, as if this life was made for him. This was a long way from the dusty fields of Prophesy, but sitting in the crew's mess, light-years from the farm, it seemed as if it was destined. He felt more at home than in the house where he'd been raised.

Not completely at home, though. Two sailors took their trays to the next table and sat down, their connectors clearly visible on the backs of their shaved heads. Unlike the other sailors, navigators, as these two were, and gunners never wore covers. The interfaces they needed to connect to the cybercomps that kept the ship's bubble whole and the ship on course, or in the case of the gunners, that enabled them to control the ship's weapons systems, were surgically implanted into their brains through the back of their skulls. The "cybos" generally kept to themselves, an elite among the rest of the crew. They gave Ryck the creeps, though. The Marines also used biofaces, of course, but theirs were patches that were placed on the skin, not drilled through the skull.

Ryck tore his gaze off of their heads and speared his last piece of bacon, mushing it around his plate to mop up the last of his sauce. He popped it in his mouth and contemplated going back for another serving. There was nothing to stop him, nor would anyone even care, but he decided against it as a show of inner discipline.

Sergeant Piccalo-Tensing entered the mess decks, spied the Marines, and made a beeline to them.

"Shit, what's PT got for us now?" Wan asked, quickly pushing more of his food into his mouth as if afraid he wouldn't get the chance to finish.

"What's up, Sergeant?" Pallas asked.

Corporal Pallas and Sergeant Piccalo-Tensing were both NCOs, but Pallas seemed more at home with the non-rates. There seemed to be an underlying tension between the two men that Ryck didn't understand.

"Word just came out, and I thought I would pass it to you. We're dropping out of bubble space at 1400. At 1800, liberty is being called. Vegas."

There was a moment of silence before whoops of joy rang out, not just from the Marines, but from the sailors who had been sitting within earshot. Vegas! Some Marines might go through an entire enlistment without getting to any of the fabled four liberty ports of Vegas, Kukson, Ramp it Up, or Pattaya.

"Liberty brief will be at 1700 in the chapel. And there will be an inspection. No raggedly ass Marines will be allowed off the ship," the squad leader said before turning around and leaving.

"My fucking grandmother! Vegas!" one of the sailors said.

Ryck didn't quite understand the reference of that, but he understood the tone of the sailor's comment.

"Vegas! This is going to be epic!" Sams said.

"What do you mean, there, brig rat?" T-Rex asked.

"No, no, I've got my brig time back on the Dirtball!" Sams protested.

"You sure? Seems to me you're not in the brig now because this ship doesn't have one. I think you're restricted to the ship," Corporal Pallas told him.

"No fucking way! I gotta go see England," Sams said, jumping up, half-eaten breakfast still covering his tray.

He jammed the tray into the galley window and rushed off to see the staff sergeant, almost at the run.

"They really going to keep him on the ship?" Wan asked.

"Nah, they won't, but it's good to yank his chain. He's been bragging about nailing that miner so much, he needed to be taken down a notch," T-Rex told him.

"That said," Corporal Pallas added, "your civvies really need to pass muster for a place like Vegas. I don't know about you all, but I didn't expect this, and I think I might need to hit the ship's store for something better than my ripped t-shirt."

Even on a combat mission, Marines always traveled with at least one set of civvies. Ryck's were brand new, so he thought they would be fine. It wouldn't hurt to check them, though. No way he wanted to be delayed in getting off the ship.

Vegas!

Chapter 18

"You're really trolling for more brig time, aren't you?" Pallas asked Sams as the private showed off the new tattoo on his upper arm, a Star, Globe, and Anchor with "Third Marine Division" written below it.

Ryck took another swig of his Bud while he examined Sams' bodywork. Tattoos were against Marine regs. It has something to do with how tattoos could affect both regen and how biosensors monitored the body's readings. There was no such restriction in the Navy, and many Marines got them when they left the service, but active-duty Marines were required to keep their bodies clean. No tats, no genmods.

"Ah, that's the beauty of this. Look!" Sams said while flexing his biceps.

He reached across with his left hand and pushed at something. To Ryck's surprise, the tattoo disappeared. That caught his interest.

He leaned closer to look and asked, "How did you do that?"

Wan, Pallas, Hu, T-Rex, and Smitty leaned forward, too, Hu knocking over his Slicer Lite to spill on the peanut covered floor of the bar.

"Alcohol abuse!" was shouted out by the rest of them in unison, as was expected, but their attention was on Sams as he did something else with his left hand that caused the tattoo to re-appear.

"It ain't a tattoo. Me and Aesop here," he started, tilting his head back on the lance corporal who'd come in with him, "saw this place over on Sahara, by the Poseidon Club, and we went in. This is what they call a 'refractive body art,' or some bullshit. It has to do with light waves and such, and when I touch this point here," he said, indicating a small point at the top of the anchor, "it polarizes so it goes stealth-like."

He pushed the spot, and the tattoo disappeared again. Corporal Pallas grabbed the bigger Marine by the arm and pulled him closer so he could see the arm better. He ran a finger over the spot where the tattoo had been visible only a few seconds before.

"No shit!" Hu said, reaching out to touch Sams' arm as well.

"I don't know," T-Rex said. "It looks like a tattoo, and I bet the first sergeant's going to have your ass over it."

"It's not a tattoo," Aesop said. "They had it all explained. This is brand-new techno."

"So, where's yours if it ain't a tat?" T-Rex asked him.

"Well, they said it wasn't a tattoo, but like you said, you think the first sergeant's going to buy that? I've got seven more months in this green machine, and I'm getting out with the stripes on my sleeves. I need my VSEB[18] if I'm going to go to school."

"Chicken shit excuse if you ask me. You're out with your liberty buddy, and you let him do that if you think it might be illegal? Sams might be a busted-down private, but all that means is you still outrank him," Pallas reminded him.

Marines and sailors were not allowed to wander alone while on ship's liberty. Vegas was a safe haven—other than losing your money, not much else would happen as the police kept a pretty tight lock on the tourist spots on the planet. Almost "anything goes" in Vegas, but the police kept violent crimes at a minimum. They wanted tourists to come back again and spend more. It was common knowledge that for a place such as Vegas, the liberty buddy concept was more there to protect Vegas from Marines and sailors than the other way around.

The two newcomers grabbed seats as Sams ordered another round for everyone. Hu, Sams, and Wan continued to discuss the regulatory ramifications of Sams' "refractive body art." Hu was debating on getting one himself. Pallas and T-Rex were discussing the GFL and the upcoming season. Smitty, getting deeper into his

---

[18] VSEB: Veterans Service Educational Benefits—payments made to approved schools for veterans who were received Honorable Discharges.

cups, was softly singing to himself. Ryck just leaned back to watch the dancers on the stage. To say they were hot was an understatement, and Ryck had been socially and physically celibate since leaving Prophesy. The tall redhead on the left was particularly stunning. Like all the rest, she had on bikini bottoms made with the same flashing LED fabric as Lysa used to wear while "working," but while he hated Lysa wearing the fabric, on this undulating goddess, it seemed pretty natural. Of course, he rather liked the rest of her body better where nothing was left to the imagination. What he was able to imagine was what he would like to be doing with her.

"I see you enjoy what a woman can offer," a soft voice said in his ear, startling him out of his reverie.

He looked back to where a blue woman was standing. Blue skin and yellow hair. Very little clothing.

"May I sit down?" she asked.

"Uh, uh, sure," Ryck stammered out, pulling a chair from the next table to beside him.

"Your buddies seem to be interested in other things," she said, pointing a long blue finger at them.

They might have been discussing other things a moment before, but as she sat, she had all of their undivided attention. When she smiled at them, her teeth dazzling white, before putting one hand on Ryck's arm and turning her body to face him, they shrugged and went back to what they had been doing, even if glances kept being shot her way.

"So, what's your name?" she asked Ryck.

"Private First Class Ryck Lysander," he told her.

She leaned her head up and gave a trill of musical laughter. "So, your mother named you 'Private First Class'?"

"No, no. My mother and father named me Ryck. I'm a private first class in the Marines."

"OK, Private First Class Ryck Lysander, sorry for teasing you like that. It is just that you are so cute!"

She put her hand back lightly on his arm. It was barely touching him, but he was extremely conscious of it.

Ryck stared at her hand for a moment, then followed the arm up to the rest of her. She was blue, all right. That was her skin color, not some tight-fitting clothing. She was a deep, almost incandescent blue. Her hair was bright yellow, and her eyes seemed to glow with the same shade as her hair. She had on a small v-neck halter and nancishorts, both the same shade of blue as her skin, but with the lights in the bar, it was hard to tell where fabric left off and skin began. Ryck thought back to his Grand Lit class back at school. They had spent a week on comic books, anime, and shorts, and one of the comics had been an old 20th Century volume of X-Men. This woman reminded him of one of the characters in that comic named Mystique. She didn't quite look like what he remembered of the fictional character, but the blue skin color trumped other aspects of their respective appearances. He wanted to ask of her skin was a genmod, or if it was superficial. He knew he shouldn't stare, but she didn't seem to mind his attention.

"Are you enjoying Vegas?" she asked.

"Uh, yeah, sure. It's great. We've only been here a few hours, though. We're on the . . ." he started, then realized that he shouldn't be talking about military details.

"You're on the *Adelaide*, and you are just back from Atacama where they had a tax revolt. Yes, we know all about the comings and goings of ships here in Vegas," she said as her face broke out in a dazzling smile.

That took Ryck by surprise. Was she grilling him on military secrets? He glanced back at the others. Corporal Pallas was sitting on the other side of him, and the NCO seemed to have heard her, because he was looking back at Ryck, a smile on his face. He lifted up his bottle of Bud in a mock salute to Ryck, then turned back. The lack of security awareness seemed weird to him, but if Sparta didn't think much about it, it had to be OK.

"By the way, I'm Purety," she said, offering her hand.

"Uh, hi, Purety."

There were a few chortles from the others and one sarcastic-sounding "smooth move, there." The other Marines had given him the field of battle, but they still had the two of them under reconnaissance.

"So, you boys have been deployed for a while with nothing to do. Saved up all your pay, right?" she asked him.

"Yeah, you've got that right. Nothing we could spend it on there. But Vegas, you know, this place can suck it out of you. I've already contributed to your economy on the blackjack tables," he said, trying to be funny.

He didn't quite get the reaction he'd expected.

"Lost it already? Everything?" she said, pulling back ever-so-slightly.

"Oh no, nothing like that," he said hurriedly. "It wasn't much. I've got most of it here," he added, patting his back pocket and wallet.

Seemingly mollified, she leaned back into him, took his arm, and said, "Good. There are better things to do with your money. Much better."

As she said the second "better,' she leaned even farther forward, pushing her left breast up against his arm.

Ryck wasn't naive. He hadn't needed the liberty brief where the sailors and Marines had been warned that while prostitution was legal on Vegas—as it was throughout the Federation with a few exceptions, as a matter of civil rights—it tended to be a very costly proposition. There would be no pay advances for anyone who spent all of his money, so making sure it stretched out for the entire four-day liberty was up to each individual.

Still, it had been a long time, and she was a very sexy woman. Her blue skin added to the attraction. It seemed more appropriate, somehow, that if he was going to enjoy the company of a working girl in Vegas, she should be rather unique, and Purety certainly fit that bill. He hadn't planned on doing anything other than drinking and gambling, maybe taking in a show. But sitting next to Purety, he felt his resolve begin to falter. This was Vegas, after all, with their hundreds-of-years-old motto of "What Happens in Vegas, Stays in Vegas."

She scooted a little closer, this time pressing her leg up against his. Her leg was bare, but he had on full Dekes. Still, the heavy fabric of the Dekes did nothing to lessen the electricity that flowed into his leg.

"So, you interested in partying?" she asked him in a husky voice.

Ryck was just about to give in when the recall button on his collar sounded. Groans and curses sounded from other sailors and Marines as they realized what the buzzing buttons meant. Their liberty was cut short. Something was up, and they had to get back to the ship.

"You heard it, gents. Let's get going," Corporal Pallas told them as he stood, swiping his card to clear his tab. "Pay up if you haven't already, and we've got 20 mikes to get back to the shuttle. Wan, you and T-Rex make sure Smitty gets back. OK, move it!"

Ryck stood up and looked back down at Purety.

"Uh, sorry, I mean, I wanted to, but I've gotta go."

She shrugged indifferently. "I know. Go ahead."

Her voice had lost some of the sultriness. Despite her still exotic looks, she suddenly sounded like anyone else at a humdrum job; bored and wishing she was someplace else. He wanted to say something more, but as the others started to rush off, he simply turned away and sprinted off to the shuttle port.

Chapter 19

The entire company was crowded into the ship's mess, the only place large enough other than the shuttle bay where everyone could gather. The *Adelaide* was only a destroyer, not one of the larger troop transports. Major Paulan, the detachment commander, stood up to speak, and the room quieted. Something big was up.

"Listen up, Marines," the skinny major said, his voice surprisingly deep for coming out of such a small frame. "We've got a real situation here. The passenger ferry *Robin* was hijacked two hours ago. We are at full throttle now to try and pick up the spoor. If we find it, we will track down the ship and rescue the crew and passengers."

That caught their attention. Anti-piracy was part of the Navy's mission, but that usually meant blasting pirates or their bases into their component atoms. Sometimes, though, that meant a rescue, and that required Marines. The *Adelaide* was probably the closest ship in the immediate vicinity with embarked Marines, so that had to be why the ship was given the mission.

If the pirated vessel was a bubble ship, then time was of an essence. When a ship entered bubble space, there was a warp in the fabric of real space, but one that faded with time. If a Navy ship could find that spoor, they could somehow follow the ship, even through bubble space, and track it down.

Ryck didn't understand how they could do that. In a class back at recruit training, it was explained that it worked the same way as hadron communications. That confused him, though. He understood the concept of hadron comms. The physics of it was that the key components were split-manufactured by twinning. Up to 32 receptors could be made, and they reacted to any outside stimulus in unison, even when separated. Push one up, and the other 31 would instantaneously go up in the exact same manner, even if light-years apart. Make communicators out of these receptors, send them across the galaxy, and camming was possible from one to the other. Cross-connect to other comm hubs, and a person could cam with pretty much anyone in the known galaxy, at least within Federation space. That was intrinsically obvious to Ryck and made perfect sense.

He didn't, though understand how a Navy ship could sniff out the bubble spoor, "taste" it (the term used by the class instructor), then lock it in. They weren't twinned, after all. There was no connection between them at the hadron level. It didn't make any sense, and Ryck wondered if there wasn't another explanation, one highly classified. Regardless, he just had to accept that this was within the Navy's capabilities.

"It looks like the pirates are SOG," the major added, eliciting a murmur from the Marines.

Soldiers of God were criminals, their religious-sounding name notwithstanding. They had rained terror on the Reaches, wiping out entire communities, recording their torture and rape and sending those flicks out over the open net. Their leader, who went by the name of All Seeing, narrated each flick, explaining that God told them to kill and pillage. When they entered the inner core, hitting planets, stations, and ships, the leeward edge of both the Federation and the Brotherhood started to panic. No one knew where SOG originated nor where they got their ships.

They were not always successful. Several ships were destroyed by Federation or Brotherhood Navy ships, and DNA regression studies on what human remains could be gathered showed that there was no single ethnic or regional source. It seemed as if SOG came from a wide variety of worlds and people, probably recruited from the flotsam of society.

The Reaches, by definition, were widespread and sparsely populated. Even with modern technology, the SOG's homeworld remained hidden. That was until an SOG pirate mothership was purposefully damaged, but not destroyed, and allowed to "escape." Two Shrike pilots, operating well beyond the range of the little fighters, followed in trace, stealth projectors at max output. One disappeared into bubble space, but the other found the homeworld and torped back the coordinates to the waiting combined fleet. The fleet arrived, and with the main guns of the FS *Russia* and the Brotherhood battleship *Retribution* slaved together, the admiral of the Federation fleet and the archbishop of the Brotherhood fleet jointly pushed the firing button, sending no less than twelve planet busters to destroy the homeworld of the SOG.

Unfortunately, within a year, SOG was back. All Seeing was probably killed when the planet was destroyed, but others rose in his place, and SOG was back in the space lanes. They started taking freighters, disappearing with valuable cargos. They took some planetary militia ships, and even a destroyer from the independent Greenworld. Finally, they had started taking some passenger ships. No ransom was ever requested. The rumors were that the men were made into slaves, the women into wives and breeders.

The major let the rumble die down before continuing, "I don't need to tell you what happened three years ago with the SOG and the *Mount Ranier.*"

It had been widely publicized, so pretty much the entire Federation had followed the story. The SOG had gotten aboard the ship as passengers, then taken over the bridge while the rest of the pirates boarded from small shuttles. Over 600 souls were taken captive. The *Ranier* was not a bubble ship but an old fabric ship. The FS *Wuhan* caught them before they could align for their jump. The Marines assaulted, but when they entered the *Ranier*, they found all of the passengers murdered, most horribly mutilated. The 30 pirates themselves had committed suicide.

"I was part of the boarding team, and I am not ashamed to admit to you that I broke down when I saw what they had done. Rest assured that this is not going to happen during my command."

Several "oorahs" echoed within the mess deck, only to fade in an awkward silence.

"I'm going to turn this over to Lieutenant Silverton for a moment. He's the ship's intel officer, and I think we need to listen to this."

Several Navy officers and crew had arrived with the major and Captain Light Chaser. One of them, obviously a heavy-worlder from his physique, stood up to face the Marines.

"As the major said, I'm Lieutenant Silverton," he started. "There has already been a release that the hijacking is the work of the SOG. However, a couple of things stand out. First, this is the farthest into Federation space that the SOG has ever struck. Second, the announcement that they were the SOG came quite early, sooner than what they normally do. They are still vulnerable, and usually the SOG waits until they are safely away. The Admiralty gives it a very high probability that this is not the SOG, but rather a copy-cat group that is using the *Ranier* incident to forestall pursuit."

That elicited another round of rumbling, and the lieutenant had to hold up his hand to get everyone to quiet down.

"The decision has been made, and this is at the *highest* levels, that SOG or copycat, the *Adelaide*, if at all possible, will track down the *Robin* and take it back, no matter the consequences. The pirates, whether actually SOG or not, will be given the same summary treatment as authorized by Joint Communique 2005."

"Joint Communique 2005" was an official understanding between the Federation, the Brotherhood, the Confederation, and seven independent planets that all civil rights with regards to SOG members were suspended, and summary executions would be conducted on every captured member. The Federation had issued similar rulings before, but those were only in effect in Federation space. This was the first time, to anyone's knowledge outside of it, at least, that the Brotherhood had done away with due process.

The lieutenant sat down, nodding to the major, who stood back up.

"To repeat what the lieutenant said, even if these are copycats, they will be treated like the real deal. You want to play with us, then accept the consequences," he said.

This time, the chorus of "oo-rahs" was louder and sustained.

"According to what I've been told, we should arrive on station in about, uh . . ." he started, then looked down at his watch, ". . . about 45 minutes. Then our Navy brothers need to find the spoor and lock on the trail. Even if successful, the soonest we could possibly launch is in two or three hours. Not much time, so I'm going to turn it over to Captain Light Chaser for the op order. Listen up. We won't have time for a real rehearsal, but we're Marines. We make do, and do it in a most *outstanding* manner! So, listen up and get it down, then we've got to get suited up and ready to go. Captain Light Chaser?"

Major Paulan was actually the battalion ops officer, but when the mission to Atacama came up, he'd been given command of the task force of the ground element, the single Stork of the air element, and the small logistics element. Captain Light Chaser was the Fox Company commander, and as such, commanded the company along with the arty and engineer detachment. Navy Captain Webber, the Aidelaide's skipper, was the overall commander, and Major Paulan the Marine commander, but Captain Light Chaser would lead the assault.

As the assault force commander, Captain Light Chaser stood up to give the order. He had everyone's undivided attention. Two hours was no time to plan and kick off a ship-to-ship mission. But they would march on and complete the mission. Ryck joined the others, all business, as they received their op order.

Chapter 20

"Team B, pass through C, but keep it tight," the lieutenant's voice came over the platoon circuit.

"Team B" was the assault element, the bulk of it made up from First and Second Platoons. Third Platoon was the security element, Weapons and the attachments the support element. The support element's job was to make the initial crossing to the *Robin* and secure the breaching chamber. The security element's mission was to breach the ship, then secure the breach. The assault element would immediately follow, pass through Third, and rush to take out any pirates and secure the captives. Speed was of an essence.

"Assault, assault, assault," the Marines of the assault element muttered as they shuffled through the line of security element Marines. The movement was complicated even further by the Stork and the *Aidelaide's* two shuttles filling the hangar deck. The Marines shuffled to the far bulkhead and stopped, still facing outwards.

"This has got to be quicker," the first sergeant broke in on the company circuit. "Much quicker. If we are too slow, those fuckers will smoke check each and every captive."

"You heard him," Captain Light Chaser's unique voice cut in. "Element leaders, get them back and go through this again. Time's getting short, and we could get the go-ahead any minute now."

The company had given out the op order in record time, and the Marines had gotten suited up and were ready to go within an hour. Staged in the hangar bay, the company commander had started rehearsals. Walking around in the bay was a far cry from actually flying through space and breaching a hostile ship, but Ryck had to admit that it still helped.

Because of the imminent threat to the captives, a decision had been made to conduct the assault in bubble space. This was highly unusual and extremely risky. Normally, a vessel would be tracked through bubble space, then taken when both ships emerged back into real space. However, once they were in real space, at distances close enough to board, the *Adelaide's* presence would be extremely difficult to mask, and with any warning, the SOG could massacre their prisoners. So it had to be surprise. The SOG would not be expecting it, and their first indication that something was up would be when the breach was made. The fact that a ship takedown could even be accomplished in bubble space was something kept under wraps. Some rumors had leaked out, of course, over the years, but the Naval Civil Information Service had counter-propaganda employed to make those rumors seem ridiculous.

They had been putting on their EVA suits when the word was passed that the *Robin's* spoor had been acquired, and a cheer had echoed throughout the armory. EVA suits were custom made for each Marine, and one of CWO2 Slyth's primary missions in life was to make sure the suits were continually adjusted to keep the fit right. Ryck had just gone through his standard 30-day check two days before they had pulled into Vegas, so his was pretty much right on. But the chief warrant officer, his gunny, and his two sergeants had been pinging back and forth in the crowded armory, taking readings and making last-minute adjustments. Ryck had gotten out of there as soon as he received his OK and made his way to the hangar deck.

Normally, the bay was pressurized, with the Stork and the shuttles passing through a magelectro field. However, with speed as a priority, the only way to get so many Marines and sailors out into flight was through the hangar bay doors. The ship's two airlocks just couldn't cycle the assault force quick enough. And with the shielding of the EVA suits not sturdy enough to fend off the field, it had to be turned off. So, the hangar bay was open to bubble space. The Navy deck crew, the assault force, and the Navy prize crew were all suited up, ready to step out the door.

Ryck couldn't help glancing out the huge doors. No stars were visible, of course. There was only a murky, greenish glow. Like every single sailor and Marine there, he knew that no matter what happened, he had to stay within the glow. Drift out, and he would be lost in the emptiness of space, probably lost for good. He didn't have the luck of Derek Housa, a Legionnaire who had gotten thrown out of bubble space, only to be picked up by an ore miner who happened to read his distress beacon, something that had to be a million-to-one shot. Ryck had seen the flick about that when it had come out a few years ago, and the scenes of the Legionnaire floating around all alone in the vastness of space still gave him the heebies.

The *Robin* was not in view yet, either. As soon as it was, the assault would be launched. The Navy bridge crew would be maneuvering the ship closer to the *Robin*, then if they were successful at that, the external projector pods would be extended, effectively spreading the bubble. The pods would move toward the *Robin*, eventually enveloping it, where like two bubbles in a bath, they would merge.

This was the most difficult part of the mission from a technological standpoint. Ryck had heard the process likened to balancing a maglev car on a string of straws, one straw jammed in another until the car was a kilometer in the air. The cybos might weird Ryck out when he saw them out and about the ship, but he wished them well as they tweaked and shifted the pods, more by feel than any hard and set calculations.

Ryck shuffled with the other Marines back to the far side of the bay for another rehearsal. The ship had stopped its rotation in preparation for the assault. Having centripetal force as they exited the hangar was not a good idea. The ship had rotated so the hangar faced the expected direction of where the *Robin* would be, then stopped. With no gravity in the hangar, which unlike the bridge and many of the other spaces had no artificial gravity, the Marines and sailors shuffled their feet to keep in contact. It was considered poor form to have to turn on the EVA's jets to get back into place.

Ryck had just gotten back to his starting point when a voice came over the circuit, "Look, there she is."

Ryck looked out the bay doors, and off in the distance, the *Robin* was appearing as if through a mist. She was nothing out of the ordinary. Like all bubble ships, she was round. A ship did not have to be round to project a bubble, but the shape was far more efficient, and it took far less power to keep the bubble formed around a sphere than any other form. Inside the greenish light of the bubble, she took on a somewhat eerie tone. This appearance was why some people referred to a ship traveling through bubble space as "ghosting."

As expected, the ship was not under rotation. Pirates usually kept captured ships in null G as it kept more passengers uncertain and unwilling to resist.

"Element leaders, get your men in place. Stand by for the go," Captain Light Chaser passed.

"All hands, this is Major Paulen. Do us proud. It's time to earn your big paychecks."

Ryck knew the major had to be chomping at his bit. He would be coming over with the Navy prize team, the sailors necessary to run the *Robin* and effect any required repairs. This would be Captain Light Chaser's assault, and the major had stepped back to allow it, but he had to have been tempted to take the assault himself.

The hangar crew moved into position. They had their own EVA suits, unlike the prize team who were in standard suits. The two officers had their suits shifted to yellow, the enlisted to green. Ryck had thought the colors a bit odd at first, but with all the men in the hangar, it really did help to sort things out.

The support element made their way to the front of the open doors. Two Marines had their hands on each of the four breaching chambers, ready to fly them across to the *Robin*. The other Marines in the team flanked them. Directly behind them, the security element was lined up. They would actually enter the breach and hold it for the assault element to exploit. Ryck took his place behind them, about two meters from the edge of the door. Two meters from open bubble space.

Between the Marines in front of him, Ryck could see the Robin looming larger. It was difficult to tell in space, but it couldn't be more than a couple of hundred meters away. That thought alone was mind-boggling. Both ships were hurtling through bubble space, covering light-years in real space, yet they were just meters apart. Real space speed meant nothing.

Ryck felt his excitement rise. This would be his first EVA since the near-disaster during recruit training. He popped his M99 free, checked it, and popped it back into the holster.

Suddenly, the yellow-suited deck officer wheeled and pointed out the doors. For some inexplicable reason, he could not talk on the Marine circuits. The Navy working and Marine tactical circuits were incompatible. The Marines knew the signal, of course, and the first rank stepped off and started flying.

Thousand-one, thousand-two, thousand-three, thousand-four Ryck counted in his mind. On "four," the next rank stepped off.

Now was the wait. If all went well, the breaching teams could set up and breach the ship within 30 seconds after reaching it. The breaching chambers were adjusted to their shortest length as they were not going to be acting as airlocks. They would be opening the ship up to space.

The security element was given another 30 seconds to secure the breached rooms. The breaching points had been selected compromising between where the air loss would be minimal and where the assaulting Marines could quickly reach where captives were probably being kept.

At 60 seconds, the assault element would be arriving at each of the four points, ready to dive through the breaches. As the assault element arrived, the breaches would be closed off, extended, then converted to airlocks for the follow-on forces.

It was a long, long minute until the deck officer wound up and sent them on their way. Ryck stepped off into space. Ryck was on the left flank of the assault element's line, with only T-Rex outside of him. They would be flying to breach "Tennison." Inside bubble space, it was almost impossible to tell exactly where the bubble "skin" was. It sort of swirled and shimmered, defying comprehension. From what they'd been taught, a person wouldn't know that he had reached the bubble until he was out of it and injected back into real space. Ryck kept glancing toward his left. He figured, though, that if they were drifting too close, T-Rex would disappear first.

Up ahead of him, the breaching teams had already reached the ship and attached the chambers. With that, the pirates would realize that something was up. This was real, now. Ryck flew on, keeping in formation with the others. What the captain didn't want was to have everyone bunching up at the ship. The four breaches were the bottleneck, and he didn't want confusion to take over.

Ryck was getting closer when the security team around Tennison started to dive into the chamber. They would be reporting back what they found, but that was not on the general assault element circuit. If there were something Ryck needed to know, he would be told.

Ryck glanced over at the other two breaches that were within his view, the fourth being behind the curve of the ship and out of sight. Marines were already inside at "Jakarta," but at "Capetown," there seemed to be a problem, with the security team still outside while the assault element was arriving.

"Team Tennison, get ready to enter. Security has cleared the immediate entry. Stick to the plan and move forward into the passageway. There are two enemy KIA and one rescued hostage," Sergeant Piccalo-Tensing passed over the team circuit.

Ryck was running pretty true, and it took only a few minor jets to correct his aim and slow down in order to get into his position in line for entry. He looked down at the telltale on his left gauntlet. Unlike the team leaders who had the positions projected onto their faceshields, just as with the PICS, the riflemen had only repeaters on the flexible patch screen that most wore on their forward shooting arm. It wasn't as detailed as those for the leaders, but it did indicate friendlies. Ryck could see the security team icons as they moved into position within the ship.

Quicker than expected, Ryck approached the ship. He fired two quick jets to slow his approach and took care not to jostle anyone else, sending them tumbling, but he had to keep on the ass of Wan as they dove through the chamber. He crashed into the lance corporal inside the ship as they hit the deck, but Wan was up and moving within seconds. Ryck grabbed his M99 and got his feet under him, pushing forward to the far hatch, which was just where he'd been briefed it would be. He took in the two dead men, both in varying degrees of undress. With their skin exposed to the cold touch of space, it was easy to see where they both had been stitched by the security team's M99s. A naked woman was inside a zip-lock, the clear, flexible emergency pouch that could keep someone alive in the vacuum of space for up to 20 minutes. She was hyperventilating, and a Marine, or probably Doc Stanton, the corpsman with the security element, was with her, trying to calm her down.

Ryck took all that in during the few seconds it took him to cross the compartment, go through the next hatch, down one deck, and turn left to his assigned position. He crouched there, weapon at the ready, waiting for the order to move. The ship's emergency reaction AI had closed off the passages as soon as the breach was made, so no air was rushing out. Gravity was gone, but nothing was trying to push the Marines back out into space. No move would be made to breach the closed hatch 10 meters down the passage until the breaching chamber closed off the initial entry and became a working airlock. Ryck silently counted down the time. The plan was that all the security and assault elements would board the *Robin* within 90 seconds.

Ryck knew his count would be off, given that he'd been diving through and moving during part of it, but the order came to move out when he hit 82 seconds. They were all in the ship and could advance.

Corporal Pallas was up and moving almost before the order was completed. Wan, T-Rex, and Ryck were hot on his tail as they rushed to the hatch in front of them. They were to breach it, then make for a berthing space on the other side while Smitty's team moved on to the ship's passenger galley another 10 meters down. Their sense of urgency was heightened. The necessity for speed had been shoved down their throats while they waited.

T-Rex placed a toad on the edge of the hatch where the locking mechanism was concealed. The toad was a small, soft, greenish lump that could stick on just about anything. EVA gauntlets or special employment gloves for planetary use were treated to be able to handle them, but as soon as they touched almost anything else, they stuck to it. There was a three-second fuse in each toad, the only solid component to the little explosive, that gave the user a very short time to move back. Toads, or the "E-559

Self-contained Slow Breaching Device," burned more than they actually exploded and could be used in a vacuum or in breathable air. They carried their own supply of oxygen with them, suspended in the combustible material, and could burn through almost any material.

"Fire in the hole!" T-Rex shouted, pushing back.

The toad hissed, then started its burn, the EVA suit visors instantly compensating for the flare. The hatch broke free, and T-Rex gave it a kick, sending it open. Immediately, a burst of fire came back at them, one round, at least, pinging off Ryck's shoulder. As it was not an explosive, the toad only opened and did not clear what was on the other side.

EVA suits could take some punishment, but they were not PICS, nor even bones, although they did give 100% coverage. A high-powered weapon would go right through it, and even a lucky shot from small arms could find an opening. All four Marines returned fire en masse, not even fully aware of the target, trusting the very nature of a ship's passageway to focus their rounds.

"Cease fire," Sparta ordered after a good 100 or more rounds were sent down the passage.

Ryck peered ahead. On the other side, a figure writhed suspended above the deck. He had an old M-8 alongside him, but he wasn't paying it any attention. Unlike a typical pirate, he was wearing body armor, or at least a hodgepodge of armor plating, and from the looks of it, the old Proskov carapace he had on had protected him from the Marines' M99s. The only problem was that he had only the torso carapace and a helmet that Ryck didn't even recognize. He had nothing on his arms or legs, and they were torn up pretty bad. One arm was almost gone, and he kept trying to sort of push it back into place with the other.

The four Marines rushed up to him with Wan kicking away his M-8. Ryck automatically started to reach for some ties to secure the man when T-Rex reached forward and pulled up on the man's helmet. He looked like a flick pirate with his unshaven, ratty face. Central casting could not have done better. He looked up at T-Rex and raised his good, or at least not as bad arm, in surrender.

T-Rex calmly put the M99 against the man's forehead and pulled the trigger.

Ryck had almost forgotten. With SOG, there were no prisoners. This went against everything they had been taught since T3 back at recruit training. Ryck didn't like it. They were supposed to be the good guys, the ones upholding law and order. But he understood the orders and would comply if put in that situation. He just hoped he wouldn't have to.

The pirate's body floated back, blood making a string of small globes that were surprisingly beautiful. The little red planets kept going for another two meters before suddenly falling and splattering on the deck to pool there.

With a clear view on where the artificial gravity was working again, the four Marines twisted around so they could land on their feet as they hit that section. Ryck took a moment to glance at his telltale. Smitty's team had already branched off, and Corporal Julio's team was in trace, ready to exploit that mission, which was the point of main effort for this section of the ship as the most logical place for captives to be held. Ryck knew that Sparta would be in pretty constant comms with Sergeant PT, Staff Sergeant England, and the lieutenant, but too many on the net confused things, so Wan, T-Rex, and he were off the circuit. The comms AI would kick in if Sparta's comms went down for any reason, or if the AIs or the command decided they needed to be brought in. On the one hand, Ryck was glad of that. He could focus on his mission and on the other three Marines in his team. On the other hand, he wished he knew what else was going on in the assault. Were the pirates killing the captives? Were they fighting back? Not like the lone pirate T-Rex had blown away, but with any semblance of tactics?

With gravity again, the four Marines rushed forward and were at the berthing hatch within moments. T-Rex reached forward and gently pushed on the entry switch. To all of their surprise, the door rose with a whoosh. It took all of them a split second to realize that they would not have to breach into the space. Sparta and Wan rushed in first, followed by T-Rex and Ryck. Sparta and Wan split to each side, getting down low while Ryck and T-Rex went in high.

The space was chaos. The bunks were all deployed. This was Berthing 4-19, one of the two male third-class berthing spaces. The bunks folded up and were retracted into the overhead during waking hours. This left space for the passengers to relax, watch flicks, read, or whatever. During sleep hours, all or some of the berths would be lowered, three bunks to a column. With the bunks deployed, there was only a narrow passage between the bunks, a small common area, and a hatch to the heads.

From the main hatch, the passage was twice as wide as those between the bunks, and it led right to the common area. The first thing Ryck saw was the body of a man, hands tied behind him and a blindfold over his head, lying on his side. The blood pooling under his head did not bode well for his condition.

Ryck jumped when someone, or something, slammed into his legs. He swung his weapon around, ready to blast, barely holding back when the hands tied behind the man's back and the blindfold that had fallen to around his neck registered. The man looked up in resigned despair, a look which slowly shifted as he took Ryck in.

"Help me!" the man shouted, wiggling out from between the bunks and scooting in back of Ryck.

Wan was just in front of Ryck, and when the man appeared, he turned back. He and Ryck caught each other's eyes, then hunkered down in unison, looking for the reason the man was asking for help. In front of them, cursing as he struggled to get through the bunks, was an armed, armored man. He fell between the bunks with a thud, only one bunk's width away from the two Marines. He started forward again, only then seeing that it wasn't his target in front of him, but two Federation Marines. With a curse, he struggled to bring up his Freelancer, the muzzle catching on the bunk in front of him.

With him prone like that, not much of what was facing the two Marines was unprotected. Except for his neck. If he'd been standing upright, his neck would have been protected by his armor. However, on his belly, under his visor, there was a gap. Ryck and Wan opened up on that gap. At a meter or so, there was no way they could miss.

The man's armor was pretty good quality, from the look of it. It wasn't Federation-made, but then, pirates didn't recognize borders. Being well made, it could stop a dart—from the outside, as designed, but that meant also from the inside. The two Marines each put several darts into the man's neck where they ricocheted back and forth inside the armor, slicing him to ribbons. He simply collapsed like a deflating balloon.

"To your right!" shouted Sparta, the circuit compensators bringing his volume down a few decibels before the two Marines heard it over their helmet speakers.

The command was not very exact, and he hadn't addressed it to anyone in particular, but both Wan and Ryck reacted, ignoring the still-tied captive as they rushed forward to a passage, then tried to force their EVA suits through it. The suits were not particularly bulky, but what they added made pushing through the bunks difficult. As they swung to the right, they flanked a pirate who was holding a man in front of him, an unrecognizable handgun of some sort to the man's head. Like the other two pirates, he also had on armor. This was out of the ordinary. From pirate culture, armor was considered coward's gear. In the flicks, pirates thought that armor was not manly. Fiction or not, flicks impacted opinion, and pirates tended to ape what was shown.

Unlike modern Federation personnel armor, which tended to be flexible plates that were attached to or inserted inside of clothing, all three pirates had outer shells. That didn't mean the armor was not effective. All that meant was that they probably acquired it outside of Federation space.

The pirate to their left had what looked to be newer armor, but either he didn't have a helmet or hadn't a chance to put it on before the four Marines burst the space. His clean-shaven face and perfectly-groomed blonde hair gave him a look far different from that of the first pirate, an indication that this group was multi-cultural.

As Ryck and Wan arrived, the man spun first toward them, then back toward Sparta and T-Rex, who had their weapons trained on him.

"Stop, or . . ." he began.

"Or" what, the Marines could guess, but never know for sure as Wan calmly put a couple of darts over the shoulder of the captive passenger and into the pirate's handsome blonde head. The tiny turn the pirate made back to Sparta and T-Rex had given the lance corporal all the opening he needed.

The captive stood still as the pirate fell back. He slowly turned around, hands still tied behind him, and stared at the dead man for a moment before taking a step forward and leveling a powerful kick at the corpse's head.

"There's three more," he said matter-of-factly to the four Marines.

"Wan, did you get anyone else?" Sparta asked.

"One down," Wan replied.

"Where are the others?" Sparta asked, his external speakers broadcasting his voice into the compartment so any captives could hear.

It was only then that Ryck really noticed the other four bodies on the deck, all with their hands tied, all executed. He hadn't been able to see them from the front hatch, and his attention had been on the pirate when they'd gotten up there.

"Over here!" a voice shouted out from within the deployed bunks to their left. "There's one of them here!"

A heavy report sounded out from that direction, followed by a cry of pain and sounds of somebody crashing around the bunks. At the same time, a finger of lightning reached out from between the bunks to their right, splashing across Sparta's EVA suit.

Someone had a plasma weapon over there, but this was a case where the EVA suits had an advantage over skins and bones. All the plasma had to do was to touch open skin, and it would essentially short-circuit the body's nervous system. It acted like it had a life of its own when it stuck, seeking out the ground through a living body. It could be devastating to Marines in just their standard combat armor. To an EVA suit, though, it had no effect.

The crewman they'd just saved dropped to the ground, whether kissed by the plasma or not, Ryck couldn't take the time to check as he and Wan instinctively spun toward the sounds on the other side of the space. They split on each side of a line of bunks, then sprinted forward, trusting the other two Marines to take out the plasma pirate.

The berthing space was not really that big. Any hangar was much larger. But with the bunks deployed and blocking the view, it seemed pretty vast. Ryck tried to keep abreast with Wan, glancing through the bunks to keep even with him. Blood covered the deck about eight or nine bunks down from the common area. Ryck took a quick glance at the bottom bunk where a man had dragged himself. A huge chunk of the man's side was simply gone. The man was struggling to breathe, and Ryck knew he needed medical care ASAP.

"One friendly WIA, needs immediate care," he hit on the medical circuit, knowing the AI would add Ryck's position.

That was about all he could do for the man at the moment. A sudden boom sounded, and the rack between Wan and him simply exploded. The concussion hit Ryck, actually pushing him aside a few centimeters.

"What the hump was that?" Wan asked on Ryck's direct circuit as both Marines hit the deck.

Even though the EVA suits were not particularly bulky, they were not made for crawling around under gravity. The helmet's design made looking forward while prone difficult, and the power packs, thrusters, and oxi cells added bulk to the back. Ryck wished they had stopped to get out of the EVA suits and into skins and bones after the breach, but with the time crunch, EVA suits in the attack it was.

Another blast sounded over them, raining bits of bunks down like dirty snow. Whatever the pirate had for a weapon, it was pretty big.

"He's heading for the front hatch!" Wan said. "We've got to stop him before he gets there."

"Corporal Pallas, can you cut this guy off? He's trying to get out the front," Wan passed on the team circuit.

"Negative, Wan. We've got our hands full here. You two take him," Sparta responded.

Wan glanced over at Ryck across the bottom rack that separated the two of them and said, "You heard the man. I don't know what the hump that bastard's got with him for sure, but I think it's like our bunker buster. Whatever it is, we can't let him get away. I want you to flank him. On three, you scoot through these racks, keeping your ass low. I'm gonna get up, hit the bulkhead up ahead, and rush the arsehole. Iffen you get a shot, take him out while he's glommed onto me."

"Oh, man! You sure? Maybe we both need to rush him, so he has to choose a target, you know, confuse him until we light him up," Ryck said.

"Nah, this is the way it's gonna be. Iffen what he has is a bunker buster, you know the range is limited, and it's about as accurate as throwing rotten apples. And you know the Wan man. I can move it. I'll be juking and jiving, so no way he hits me. You just be sure to nail him."

He slowly reached up and hit the helmet release. There was a hiss as the slight overpressure inside the suit puffed out into the ship. He lifted the helmet up and placed it on the deck, detaching the comms buds and sliding them into his ears. This was against policy. If the ship suffered a catastrophic breach, Wan would have only seconds to find a pressurized space.

He shrugged at Ryck's questioning look and whispered, "Gotta be loose and light, you know."

He held up his hand, then counted down three, two, one with his fingers. On one, he stood up and rushed forward to the compartment bulkhead, five more bunk-lengths ahead. At the same time, Ryck turned to dive over the bottom rack next to him. After clearing it, he gathered his feet to dive over the next one. He barely noticed another body as he passed it. At least the guy hadn't died like a sheep at the slaughter. He'd tried to get away.

Just as he cleared the third rack, a huge boom sounded, and flames shot down the passage along the bulkhead. That pinpointed the pirate for him. He was just on the other side of the next line of bunks. Ryck slid over the next bunk and looked up.

The pirate standing in front of him was not in some hodgepodge body armor. He was fully protected with black, interlaced, external plates that looked like ceramosteel. Ryck didn't recognize the actual make, but it was doubtful that is was Federated or Brotherhood-made.

There were two main trains of thought on body armor. The Federation went with flexible inserts that reacted within a split instant upon impact, hardening to stop a projectile before reverting back to its original state. The armor was far more comfortable than plate armor and was better at stopping solid projectiles. Plate armor, on the other hand, relied on sandwiched materials that were strong enough to withstand modern projectiles. The PICS relied on plate armor, but they were big enough and powerful enough to carry pretty heavy plates. It was easier to make plate armor, and it didn't have to be custom made for each soldier. It was actually better for protection against some energy weapons. However, it was bulky and heavy, and even with exoskeletal assists, it limited mobility.

The armor was the first thing Ryck noticed. The second thing was the stubby tube-like weapon the pirate was holding. Wan was probably correct in that it was the pirate version of the Marine's M-77 Bunker Buster. The bunker-buster was designed to break or penetrate hardened targets. It sent a focused energy "shell-less shell" that would shoot forward and either re-focus that energy into a shaped charge or simply explode in a blast ring. Due to the physics of energy dissipation, it had a very limited range of about 5 meters with a huge drop off in effectiveness beyond that. Within 5 meters, not much could withstand its power. It could even take out a Davis from point-blank range. Due to its power, it was almost never used aboard a ship. It could easily rupture the ship's skin, opening it up to vacuum.

Evidently, the pirate was not too concerned about that. They were only a deck away from the skin of the ship, but that was far enough, along with whatever was between the weapon and the ship's skin, to keep the pirate from creating the rupture.

Bunker busters were not made for man-to-man fighting. The weapon was not very accurate, and there was a considerable re-charge time. The Marine Corps M-77, for example, carried six charges in a load, and each one took approximately 12 seconds to cycle and recharge. That was fine when taking on a hardened target, but not so fine when the shooter's target was men who were attacking him.

The pirate was looking down the passage alongside the bulkhead. Even with the pirate in his armor, Ryck could see that he was focused on something, yet he was not scrambling to either move or fire again. The only conclusion Ryck had was that Wan had been hit.

Ryck didn't know how much time he had before the pirate's weapon would be re-charged. Just because the Marine Corps weapon needed 12 seconds didn't mean that the pirate's was the same. Instinct took over. He knew time would be tight, so he got to his feet and started charging the pirate, M-99 on full auto. He could see the impacts of the darts on the pirate's armor as they ricocheted off without effect. Ryck needed something heavier, but as the assault element with speed of an essence, they had gone in light. T-Rex had an M-72 on his back, and that might be able to knock out the pirate, but T-Rex was otherwise engaged.

Ryck kept charging as the pirate swung ponderously around to see who was attacking him. Ryck couldn't see the man behind the dark helmet visor, but he kept pumping out rounds in hopes that one would find a crease or weak spot in the man's armor.

The pirate brought up his weapon, aiming from the hip, the 20-centimeter barrel looking huge as it pointed at him. For a moment, Ryck thought he'd be able to reach him before he fired, physically tackling the man. Just a step away, the weapon went off, a flash of light blinding Ryck as something struck him hard along his right side. He wasn't even aware of being thrown back, of his right arm and two fingers of his left hand being turned to hamburger. He wasn't aware of when his EVA, acting on the breach, closed the torn sleeve and gauntlet, slicing away the mangled flesh that used to be his right arm and left fingertips. The EVA didn't care if it was in a vacuum or on a pressurized ship. If the suit was breached, it acted to seal the breach and keep integrity.

A sense of lassitude crept over him as drugs were injected into his body, drugs meant to calm him and slow down his respirations. In space, this made sense, lowering a Marine's oxygen intake until someone could rescue him.

He looked up to see the black-armored creature approach him. The huge dragon stood over him, ready to breathe fire again.

Jonathan P. Brazee

He settled back to watch the show, but something wouldn't let him relax.

NO!

He fought the pull into the cottony dreamland. That was not a dragon. That was a pirate, a man just waiting until his weapon cycled before he would end Ryck's life. Ryck had to do something. He tried to push back, to get away, but he barely moved a few centimeters before the pirate stepped forward, foot on Ryck's leg, holding him in place.

The pirate held up his weapon, looking at something, probably a gauge that would indicate when the thing was charged. Ryck reached out to grab his M-99, but there was nothing with which to reach. It was only then that he realized his right arm was gone. Surprisingly, that didn't bother him. He knew it should, but he just brushed it off. Those had to be some pretty good drugs.

Ryck was at a loss. Would T-Rex come charging in, M-77 a'blazing to save the day? Or would the fire from the pirate snuff out Ryck's life?

Fire. T-Rex. What was the connection?

Then it hit him. As the pirate stared at his weapon's display, waiting, Ryck reached with his left hand to his hip magazine. He flipped it open and reached inside. Something was off with his touch, how his hand was working, but he wasn't sure just what. When he felt something give, though, he knew he had it.

Pulling out his toad, he thumbed the fuse just as the pirate nodded and started to lower his weapon. Ryck casually flipped the toad up into the air. Even drugged, though, he realized he'd thrown it up behind the pirate, where it would fall behind the man, not to where it would hit him. He had lost. But the pirate was not going to shoot Ryck from point-blank range. He took a step back. Ryck was looking up as the toad started its descent. It passed just behind the pirate's head and out of sight. Ryck knew the entire sequence was only three seconds from when he had thumbed the toad, but with the drugs, time was extended. Everything was in slow motion.

The pirate finished his step back and raised his bunker buster. Ryck watched dispassionately for the fire to erupt from the weapon, and when he saw a flare of light, his muggy brain thought it

146

was from the pirate's bunker buster, that Ryck had lost. But the light was from behind the pirate's back, up around the shoulder level. The pirate hesitated and tried to turn, one hand reaching up and in back of him. The next flash was when the toad ate through the armor plate. For an instant, Ryck thought he saw the pirate's face through the man's armor visor, lit from within as a small, intensely hot star burned through his body.

Then Ryck went to sleep.

Alexander
Camp Kolesnikov

Chapter 21

Ryck opened his eyes. His stomach was growling, crying out for food. He had to get some breakfast to quiet it down. He tried to stretch, but his hands would not move. Confused, he turned his head to his left. His hand stretched out from him, but imprisoned in some sort of restraint. Thoughts of pirates, of fighting, of death suddenly flashed through his head. He had to get out of there!

"Easy there, cowboy," a familiar voice called out as Ryck struggled to get up.

It wasn't until the person who spoke moved forward that he realized who it was. T-Rex, put a hand on Ryck's chest, calming him.

"What . . . ?" Ryck stammered as it all came back to him—the mission, the fight, him being hit.

He quickly looked over to his right arm, or at least to where his right arm should have been. Instead of an arm, the stubby chamber of the regen seeder was attached to his shoulder. A steady green light was the only sign that it was doing its job.

He looked back to his left arm. Most of the arm was intact, but the hand itself was covered by a small regen chamber. To his surprise, he wasn't horrified. He knew he was drugged—the chance for a successful regen was significantly increased when the immunosuppressants were employed. Still, he felt he should be more shocked instead of just mildly curious.

"You OK, there?" T-Rex asked.

"I . . . I guess so. Where are we? We on the *Adelaide*?"

"Not hardly! We're back on the Dirtball. Home sweet home. You've been out of it for two weeks, and they just let you wake up now," T-Rex said, nodding toward the foot of the hospital bed where a nurse stood, watching Ryck closely.

Ryck tried to organize his thoughts. Of course, he would have been put into an induced coma. They'd been well-informed on what would happen if they had to go through regen. A coma during the initial stages of regen helped the process catch better and helped ensure a more complete outcome.

"A couple of the guys came to see you wake up, but you took your own sweet time with it. They went to the geedunk[19] and the head while you were napping," he told them.

"So, what happened?"

"With you?" T-Rex asked. "You took on that pirate, zeroed him, but he kind of got you, too. Doc Silvestrie came in, got you stabilized, and you were zip-locked back to the *Adelaide* even before the ship was secured."

"What about Wan? Is he OK?"

Some of the spark left T-Rex's eyes as he said, "Wan Man didn't make it. Doc got him out before you, and he was put into stasis. He made it back here to the Dirtball, but he just couldn't hang on."

Ryck looked up at T-Rex uncomprehendingly. People just didn't die if they made it to stasis. "Stasis" wasn't really an actual suspension of the body, but it came pretty close. Fluids were pumped into the circulatory system, and the body was cooled, taking it down to a bare minimum of metabolic activity. If a wounded person made it that far, then he could almost always be saved once he reached a full-service medical facility. The Dirtball, as home to both a Navy fleet and a Marine division, had one of the best.

"The Wan Man fought, but the docs, they just couldn't save him," T-Rex said.

Ryck needed to change the subject until he was able to digest that, so he asked about the mission itself. T-Rex gave the nurse a

---

[19] Geedunk: Snack bar.

pointed stare. The nurse checked Ryck's vitals, then took the hint and left. Technically, the nurse was Navy, but he almost assuredly did not have a clearance for tactical operations.

"We took back the ship," T-Rex started once the nurse was out of the room. "Two Marines KIA, Wan and Staff Sergeant Piers over in Second Platoon. Another 12 WIA, three others like you going through regen."

"The passengers?"

"Three-hundred-and-twelve passengers and crew out of three-seventy-five rescued. Most OK. The dead, well . . ." he began, stopping to look around to see if there was anyone within earshot before continuing. "Sergeant Marc's squad from Second, they might have taken out five or six passengers, from what I've heard. The pirates had them dressed in that shitty armor, and they got zeroed when Marc took that compartment. The pirates, they got dressed like the tourists, trying to blend in. There's an investigation going on, and Marc's ass is on the line."

"They tried to blend in, to get away? That doesn't sound like SOG."

"No, it doesn't. And that's not all. Some of their combat armor, it was Alliance gear, new stuff. The scuttlebutt is that they weren't SOG at all, even if that's what's on the news feeds."

"He's awake! About fucking time," Sams said as he came in with Hu, Sparta, Smitty, and another Marine Ryck didn't recognize.

"Eat me," Ryck said automatically. "And who's that?" he asked, pointing with his chin at the new Marine.

"That's our new boot. Private Hamburger. Came in to take your place while you fuck off," Sams replied.

"I keep telling you, it's Helmesburgen, not Hamburger," the private objected.

"Shut up, boot!" the other Marines said in unison.

"You OK?" Corporal Pallas asked.

"Hungry as shit. You got anything there?" Ryck asked, looking at the burger Hu was munching.

"Yeah, don't I know it. I thought I would die of starvation when I regened my foot, but you got to eat their puke-slop to make your arm grow nice and strong. Just be glad you're not Lieutenant

Badalato. He lost all his guts, everything from the belly button down. Cut in frigging half. When they let him wake up, it's IVs in the arm for at least a year before his new stomach can take real food."

"You're quite the talk of the town, you know," Sams said. "Burning pirate ass with a toad. That's some freakin' shit. Most copacetic!"

"Well, he burned out his neck, at least," Hu corrected.

"No, I was there, and I saw the body. Sams has it right. Burned his *ass*. The armor that bad boy was wearing kept his stinking corpse upright enough for the toad to burn all the way down to his ass, then out the armor again. It looked like he farted fire! Unbelievable!" the fire team leader said.

"How did you decide to use the toad?" Hamburger asked.

"Shut up, boot!" the others chorused again.

"That was pretty bitchin'. No fucking arm, and you decide to play catch with him," Sams said.

"You didn't do too bad yourself, PFC Samuelson," Sparta said.

"PFC? You just got busted down to private." Ryck said.

"Ah, no big deal," he said before Hu cut in.

"Our esteemed dickwad here led the charge into the galley just at the pirates started to execute the captives. He took out two of them with his M77, then tackled the third, I mean bam!" Hu said, getting excited. "He's going all psycho on the guy. And this guy, he's got some of that new Alliance combat armor, but he can't do nothing, 'cause this beserker's all over him. Sams here, he saved a bunch of the passengers, and the captain, when he comes in and we show him the vid, he promotes him on the spot. Takes away his brig time, too."

"No shit?" asked Ryck in wonderment.

"It wasn't quite like that," Sams protested.

"I'll show you the vid next time I come," Hu said.

"OK, OK. We've got to get going. Someone will come back to check on you after evening chow, but you need anything now?" Sparta asked Ryck.

"Uh, yeah, but this is sorta weird. I can't move my arms now, and my nose is really getting to me. It's itching up pretty good. Could one of you, you know, give it a scratch?"

The other Marines broke out laughing, but the corporal moved forward, reaching up to gently scratch Ryck's nose.

"None of you've been through regen, so you don't know what it's like," he said.

"Just make sure that's all you do, there, corporal. Ryck never got to get that ho in Vegas, and it's been a *long* time, so don't you go getting any ideas on getting him off, what with his hands out of action like that," Sams shouted.

"Oh, man, he can't even jack off!" Hu joined in. "I bet that nurse out there, he'll do it for you, Ryck, so don't you worry. I'll go ask him now, to make sure he takes good care of you!"

That brought out howls of laughter, even Ryck joining in. He hadn't yet really thought about life without his arms for a good amount of time, but leave it to Marines to bring it up and then take it down in the gutter.

"Something funny in here?" a voice broke through the din.

"Attention on deck" Hu shouted as the battalion commanding officer and sergeant major stepped into the room.

Despite himself, Ryck struggled to get up.

"At ease," the colonel said as he walked up to Ryck before turning around to face the others. "Sergeant Major, I think these men want that nurse out there to come in. Did we hear that right?" he asked the Marines.

There was a heavy silence as the men seemed afraid to catch anyone else's eyes.

The sergeant major glowered at them for a moment before breaking out in a laugh.

"Sorry, sir, I couldn't hold it in any longer. You had them shitting in their pants," he said to the CO.

"Just Marines looking out for each other, as it should be, Sergeant Major, as it should be. PFC Samuelson, though, seems to have a thing with the ladies, so maybe he could do better than that fat nurse out there."

There was more dead silence, and Sams snuck a look at Sparta.

"The colonel told a joke, men. Laugh!" the sergeant major said.

There was a ragged volley of forced laughter.

That elicited a hearty laugh from the colonel himself.

"OK, sergeant major, you've had your fun, so enough yanking on their chains. We're here to check on Lysander, after all," he said, turning back toward Ryck. "You've just been brought out of your coma, right? Still a bit murky, I bet, and you're probably starving."

"Yes, sir," Ryck answered.

"I've been through it myself, three times, so I know what it's like."

Everyone knew the colonel's history. He was a mustang, up from the ranks, from private to first sergeant, then to lieutenant and on up to lieutenant colonel. He wore the Navy Cross, the second-highest award for valor. Earning that medal had cost him both arms and legs as well as a good portion of his torso. That the Navy docs had saved his life was something of a miracle, and he had spent a full two years in regen and therapy, so yes, Ryck was well aware that the colonel "knew what it was like."

"You'll get fed after we leave, but it won't be good. These Navy docs must think that decent taste ruins the process. Before that starts, though, the sergeant major has something for you.

"Sergeant Major, if you will, and let's bring in these reprobates here, too."

The sergeant major pulled a stack of paper cups from his cargo pocket and passed them around to the Marines. He took a tube from under his sleeve and poured something out of it into each cup. He gave another to the colonel and took one for himself before moving to Ryck and offering him the end of the tube. Just before Ryck put it in his mouth, he pulled it back a fraction of a centimeter and waited.

"Gentlemen, needless to say, this does not go beyond this room.

"Lift your glasses for a toast. To Private First Class Ryck Lysander, *Audaces Fortuna Iuvat*."

"Here, here!" they all chorused as the sergeant major slid the tube into Ryck's mouth.

Ryck took a long swallow, the cold beer feeling wonderful as it slid past his tongue and down his throat. Alcohol was explicitly prohibited throughout the regen process, but if the colonel, with all his regen, thought it was OK, Ryck was not going to argue.

The colonel leaned forward and quietly said, "You're going to be OK, Ryck. Semper fi."

And Ryck knew it was true. He *was* going to be OK.

Chapter 22

Ryck sat at the test bench, watching the results on the PI-530. He didn't really need to be there. The process was automated. Once the test was initiated, each PICS was pulled out of its locker, trundled over to the bench, and subjected to the tiny pulses the 530 threw at it.

The PICS was high tech. It might be over 50-year-old tech, but high nonetheless. And that required constant maintenance. The 530 was just one of the tools in the armorer's box to keep the PICS in top working condition. This piece of test equipment sent tiny pulses into the skin of the PICS, testing the kickbacks. Each kickback had to react within 10,000[th] of a second, firing back at the incoming projectile or pulse. Coupled with the integrity of the LTC array armor itself, the kickbacks helped the PICS to withstand 20mm cannon fire or 6mm hypervelocity rounds. They only helped marginally against pulse weapon strikes, but the PICS had other defenses for those.

The PICS being tested belonged to Corporal Timothy Brown in Golf Company. Golf was the "heavy" company in the battalion, with each Marine and corpsman having a suit. Ryck had been in Fox, where only one squad would be suited up if the mission required it. Ryck had seen Brownie out and about, but other than one group conversation on the GFL, he never really had any contact with him.

Ryck had been transferred to H & S, to the Rehab Platoon (the "Sick, Lame, and Lazy Platoon") once he had gotten out of the hospital, and while he still hung out with the guys, he did not train or work with them. Fox had been out on a routine show-the-flag mission to Barrow to help celebrate their Landing Day, so for the last two weeks, he hadn't even had them around. He knew they had returned the night before, but no one had stopped by. It was great when he was around them, but with new guys coming in, and with him going on eight months since being wounded, he felt like he was being forgotten

The green light flashed, and the numbers popped on the screen. Brownie's suit was at 98.7%, good enough for government work. Ryck reached out with his left hand and hit the approve button. Brownie's suit was trundled back to its locker, and another was taken out. Ryck knew he really wasn't necessary for the test. The lab was fully capable of automatically rejecting or accepting test results. This was make-work. This was a result of the psych docs who insisted that all servicemen and women in regen be given work as soon as it was feasible. It was supposed to make them feel needed. On the one hand, Ryck thought that was so much BS. No one doubted that Ryck was hurt. His right arm, now three-quarters grown, was proof of that. But still, the "Sick, Lame, and Lazy" label didn't make him feel very good, nor the "gen hens" nickname, even if those undergoing regen used that term among themselves. On the other hand, he could have done worse. Some of the other gen hens were pushing papers, monitoring chow, or other thrilling, exciting jobs. At least Ryck was still peripherally associated with combat, and both CWO2 Slyth, the Fox Company armorer and CWO4 Heng, the battalion armorer, had taken him under their wings, teaching him quite a bit about not only the PICS suits, but also all the battalion's weapons. Ryck was still infantry through-and-through, but the weapons were pretty brills.

It also helped that CWO4 Heng had a prosthetic hand. It had only been his second regen, and it had gone well at first, but the regen had failed at the wrist. Hands were more difficult than arms, for reasons beyond Ryck's understanding, but still, a partial regen was rare. Heng had petitioned to remain a Marine, and it was granted. His prosthetic was pretty amazing, but still, the Corps rarely approved such requests, and only when the petitioner had a mission that he could accomplish. Of course, CWO4 Heng's four—yes, four Platinum Stars—might have helped with that.

With Heng on his mind, Ryck looked at the regen sleeve on his right arm. This was his fourth sleeve. As his arm grew longer, he went up a size. This one looked to end right about where his wrist would be. He wondered if he would have problems with the hand just as Heng had. He was scheduled for a full scan in two days. Maybe the docs would tell him something then.

Actually, his regen had progressed unremarkably. Sure, he had phantom pain and itching with his missing arm, but not to any great extent. His left fingers, though, had been another story. The itch had driven him crazy. With the regen process, the nerves re-knitting caused prickling for most people, and nothing could be done to stop the cause of the itching. Only the symptoms could be treated, and that with only varying degree of effectiveness.

His regen for his left fingers was technically completed, but he wore a special glove to protect the tips. It was skin tight, so it didn't get in the way of his using the hand. Being one-handed sure beat being no-handed.

"Happy birthday, Marine," CWO4 Heng said, sticking his head in the test lab.

"Happy birthday to you, too," Ryck said.

"You know, the pageant starts in about 20, and the armory is officially off duty now. You coming?" the Heng asked.

"Uh, yeah, sure. I just wanted to get some things finished up here," Ryck said.

In all truth, Ryck hadn't planned to watch the pageant. He couldn't get out of the mess night that was scheduled for the evening, but he figured he could skip the pageant without anyone noticing. He wasn't in the mood to watch the units march in review. While he was holed up in the hospital, Fox and Echo had conducted yet another live op, the takedown of the so-called "Kingdom of Morvania." That was three live ops since Ryck had come aboard, which was pretty amazing for a "peacetime" Corps. Joshua, who had gone to the supposedly premier First Marine Division, had yet to march into harm's way. While Joshua was jealous of Ryck's experiences, Ryck had only been on two of Fox's ops. He'd been lying flat on his back in his hospital bed when the company had answered the call to battle.

CWO4 Heng was waiting, though, so Ryck stopped the 530 and powered it down. Together, they walked down the passage and logged out.

"Happy birthday, Marines," the sailor manning Post 4 said as they came up. Post 4 was manned around the clock, but for the Marine birthday, the sailors at the Naval Air detachment usually took over some of the vital posts to let the Marines enjoy the celebration.

The gunners mate who had taken the post was huge, muscles upon muscles. His obsidian skin was in stark contrast to his Navy whites, and his smile notwithstanding, Ryck got the feeling that he could take on a Marine in a PICS even in just his skivvies. He had no doubt that the armory was in good hands.

The two Marines made their way through the various support buildings, past the regimental headquarters, and out to the parade deck. They skirted the brass, Navy and Marine, the Legion reps, and all the civilian bigwigs in the center section of the bleachers and made their way to the far right to join the other peons. In front of them, the entire regiment and attachments were waiting in formation.

Most Marines celebrated three birthdays in the course of an Earth year. The first was on February 27, commemorating the founding of the Infantería de Marina back in 1537. There had been an unbroken line of service since then, so that was considered the birthdate of the modern Marines. The celebration on Feb 27 tended to be subdued, with memorials for those who had fallen over the years. The most telling moment was when the names of those who had fallen that year were "read out," that is, their names announced as they joined the list of absent comrades.

The second birthdate was November 10th. This was the date when the Federation Marines were officially stood up. That this was also the anniversary of the date of the US Marine Corps was not lost on anyone, but with the largest contribution to the new Marine Corps, the Americans had held some sway. Politics were not absent in matters of the military. This birthday was more celebratory. The pageant was one of the main events, the mess night the other. Free-flowing drink and hearty companionship were the orders of the day.

The third birthday varied by unit. With four Marine divisions, each with four regiments (three infantry and one combat support), that made 48 combat battalions in the Corps.

Coincidently, there were 48 separate Marine Corps that joined to form the Federation Marines. While not official at first, each battalion "adopted" one of the old corps. They flew the colors, they kept the artifacts, and they celebrated the founding of that corps. Ryck's regiment, the Ninth Marines, was the "South East Asia Marines." First Battalion had Thailand's Royal Thai Marine Corps. Second battalion, Ryck's battalion, had the Philippines Marine Corps, and Third Battalion had Indonesia's Korps Marinir. On their adopted corps' birthdays, they would serve traditional food from that contributing nation. During the last birthday for Second Battalion, the Philippines had even sent traditional dancers for the celebration. Ryck had been still in the hospital, but the dancers had made the rounds to all the gen hens.

Of course, First Battalion, First Marines had claimed the US Marines, and 3/1[20] had claimed the Infantería de Marina, but that was a waste, as far as Ryck was concerned. It was like having a personal birthday on Christmas.

Ryck had missed the last battalion party, but no one, if it was at all possible, missed the big celebration. Several ambulances pulled up, and most of the non-ambulatory Marines and one corpsman were wheeled out. Ryck caught the eye of Lance Corporal Jonas Greenstein and nodded a greeting over the heads of the other spectators. Jonas had badly broken his back in a hover accident and had been Ryck's hospital suitemate for several months until Ryck was discharged back to the battalion. Even with most of his body intact, it was still going to be a while until his nervous system re-knitted itself.

"Here we go," CWO4 Heng said as the regimental commander stood up and approached the reviewing stand, the sergeant major one step behind and to his left.

Back at Camp Otrakovskiy, outside of St. Petersburg, with the division headquarters and two of the regiments, the division commanding general would be the reviewing officer. This year, the assistant commanding general had gone all the way out to Camp Dneprovskiy and Tenth Marines to be their reviewing officer. That

---

[20] 3/1: Marine shorthand for Third Battalion, First Marine Regiment. 3/4 would be Third Battalion, Fourth Marine Regiment.

meant Col Pierre didn't have anyone from higher headquarters horning in on the regiment's celebration.

With the CO in place, the band slowly marched from behind the formed units. Only the lone drummer kept beat. When it reached in front of the formation, it wheeled about to face the CO. The band commander, who was actually a sergeant in First Battalion, raised his baton and waited.

"Regiment, atten . . . hut!" the adjutant shouted from off to the left of the reviewing stand.

There was the swish and slap of close to 7,000 Marines and sailors coming to attention.

"Sir, the regiment is formed!" the adjutant shouted out, his voice only slightly breaking at the end.

"Very well," came the reply, not as loud, but clear to those in the stands.

With that, the band commander's baton came down, and the band kicked into the Federation national anthem. Everyone in the stands stood up, those in uniform saluting, the rest with their hands over their hearts.

Next came the Marine Corps Hymn, then the Navy Hymn, followed by the Foreign Legion's Le Boudin. Finally, Alexander's planetary anthem was played. Ryck was glad when the last verse of the Dirtball anthem finished that he wasn't back at Camp Otrakovskiy. As the division headquarters, there would be many more foreign dignitaries, and each one would have their government's anthem played.

As the band finished, the adjutant marched out to the center and read the citation. Each year, the commandant sent out his message, and each year, it was read out at pageants and mess nights. Ryck tuned it out.

With the formalities over, the pageant itself could begin. The spectators sat down, the Parade of Marines led it off. This was Ninth Marines, so the three Marines dressed in the uniforms of the Thai, Philippines, and Indonesian Marines were the first to march by. Ryck was surprised to see that it was Sams, Lance Corporal Samuelson now, in the Philippines Marines uniform. Sams had been busted to private only a year before, but he was already back up to lance corporal and the new fair-haired child of the company. Sams and Ryck had two of the four Battle Citation 3s awarded for actions on the *Robin*, but then Sams had gone and earned a BC1 fighting the Kingdom of Morenvia. The so-called King had declared sovereignty for the island nation of Lesia on Glorywall. The only problem was that the people of Lesia had no intention of letting some outsider in, and "Merlin the First" had taken over 500 children hostage to ensure the cooperation of the people. Two Marine companies had gone in to secure the situation. Against only 30-40 "royal militia," it should have been and was a cakewalk. Despite this, Sams had managed to distinguish himself in the rescue of the kids, from all reports saving their lives. From women on Atacama to prisoners on the *Robin* to children on Glorywall, Sams seemed to have a thing for the civilians.

He was grinning ear-to-ear as he marched down in review, smartly saluting the CO as he passed. Following the three positions of honor, Marines marched by in period uniforms for each of the other corps that had made up the Federation Marines. As tradition dictated, once all the corps had marched by, the Federation colors, followed by the Marine Corps colors, passed in review. Everyone came to their feet and saluted again. Then, the mass of Marines started to march. A couple of companies were missing due to operational commitments, but it was still impressive. Ryck hadn't wanted to come, but he felt the pride stir within him. This was a pretty potent force.

After the infantry came the armor, artillery, transport, engineers, and the rest. Recon put on a good show. They had flown up on their one-man scoots in full stealth mode. One moment, the area in front of the CO was empty. A moment later, in unison, the recon company appeared, 15 meters in the air. The crowd broke out into applause.

The reception was even better for the air pass-over. First came the Marine air. The six Storks attached to the regiment did a flyover, followed by the Hummingbird aerial recon team. A big Navy planetary transport flew by, low and slow, looking huge. The Marine Wasps drew the oohs and aahs, looking sleek and deadly. But it was the Navy Experion fighters that caused the crowd to break out in applause again. The deadly dual space and planetary fighters were impressive, to say the least. The entire pageant took over an hour, with the band, the adjutant, the sergeant major, and the CO standing at attention, never moving except for the CO when he returned a salute. To Ryck, that was more impressive than anything else.

"Well, another pageant come and gone," CWO4 Heng said.

"How many of them have you seen?" Ryck asked.

"Too many to count," was the simple reply. "You going down there to say hello to your bros?"

Ryck looked to the right where all the equipment had been set up as static displays and Marines and civilians were already milling about.

"No, sir, I don't think so. I might need a little extra time to get ready for the mess night, so I think I'm heading back to the barracks."

"OK, but make sure you are there on time. You know how that is," the chief warrant officer said.

"No problem, sir. I'll be there."

Ryck made his way out of the bleachers. He said hello to Jonas and a few of the other gen hens, then quietly slipped away. He just didn't feel up to mixing with the able-bodied Marines.

Chapter 23

There wasn't a facility large enough for a full regimental mess night, so the battalions had broken off to have their own. Second Battalion had rented out the Raging River Mövenpick Resort, some 50 km outside of Rostov and Camp Kolesnikov. It was out in the middle of nowhere, but that was probably all for the best.

Ryck looked across the ballroom at the gathering Marines. Despite himself, he started feeling the esprit de corps he'd felt was missing since his injury. For some reason, he almost wanted to hold onto his feeling of isolation, but he knew that was crazy. He had to just let go and enjoy himself.

"Look, there's Captain dela Grosso," Troy Simmons said, pointing to the battalion's most decorated Marine. The captain had two Navy Crosses, one of only two Marines on active duty to be so distinguished. One of those should have been a Federation Nova, most Marines thought, but still, two Navy Crosses was nothing to sneeze at.

"He's sure got a shitload of hangers," Ryck said to Troy, watching the captain make his way to his seat.

Troy was a sergeant, but among the gen hens, ranks had a tendency to fade, and first name use between ranks was pretty common.

"Yeah, him and your good buddy, Heng," Troy said. "He's got more hangers than anyone, just no Navy Crosses."

Ryck looked over next to the bar where CWO4 Heng was standing. Troy was right. Heng had to have at least 25 hangers on his chest. Ryck looked down at his own chest. He had three. There was his Combat Mission Medal with a bronze star, his Purple Heart, and his Battle Commendation Third Class. Some of the long-time Marines had upwards of 10 or 15 hangers, but still, Ryck had more than most of the non-rates.

"Recruit Lysander! Get down and give me 20" a gravelly, unforgettable voice rang out from just in back of him.

Ryck spun around to see King Tong standing there, a grin on his face. Ryck couldn't have been more surprised had an elephant walked into the room. His heart fell.

"I, uh, I can't really, I mean, my arm!" he protested.

"Relax, Lysander! I'm just messing with you," Sergeant Phantawisangtong said. "So, how've you been doing? I mean, I can see you took some shit, but the word is that you've been doing yourself proud."

Ryck subconsciously covered the regen chamber on this right arm with his left hand and said, "I don't know. I guess so, but really, it was no big deal."

"That's not the word on the street," King Tong said.

"Don't listen to him. He's a certified ass-kicker," Troy said, holding out his hand and introducing himself. "Troy Simmons."

"Hector Phantawisangtong, or as Lysander here will tell you, they sometimes call me 'King Tong.'"

"So, what are you doing here?" Ryck asked, trying to change the subject from the King Tong nickname.

"Since this is a mess night for 2/9, I guess that means I've been transferred here."

Just then, the bugler played the call to order. The Guest of Honor must have just arrived. Marines started to move to the main ballroom where the mess night would be held. King Tong made his apologies and went his own way while Ryck followed the other gen hens to a table close to the front entrance to the ballroom where they would be sitting. Three Marines in their hospital gurneys were already there, waiting for them, as well as those in wheelchairs. Ryck took the first empty seat, next to Jonas, who was at the table in his wheelchair.

There was minimal milling about as the Marines and sailors took their seats. When the CO, who was the president of the mess, called the mess to attention, eyes craned to see the guest of honor.

"Battalion, I present Corporal Lek Gutterheim, veteran of the War of the Far Reaches!"

All the members of the mess applauded as the frail old man, on the arm of the sergeant major, entered the mess. He was bent at the back, but his head was held high, his eyes blazing with pride.

The adjutant's voice rang out as the three made their way to the head table, "Corporal Lek Gutterheim enlisted in the Marines on February 3, 256, Standard Accounting. His first duty station was with the Alpha Company, First Battalion, Sixth Marines, Second Marine Division. He participated in three operations, rising to the rank of lance corporal, and was a fire team leader at the outbreak of the war. During the conflict, he made two opposed landings, on G-12 and Felicity. He was promoted to the rank of corporal, and after the surrender of the CALCON forces, served out the remainder of his enlistment. He returned to his home here on Alexander where he married his wife Anna, and had four children: Paul, Sarah, Allison, and Horace. Horace served 30 years in the Federation Navy, reaching a rank of master chief."

More applause sounded as the head party took their seats. The War of the First Reach had been a full-scale, ship-on-ship, opposed-landing war, not like the skirmishes and police actions since then. Entire fleets had been wiped out. Very few vets from the war were still around, and it was a privilege to have Corporal Gutterheim as their guest of honor.

Once the head party was in place, the bugler stepped forward, along with the mess butler, and called forth the beating. A palpable sense of anticipation arose among the mess. It started with a lone beat of the drum outside the ballroom. A single drummer marched into the mess. A few moments later, another drummer appeared, commencing to join the first as soon as he crossed the threshold into the room. Six more drummers made their way, one-by-one, until all eight were at the center of the ballroom, right in front of the head table. They looked like robots, their arms in perfect unison as they pounded out the beating.

Ryck especially liked it when different drummers snapped their drumsticks to eye level, horizontal, and held them there for a second, before bringing them back down again to re-join the rest. This went on for about seven or eight minutes, the drummers marching in complex patterns, their beat never faltering. Ryck found himself beating out his own tattoo with his left hand on the table.

When the drummers at last finished, the mess erupted once more into cheers and applause. This was always one of the highlights of a mess night, or most any celebration. When the Federation Marines were formed, there had been some discussion on the Marine bands. The 38 Marine bands (not every corps had a band) actually performed a throw-down. The US Marine Band, with its members having music degrees, had probably been the most technically-advanced band, and it had been chosen by the brass to form the basis of the new Marine band. The Royal Marine Band, though, and in particular, the Royal Marine Drum Corps, had been the immediate favorite of the rank and file, and by popular demand, were given a place in the new corps. A US Marine Band clone was set up on Earth at Marine Headquarters, but for the divisions, it was buglers and drummers. The leopard skin worn by some Royal Marine drummers became the uniform for all drummers, something worn with pride.

Members of the band practiced in their free time. They were not professional musicians but came out of all the jobs that Marines held. The long hours they put in, all in their free time, did not bother them, and there was always a waiting list to join.

A Marine mess night was loosely based on the old Royal Navy and Marine mess nights, but the mess beating was something that was right out of 21st Century Great Britain.

The mess butler (a civilian worker for the resort) stepped up with a silver tray and two glasses of port. The senior drummer came forward to meet him at the head table. The mess president took one glass, the drummer the other. At the colonel's nod, they both lifted and emptied their glasses. Once more, applause broke out.

The colors were then marched on. Being part of the color guard was considered a great honor, but Ryck did not really know any of the four Marines who were part of this year's guard. Of course, these were all Marines who had done well in combat, and Ryck had been bedridden or worked in the armory for the past year, so that was not surprising.

With the colors emplaced, next came the citation. This could be something from past battles to great deeds, but for the birthday, it was always the same thing, a copy of the first commandant's birthday message to the Corps on its first birthday. It was read by the junior member of the mess, in this case, Private Topol Narx, all of 18 years, 256 days old. His quavering voice went through the citation, faltering twice as he spoke before the assembled mess.

There was one more ceremony before they could eat.

The president of the mess stood up, and in a loud voice of authority, ordered "Parade the beef!"

Two servers pushed a large silver tray on wheels. The top was opened up to reveal a huge prime rib roast. To Ryck, it looked like real organic beef, not a manufactured roast. His mouth started watering as the servers pushed it through the aisles. As the cart was wheeled out, the order came to take their seats.

"That was pretty copacetic," one of the Marines at the table said, someone Ryck didn't really know.

"Yeah, brills," Jonas added. "It always gets my blood pounding. Bata-tat tat! Bata-tat-tat!"

Ryck had to admit it had much the same effect on him. He looked up at the head table. Corporal Gutterheim was sitting there, his pride evident even at this distance. The man had served only one enlistment, even if it was in a full-out war. He'd had a successful career, married, had children, even grandchildren, but he seemed to hold a special place in his heart for being a Marine, to wear his old uniform, to be called "Corporal Gutterheim" again.

Ryck was proud of being a Marine, too. He'd made it through recruit training when so many others hadn't. He'd proven himself under fire. It was just that lately, he didn't *feel* like a Marine. He was missing something. Looking up there at the old man, though, tweaked something deep within his consciousness. There *was* something special about being a Marine, even if he hadn't gone on a mission in over a year.

"Hey, spaceboy! Where you at, there? You gonna eat?" Troy's voice cut through his reverie.

He looked down at the salad that had appeared in front of him. The servers were busy getting everyone fed.

"Yeah, sure. I'm starving," he replied.

And he was pretty hungry. The Mövenpick had done a pretty good job with the meal. It was all delicious. He joked with the others at the table, realizing that all of them were in the same boat. All were temporarily out of action, but they would all return to it. That gave them a bond of shared experience. They were not alone in that, though. Looking up at the colonel on the head table, with his four purple hearts, that was proof that people could get through it and on with their lives.

After the main courses, the birthday cake was wheeled out. It was immense. The colonel cut two pieces with his sword. The first was given to the guest of honor as the oldest member of the mess. The second was given to Pvt Narx as the youngest. The Mövenpick servers then descended on the cake, and in a surprisingly short amount of time, it was cut up and all 2,000 + Marines served a piece. With the meal itself finished, all the plates were cleared, leaving only the port decanters and the glasses.

"Mr. President, the port is placed," intoned the sergeant major.

This was the cue for the pouring of the port. On each table, the decanter was poured, then passed to the left, sliding the decanter along the table, never lifting it off. Three of the Marines at their table, alongside the table, to be precise, could not move their arms, and their corpsmen attendants, in their Navy full dress, were prepared to pour for them, but before the port made it around, the colonel and the guest of honor walked up, and without a word, the colonel took the decanter and poured for the three Marines. The old Marine whispered something into the ear of Chase Hannrahan, one of the immobile men. Whatever he said brought tears to Chase's eyes.

The two men walked back to the head table and waited for the sergeant major.

"Mr. President, the port is passed."

With the port passed, the toasts started. The Corps, the Marines in the corps, the sister service of the Navy, the president, the Federation, the guest of honor, the good wives of Marines . . . pretty much everyone received a toast.

The conclusion of the toasts marked the end of the formalities of the mess. The colors were marched off, and the officers and staff NCOs made their rounds, shaking hands, before leaving. For smaller unit messes, everyone might stay together for drinking and mess games, but the common understanding was that it was a little difficult for a private to let loose and have fun when there was a colonel standing there at his shoulder. The senior Marines slowly filtered out, off to drink and do whatever officers or SNCOs did in another room, leaving the main ballroom to the NCOs and non-rates.

"Gentlemen, the bar is open for an hour, courtesy of the officers," the battalion sergeant major said, pausing at the door. "Enjoy, brothers, and *audaces fortuna iuvat.*"

The cheer was deafening. Some Marines rushed the bar, ready to maximize the hour. One of the servers came over to take orders for the gen hens, which made it easier. Ryck was tempted to order a glass of wine, but after the heavy port, a beer sounded better.

He was sipping on the beer, chatting with Jonas, when a voice interrupted him with, "Is this a private party, or can anyone join?"

Ryck looked up to see Sams standing there, beer in hand. He looked good in his dress blues. The BC1 he had, along with his Combat Mission Medal and BC3, especially made him stand out. It wasn't hard to see why the guy was so popular with the ladies.

"No, take a seat," Ryck said eagerly.

"Well, actually, some of the guys sent me here to see if you wanted to join us. We don't want to take you away from your new buddies," he said, indicating Jonas, "but we kinda miss your sorry ass and want to catch up."

Ryck looked to Jonas who said, "Nah, you go. I'm about ready to call it in. The buses are going to start the runs back, and I think I'll get on one."

Ryck wished Jonas a happy birthday, then followed Sams back to the Fox Company area.

"'Bout time you showed up, you limp dick!" Smitty shouted, already well on his way to a horrendous hangover in the morning. "Let me get you another beer!"

The others shouted their welcome as well. Hu kicked out a seat which Ryck took. There were several new Marines that Ryck barely knew or didn't know at all.

"You hanging in there?" Sparta asked.

"Yeah, no problem. All's good."

"Ryck's been fingerfuckin' all the PICS," Smitty yelled out. "He's gonna jump ship and go back to fuckin' Golf, no offense," he said over his shoulder in the general direction of the Golf Company tables, "when his arm grows back."

"Hey, Smitty . . ." Sparta began, putting his hand on the other corporal's shoulder.

"You think I'm going to Golf? No, they only take the most stellar Marines, so I guess I'm stuck here with all you asshole rejects," Ryck said.

Smitty was a good guy, but a drunk was a drunk, and it was hard to know how he would take some trash talk when seven sheets to the wind.

"Hah! Yeah, motherfuckers! Fox asshole rejects! We rejected that fuckin' dumbass king, though. Let me tell you, Ryck, you are always welcome back here to Fuckin' Fox Rejects! Here, let me get you another beer."

Ryck hadn't even opened the last one Smitty had given him only a few moments before, but he took the next one, too. Sams came back with yet another beer, saw Ryck had two unopened, shrugged, and opened the one he brought and took a swig.

"You should have been with us on Barrow. I mean, it was just for a celebration. You wouldn't need your arm for that. They treated us like kings!"

"Fuck, yeah," Smitty added.

"And there was this . . ."

"No, wait," Ryck interrupted Sams. "Let me guess. There was this redhead, 20 years old, about 1.6 meters, big tits, who just wanted to show you around town."

"Uh, well, she was a brunette, and she was 25," he protested as the others hooted in laughter.

"He's got you pegged, Sams," Hu shouted.

"He got her the first day, but don't forget that heavy-worlder, the teacher, just before we flew out," Mabala, one of the new Marines added.

"A heavy-worlder?" Ryck asked Sams.

"And what's wrong with a heavy-worlder?" T-Rex asked.

"Nothing if he's a Marine beside you? But what, she had to outweigh him by 30, 40 kilos?"

"Ah, just remember, my mother's a heavy-worlder. Sister, too," T-Rex said without rancor.

"Well, yeah, she was heavier than me, but only by maybe 10 kilos. Real good in the sack, though," Sams said.

That started a conversation on the relative merits of women from various worlds. Ryck sat back, just happy to take it all in. It was like he'd never been gone.

In the middle of the ballroom, some Marines were playing VSTOL. They had looped a rope around one of the ballroom's rafters (a Mövenpick staff had tried to stop that, then wisely retreated leaving the Marines to the field of battle) so Marines could grab the running end while another end, the one coming down from the rafter, was tied onto a very drunk sergeant. A table was set up under the sergeant. The goal was to lower the sergeant so he landed on the table, not touching the floor. This was the VSTOL part of it, the Vertical and Short Takeoff and Landing. Not too hard. Except that other Marines were the "crosswinds." They pummeled the sergeant, grabbed and swung him, threw drinks and chairs at him, anything to get him swinging and missing the table. The landing crew had to time the swinging in order to drop him on target. Ryck watched as the landing team almost made it, only to watch the hapless sergeant bounce off the edge of the table to land hard on the floor.

Mess games had been going on for hundreds of years, although in the days of ocean navies, VSTOL was most likely not one of them. But the mess night, the celebration of who they were and of their brotherhood, that hadn't changed over the centuries.

"Hey Ryck, you had some of those conservative religious groups on your home planet, right? Didn't you tell me that? Mabala here, he says the religious girls are conservative on the outside but tigers in bed. Is that true?" Sams asked.

Ryck laughed and turned back to his friends, his brothers. He'd been down and out, a little lost at sea over the last several months. His fellow Marines had dragged him back, and he was good to go.

"Well, it's like this. Those religious girls, in their long clothes, that gets them hot in more ways than one," he started on a sea story, one probably only 10% based on truth, which for a sea story, made it practically gospel.

Luminosity

Chapter 24

"Biofeedback, 100%. Tamberhall, let's get the weapons pack on and run it through. Time's getting pretty short," CWO3 William Weston, the Golf Company ordnance officer told Corporal Jasper Tamberhall, one of his enlisted armorers.

Lance Corporal Ryck Lysander patiently waited while Tamberhall pushed the button that lifted and attached his weapons pack. While each PICS' longjohns, the tight inner, sensor-laden skinsuit that a Marine wore while in his mech, was individually fitted to each Marine, the PICS themselves, although specifically *assigned* to an individual Marine, were still one-size-fits-all. That required regular maintenance to ensure the longjohns were communicating with the PICS' brain. This was not often a problem, but the weapons pack was a little different. Weapons packs were mission-loaded, and a Marine could get any of the normal loads and some custom loads, depending on the mission and his specific task in the mission. As a Marine could get any weapons pack, the connections had to be checked and re-checked before he was sent into harm's way. In an emergency, a Marine could just suit up and go, but when there was time, a partial, or preferably, a full check was made.

Ryck, as a semi-trained armorer, had helped CWO3 Weston as the testing commenced, but now it was his turn. He had to get back to his squad and get ready for the landing.

"Pack 2, attached. Commencing analytics," Tamberhall said as the chief warrant officer walked down the line to the next testing station.

Corporal Tamberhall had all the information in front of him, but the armorers always vocalized. Mix-ups could happen, and an assaultman who showed up to blow a door with a Pack 1 instead of the EOD Pack 5 would be useless, and the mission could fail. It was up to the Marine himself to listen to the armorer and to check the readout on his visor, to make sure he had the correct pack.

Ryck was the fire team's heavy gunner for the mission, so Pack 2 was correct.

"Weapons pack check, 100%," Tamberhall said about 20 seconds later. "You are cleared for combat. Next!" he shouted.

Ryck stepped off the platform, went to the walk-in, and popped the PICS, wiggling out the back and leaving the empty suit standing in its assigned spot. As always, Ryck pictured the empty combat suit as the shell of a cicada as the adult insect, Ryck, in this case, wormed free of it. Ryck was in the longjohns for the duration, but the PICS would sit there, an armed Navy bosun in the walk-in for security, until it was time to launch.

He checked his watch. There was just enough time to get some chow before he had to be at the final brief. He was actually a little too excited to eat, but a good Marine ate when he could, not knowing when the next opportunity would arise. He could be inside his PICs for quite some time, and the nutritional base fed to them while in the PICS, the "ghost shit," did little to assuage hunger even if it kept the body going.

He thought back to Smitty back on the Dirtball, who had accused him of wanting to go to Golf when he returned to full-duty. Ryck had been serious at the time that he wanted to come back to Fox, where his friends were. He was surprised, then, when his orders were to Golf. His time in the armory probably had something to do with it. Golf was the battalion's heavy company, with two platoons being heavy and only one being light instead of the other way around. Even then, the "light platoon" spent more time training in PICS than the lights in the other companies and could suit up if the need arose. Ryck wasn't assigned as an armorer, even if CWO4 Heng had hinted that Ryck could make the switch if he so desired. But Ryck wanted back into a fire-team. So, he was with the Second Fire Team, First Squad, First Platoon. Corporal Nimoto was his fire team leader, Sergeant Phantawisangtong his squad leader. At first, Ryck thought it just the worst coincidence he could imagine. But it wasn't a coincidence. King Tong had specifically asked for him. And it really hadn't turned out to be that bad. Squad Leader King Tong was not the same man as Drill Instructor King Tong. "Hecs," he was called by the other NCOs, but to Ryck, he was still King Tong.

Ryck hustled to Enlisted Galley D. This was not the little *Adelaide*. This was the *FS Praecipua*, a Prion Class battlecruiser, named for the battle during the War of the First Reaches. It was a modern dreadnaught, a huge ship, and the entire battalion was embarked. The ship itself was probably overkill. It wasn't like it could unleash its planet busters in this case. But the brass probably hoped that just the appearance of the big ship would quell the situation. If that happened, then the Marines would just have been passengers. Ryck knew he should wish for that. But after a year-and-a-half of inactivity, he hoped for some action. He knew he should feel ashamed about that, but the fact was that he didn't.

Galley D was the unofficial Marine galley. Technically, a sailor, Marine, or members of the FCDC advance party could eat at any enlisted galley, but in practice, the enlisted men and women tended to segregate themselves. The Marines took over Galley D as it was close to their main berthing. Ryck and a few others had eaten breakfast that morning at Galley B, just to see if there was a difference between "Navy food" and "Marine food." There wasn't.

There were at least 150 Marines with the same idea as Ryck in the galley, grabbing hot chow while they could. Over half were in skins. These would be the light infantry Marines, both from Golf and the other companies. The rest were in their longjohns. The longjohns were *extremely* tight and left absolutely nothing to the imagination. The Marines in their skins kept a running commentary about the various attributes, or lack thereof, of the PICS Marines. Fox was embarked on the ship as well, but a quick glance showed that none of Ryck's friends were there at chow. The company must have been in the middle of something. With only four hours before launch, Ryck thought that would have been a good guess.

"Hey, Ryck, you think we're going to launch?" Lance Corporal Naranbaatar Bayarsaikhan, asked as Ryck sat down.

"Ghengis" was from Larudi, the extremely homogenous world settled by Mongolians, and take away his longjohns, fit him out with furs and sit him on a horse with a "larudi" on his arm, and he could pass for his ancient forebearer and nicknamesake, Ghengis Khan himself.

"Don't know," Ryck said. "Would you want to fight if you looked up and saw the *Prake* over you?"

"Well, they know we're about there, and they know what we've got. They haven't surrendered yet," Ghengis said.

"Wait until we launch," Private Courtland Prifit said. "Iffen they don't we'll kick their perking asses."

Ghengis just looked at Ryck and raised his eyebrows. Ryck shrugged. Courtland was a boot, and this was his first operation. Boots were better seen and not heard.

Their mission was to restore the government of Luminosity. Luminosity was not a corporate world, but one founded by a freespeaker society at the height of the movement some 200 years ago. Over the years, it had grown economically, but with keeping in line with their founding philosophy, had minimal government and no armed forces. Even the police were only part-time deputies.

During the planet's third immigration wave, according to the brief the Marines and sailors had received, refugees from Kyber had arrived, settling in the main mountain range. When they started their own militia, the planetary authorities had objected, but as this was a "free" world, having a private militia was technically considered a matter of personal choice, and therefore legal.

That may have been a mistake, because over a month ago, that "militia" took over the government, declaring themselves in charge and the "protectors" of the citizens from both crime and outside influences. When people objected, they were arrested and thrown into hastily-constructed jails.

That created a call for assistance from the Federation. Two weeks later, the Federation voted to intervene, skirting the law by declaring that this was merely a "police action." The fact that the rare earth mines, especially the scandium and gadolinium mines, were closed by the new rulers, couldn't have had anything to do with the extremely quick response by the resource-hungry central planets of the Federation.

With somewhere close to 3,000 in the militia, the powers that be determined that one reinforced Marine battalion, with 2,000+ Marines, would be enough to defeat them and get things back to normal. The reports that the militia might have both armor and combat suits were largely discounted.

The battalion was assigned the mission and given two days to embark. The *Prake* was pure Navy and didn't often carry embarked Marines. But as modern bubble warships generally differed primarily in size alone, it wasn't that difficult for the ship to accommodate the Marines.

It actually took three days before they could get underway, and then another three days of bubble-space time to reach Luminosity. The ship had come out of bubble space an hour before. In another three hours, it would be in orbit around the planet.

The ship had an immense capability with more firepower than the entire Marine Corps and a good portion of the Civil Development Corps. (Not many people realized it, due to planned disinformation, but even the Civil Development Corps, which was actually an occupation army, had much more firepower than the Marines.) Using the ship's firepower on Luminosity, though, would be difficult if not impossible. Not only was the bulk of the population on the side of the Federation, but also the mines themselves could not be damaged if shipments were to commence immediately.

Marines started leaving the mess decks. Ryck looked at his watch.

"Hey, eat up. We've got to go."

They crammed down their food and got back to their staging area, a large space that they shared with crates of some sort. Then they waited. And waited. The lieutenant gathered them all together to go over their ops order, but in reality, that was busywork. They had gone over it ad infinitum, and no plan lasted past the first few minutes of contact, anyway. So, it was hurry up and wait, which was par for the course.

It was a relief when the word was broadcast throughout the ship that the landing was on. Most of the Marines gave an "ooh-rah" as they scrambled to their feet and rushed to their respective walk-ins. Ryck rushed to his PICS and slithered through the back. This actually took some effort as the weapons pack was still attached, so Ryck had to get low, over the butt of the PICS, then worm his way through the opening and up the suit, then pulling his legs up until he could slide them down inside. Some of the other Marines were having problems, but there was enough assistance, Marine and Navy, to get them suited up. An armorer ran a quick check on each Marine and initiated the cold pack.

One of the problems with any type of armored suit was getting rid of built-up body heat. The old-fashioned fins that dissipated heat into the atmosphere made it easy for heat-seekers to pick up a suit's signature. The PICS were the first Marine mech suit to use cold packs. A cold pack was a surprisingly small mass of a molecularly-arrayed synthetic heat sink. To the layman, it looked like jelly. What it did was capture heat. It had to be controlled carefully, though. If left unregulated, it could literally suck all the body heat from a Marine, killing him from hypothermia. If it didn't work efficiently, it could kill a Marine from heatstroke. Any damage it received in the field could have deadly consequences, which was why each cold pack had a small jettison command that could be sent to eject it from the PICS. The same access could be used to exchange the pack as each pack was only good for 24 to 30 hours, depending on the weather and other factors.

Finally, they were ready, and the lieutenant was given the OK. He ordered the platoon out and to the hangar. The Stork waiting for them was configured for PICS. It had no enclosed cargo bay. Marines and their corpsmen backed up to the overhead racks, and the back of their PICS married to the "clothes hooks." With a click, they were attached.

Within moments, the Stork lifted and flew out the hangar. The Stork was dual-purpose, but it was better designed for air operations. In space, it was a little slow. So, the Storks took off before any of the support craft, the fighters and attack craft.

With no deck, the Marines were suspended "above" open space. Some Marines didn't like the "dangle," even Marines who could do EVAs without a problem, but Ryck rather liked the sensation. He'd only had two training lifts, and this was his first combat launch. Without having to fly an EVA suit, he could just sit back and enjoy the ride.

The Stork rotated, and the *Prake* fell out of view behind them, the planet filling their field of vision. Ryck knew that it would be another 30 minutes until they landed. He looked around, trying to catch sight of one of the other Storks or fighters, but space was big, and he couldn't see anything.

It was obvious when they reached Luminosity's atmosphere. It started with a glow, then a burning fire that filled the space with light as the gasses of the atmosphere compressed in front of the vehicle. Ryck knew that if the diversion field on the Stork failed, they would all burn up within moments, but that really was not a concern of his, any more than if the powerpack on his PICS would explode, or if his Navy chow was contaminated. He just didn't think about odd possibilities.

"Fifteen minutes to touchdown," his comms' AI intoned.

Ryck looked, trying to see through the flaring of the atmosphere, trying to pick out some landmarks. Nothing. It wasn't for another 30 seconds that the burning died down, and he could see the planet's surface.

The bulk of the planet's population was on two main land masses. There was a small unit of the People's Army, as the militia was calling itself, on the larger mass, holding the main city there, but they would be dealt with during the second phase of the operation. Phase 1 was to take back control of the capital and the second-largest city, rescue those being held as prisoners, and secure the three main mine sites. The militia was larger, but it was spread fairly thin. The Marines could concentrate their forces and have local numerical superiority. That, in addition to the Marines better training and equipment, should give the Marines the upper hand.

The Rules of Engagement were fairly stringent: minimize friendly casualties as well as damage to the infrastructure. For this reason, Fox (REIN)[21] had the point of main effort at the capital to dispose of the illegal Luminosity government and rescue those citizens held as prisoners. PICS were not particularly effective in combat in a built-up area, unless full-scale destruction was allowed, so the more nimble-foot Marines, in skins and bones, would be employed there, with a squad of PICS Marines in support. Weapons Company would take out the militia camp outside of the capital. Echo Company would take the first mine objective (this was a foreign-owned mine, and rumor had it that this was selected due to some very highly-placed people in the Federation government having stock in the company).

Golf's mission was the encampment located outside of Green Falls, the planet's second-largest city. This was the largest encampment uncovered, and it was well-situated to react to any threat toward the bulk of the largest mines on the planet. Without friendly infrastructure or significant friendly personnel at the camp, this was more of a free fire target, where all Marine and Navy assets could be employed. Golf, with arty and armor attached, was on a mission to destroy, not rescue or save. The People's Army at the camp was to be destroyed so that none of the forces could deploy to the mines.

As the surface of the planet became visible, Ryck tried to place their own position relative to the ground below. They wouldn't be coming straight in from above, so the target was not under them. They would sweep in from southeast to northwest, supported by two of the attached Wasps and three Navy Experion fighters. Coming in on that trajectory kept them below any anti-air defenses until the end of the approach, but it also kept them out of the way of the Navy bombardment. The *Prake* had deployed one of its monitors to soften up the rebel camp. This ball of firepower had no sailors on board; it was operated entirely from the dreadnaught. It did carry a pretty solid punch, though. Parked in orbit right over the camp, so weapons had to travel through the least amount of atmosphere, it swept the camp with particle beams, disrupter fire, and explosive ordnance.

---

[21] REIN: Reinforced with additional personnel and capabilities.

Ryck had the map pulled up on his visor, watching as they approached. At thirty klicks, though, he could actually see the flash of ionized gasses as the particle beams reached down from orbit to the camp.

Ryck ignored most of the chatter coming over the platoon circuit. It was mostly a countdown until they hit the deck. If there were anything important, he would pay closer attention. He only half-listened as he did yet one more status check on his PICS and ammo load.

As the Stork swooped in, he waited for the green light. It wasn't as if he would have to do anything. Technically, a PICS could withstand a 5-meter fall without damage, and the Stork could land on the ground so the Marines could take one step and be on terra firma. But the Storks were a valuable piece of equipment, and a land mine could take one out, so the Marines would be lowered via a hoist that was incorporated into each station. After the flare, a Stork could debark a platoon of Marines within five seconds.

The ground got closer, and a voice came over the circuit, "Fox-1, stand by!"

The go-light flashed green. Three seconds later, Ryck fell out of the sky. Five seconds was not very long, but it was more than long enough for the bad guys to take them under fire, so Ryck quickly scanned the ground, waiting to fire at any threat. They had trained to fire while being dropped, and with varying, if not very effective, degrees of success, but Ryck would go down trying if it came to that.

Nothing presented itself, though, and Ryck hit the ground, his hoist line automatically disconnecting and retracting back to the Stork, which had already begun to move out.

Ryck moved to his left, relying on visuals to get into position. His head's up display had every member of the platoon identified, and if he zoomed out, he would be able to see the entire company, but he still felt more comfortable with actual visuals.

"Fox-1, move out" the lieutenant passed.

In another time and place, the first few minutes of an assault would be taken up with getting oriented, of getting a headcount, but the lieutenant's PICS-C had even more information flowing to him on each and every one of them. The common statement was that he knew if you got a hard-on and why. Staff Sergeant Grabrowski's PICS was "C-capable," which meant it had all the bells and whistles. He could view the same incoming information on each Marine, but if anything happened to the platoon commander, the AI would switch over and give his PICS the same capabilities, not only downstream but upstream as well. Ryck's PICS was the basic model with more limited upstream capabilities.

As the platoon moved out, a Navy LCC came in carrying a tank. It had to land in order to discharge its cargo, and that took a little bit of time. Still, even if it was behind them at the moment, knowing that a Davis was there was a nice security blanket.

Ryck moved forward, trying to divide his focus between what he could see in front of him and his displays. There was quite a bit of data streaming in, and he still was not totally comfortable with watching the real world out there and the electrons symbolizing the world on his visor at the same time. He could see Greg Hohn moving up just in front and to his side, but Greg was also the first blue triangle that appeared on his visor display. He knew on an intellectual level that triangle symbolized Greg, but he hadn't yet made the leap to "feel" that it was Greg, and he needed to do that to maximize his own effectiveness, to be able to instinctively and quickly react instead of having to think things through.

The platoon had about 900 meters of forested land through which to move, then there were another 400 meters of cleared land to cross before reaching the outer defenses of the camp. It wasn't as if this was a surprise, either. Storks in the air and PICS on the ground were somewhat hard to hide. Tactical "surprise" in the assault had to be how the Marines were employed, not in trying to hide the fact that there was going to be an assault in the first place.

He looked up to the upper-left section of his visor and blinked twice. The feed there switched positions and filled the center of his visor. It was a visual of the camp. A recon Marine out there somewhere had the camp under surveillance and was beaming the view to every Marine. There was the tiniest hint of a flicker, which was a good sign that the enemy was trying to jam the signal, but the AIs kept switching the frequency every micro-second, both for the broadcast and receiving, faster than whatever equipment the rebels had could catch up.

The vid showed a devastated landscape. There were no intact buildings. The Navy had leveled them. Ryck was not complacent, though. He knew the rebels were still there. He quickly switched back to visual, scanning the area in front of him. His PICS was moving smoothly, just an extension of his movements. He moved his leg, the PICS moved its leg. It was all done without thinking. His head being almost three meters up, his "hands" reaching out over two meters, had taken a little getting used to during training, but now it was second nature.

For the thousandth time, he checked his HGL. The "Heavy Grenade Launcher" was his prime weapon, the principal weapon in any Weapons Pack 2. Greg, to his right, had Weapons Pack 1, which gave him the hypervelocity rifle, similar to the M99 Marines carried when on foot, but at 8mm, packing a much bigger dart. The HGL, though, fired a 20mm grenade. A combat load of the grenades was 250 and could be anti-personnel or anti-armor. The anti-armor could take out almost any tank if employed correctly, and the anti-personnel had an ECR of 30 meters. It could fire 60 rounds per minute, so it packed a pretty powerful punch.

Second Platoon was heading right up the gut of what had been determined to be the brunt of the defenses. They were doing this to set the defense, to get them to commit while First Platoon swept up their flank. Weapons Platoon was supporting both heavy platoons, and Third, the light platoon, was in reserve, ready to exploit any advantage.

Ryck's visor lit up with activity. Second was being hit. As a grunt, he was not privy to all the comms, but it was obvious from the display if not from the sounds of explosions a klick to his right.

"All hands, be advised that the enemy forces are employing both Boost-Assisted Anti-Armor weapons as well as anti-armor mines," the lieutenant's calm voice came over the platoon circuit.

That was a surprise. Mines were part and parcel to modern combat, but Boost Assisted Anti-Armor rounds could take out a PICS. Only one power used those weapons: The Congress of Free Worlds. The Congress was a loosely allied group of 14 planets in the

Third Quadrant, a long way from Luminosity. If the People's Army had Congress weapons, that meant either the Congress was sticking its nose into Federation space or that arms dealers were supplying them to the rebels. Congress weaponology was no match for Federation, even the older Marine equipment, but still, getting hit with a BAAA round was sure to spoil a grunt's day. The Marines had to trust their PICS to deflect the rounds as they were "dumb" ordnance as the PICS' defenses could not fool a round that had no brain. All suits could do was to confuse the sighting of the weapon and hope for a glancing blow that the LTC armor could deflect.

Ryck started to blink up his scheme to change it, but the platoon sergeant beat him to it. With the command capabilities, he could switch each Marine's paint, and with visual sighting the norm for BAAA weapons, the "LSD" mode was the book answer. The LSD was the nickname for the Fractured Array. It didn't make a PICS actually invisible, but rather "fractured" the light waves, making visual sighting difficult, even causing headaches for those looking at them. An observer knew something was there, but exactly where and what would be difficult to determine.

The sounds of war to his right grew in intensity. Second was getting into it. They wouldn't be closing unless the opportunity presented itself, but that meant First had to step it up and breach the defenses.

A Wasp showed up on his readout. Ryck hoped the platoons were showing up on the pilot's readout as well. There was the incoming icon, but in flashing amber instead of the flashing red of a near-miss by friendly fire. Ryck didn't hesitate in his advance as the sky lit up in front of Second's position as the Wasp's ordnance hit home.

Ryck's visor flashed green twice, signaling that Phase Line Liverpool had been reached. This was when First Squad changed their advance to a new heading, slightly oblique of the other two squads. No verbal orders were given as the new heading was centered in the nav panel.

They had reached the rise leading up to the outer perimeter of the camp. The ground was torn up from the pre-assault bombardment. This was nothing that Ryck's PICS couldn't handle, but the servos still whined a bit with each step over the rough ground as they worked to keep Ryck upright and oriented to the enemy.

Ryck didn't need the speakers to hear the blast just 30 meters to his right. The sound waves easily penetrated his PICS as Greg Hohn was lifted into the air. Ryck watched as the big PICS flew up 10 or 12 meters, then crashed back down. He hesitated a moment, then took a step to check on Greg.

"Back in position, Ryck," King Tong's voice came over the direct circuit.

The squad leader was right. Greg's fate was already determined, and he would be fine or not, but Ryck could not leave the assault. The force had to be focused. He did glance up at Greg's icon. It was still blue, but a light blue instead of the normal dark blue. He was alive and not in immediate danger, but his PICS was damaged. His weapons pack was operational, so he could still provide supporting fire if he could not advance.

The PICS were supposed to be able to locate mines, which had to be what hit Greg. Ryck wondered what happened, then started looking more closely at the ground in front of him.

They were less than 300 meters from the outer perimeter when all hell broke loose. There were at least four BAAAs facing them. They had not been sucked in to confront the frontal assault, which would have been too easy for the Marines. Going against four BAAAs with thirteen PICS should be a reasonable mission. That was, of course, unless the rebels threw something else into the mix.

The PICS could cover the 200 meters over broken terrain in about 20 seconds, and the immediate action for this would be a full charge. He started to lurch into a run as his target comp zeroed in on one of the BAAAs. He lifted the HGL and put three rounds downrange. All three hit the gun. There wasn't a catastrophic kill, but the gun went silent.

One problem with the combat visors was that there could be info overload. There were traces of incoming and outgoing fire, there were orders being given. To Ryck, though, unless he personally received a direct order to do something different, his war narrowed down to who and what was directly in front of him.

Nothing else mattered, and frankly, that was about all he could take in. He had to trust his fellow Marines to take care of business on either side of him.

He fired at another position, a light automatic weapon of some sort, but nothing that could affect a PICS. And then he was inside the outer perimeter. He was within the camp. To his left was the BAAA he'd taken out, a light plume of smoke rising from it. There was an arm visible, but most of the gunner's body was hidden from sight. His original course of action was to breach the perimeter, then force his way deeper, past the outer belt of defenses. However, with Greg out, then the 60 meters or so to his right had not been cleared. Marines were not automatons. They were trained to think. Ryck knew he had to clear the area and not leave a potential pocket of the rebels there. He veered to the right and followed the defensive line until his movement sphere intersected with that of Corporal Nimoto, who'd had the same idea with Greg's sector uncovered and had been moving to his left. As each Marine moved, the AI's determined a "cleared" area and pushed that up to the lieutenant so that he would know what areas had been cleared and what areas still had potential bad guys in them.

Corporal Nimoto pointed a big PICS arm back toward the inner defenses. Ryck didn't acknowledge, but his turning and moving out was enough. Fast dissemination of information was the key to the modern battlefield, so it was ironic that the Marines relied heavily on old fashioned-hand and arm signals. But with crowded nets and anti-comms being employed against them, the less being passed via electrons the better.

Ryck shifted back to his left to where he could cover better both his original sector as well as Greg's. He was a little behind the other Marines, so he hurried to catch up.

The turtle hatch opening up just 20 meters to his front right took him by surprise. His PICS never picked it up until it opened. The big BAAA deployed within a second as Ryck tried to bring his HGL to bear. Before he could fire, flames flew from the barrel and something big slammed into Ryck's side overpowering the PICS' servos and sending it crashing to the ground.

Ryck was stunned, certain he was in it deep. He tried to stand up, but his PICS complained as his visor started flashing different series of numbers before going dark. He tried to turn his head, and to his surprise, the PICS grudgingly complied. His comms seemed to be gone, but he could see out the visor. The BAAA was right in his sight. It was a type he'd not been briefed on before. It was obviously slaved, either controlled by an AI or by an operator off-site. It moved quickly from target to target, firing away. "Target" seemed impersonal to Ryck. Those "targets" were his fellow Marines.

An explosion rocked the base of the BAAA. That had to be the Davis, getting into the fight. The BAAA immediately spun around and let out a string of fire, faster than Ryck had thought possible. There was no return fire from the Davis.

Ryck took stock of his situation. Despite being initially stunned, he didn't seem hurt. His PICS, though, was at 10% at best. His visor occasionally flickered on, but for the most part, he was cut off from the rest of the platoon.

The BAAA in front of him was close, only 20 meters away, and it was actively engaging the platoon, but Ryck didn't know what he could do about it. Robot gun or not, he knew a string of his 20 mike-mike grenades would do it some serious hurt.

Ryck tried to force his HGL arm forward. It edged forward before stopping, still a good 40 degrees from being on target. If his weapon wouldn't move, he wondered if his body could. He tried to edge back, hoping to drag his HGL into position. That didn't seem to be happening—all he seemed to do was to roll over on his belly.

Stuck there on his side, he was safe for the moment, but his platoon was still in the shit. He was trying to figure out his next course of action when something seemed to burn his ass. At first, he thought his PICS was on fire, but he couldn't smell anything. The pain started getting intense, and it was spreading down his leg.

Then it hit him. His coldpack had somehow ruptured!

He immediately hit the emergency eject for the pack, which had its own self-contained power source. The PICS made an odd sound of grinding, but nothing happened. The coldpack was still there, spreading down his leg. Already, the right cheek of his ass was numb, probably frozen solid.

He tried the eject again. The same grinding noise sounded, followed by a pop, then silence.

Ryck knew he had to get away from the coldpack. It could literally suck the heat right out of him. If the eject wasn't working, then there was only one choice. He had to molt.

A combat molt was a last-ditch action, used when a suit had to be abandoned. He pulled back his left hand and arm from the PICS sleeve and wormed down his side. He resisted trying to feel around to his ass and grabbed the molt release instead. Once outside, he'd have no protection, but it was better than freezing to death. He gave it a hard pull. At first, he thought it had failed as well, but the molt was not instantaneous. A PICS was a pretty impressive machine that was designed to take a beating, so there were a number of steps to disconnect and break the integrity of it to get out. It normally took about a minute to go through the steps to get out of a suit, but an emergency molt was much, much quicker. It really only took about five seconds, but to Ryck, it seemed like an eternity. The suit split up the back, and Ryck scrambled out.

Once out, he flopped in back of his suit, expecting to feel rebel rounds hitting him. To his surprise, he seemed to be being ignored. Twenty meters from him, the unmanned B-Triple-A kept aiming at targets and firing. The way the gun seemed to pick targets, spinning from one to the other back and forth rather than from one, then to another close by, would indicate that the guns were being controlled by an AI, or at least a program that prioritized targets. When humans selected targets, they tended to go from one then to another that was close by the first target. Humans targeted in patterns while AIs ignored patterns based on location.

Ryck glanced in back of him. The Davis was some 400 meters back, a column of black smoke rising from it. He could see other PICS moving back and forth, taking cover when and where they could. The plan to bull-rush the perimeter was already by the wayside.

Ryck took stock of what he had. That wasn't much. In his longjohns, he had no protection from even thorny bushes, much less weapons. He had his small Ruger 2mm strapped to his thigh, but that was only good against unarmored personnel. His rocket launcher and HCL looked intact, but they were on the weapons pack and so, useless.

Or were they?

Ryck started thinking of the hours he'd spent in the battalion armory. Each weapons pack was powered by the PICS. However, there was a small battery in the pack that kept the electronics alive and functioning while the pack was not attached to a suit. For energy weapons, that little battery wouldn't do much. But Ryck's weapons pack was Number 2, and the pack only used power for the electronics, which included the trigger for both the rockets as well as the grenades. Both weapons were self-powered in flight to the target.

Could he jury-rig the pack to fire?

Ryck scootched forward, his ass and thigh numb, and looked over the pack's connections. It should be easy to release the pack. Throwing the cover lever should do it. Without even thinking, he crawled up on the back of the PICS and pulled on the lever. It barely budged. In the armory, the loader mechanically opened and closed the lever. Ryck's muscles did not match that power. Mindless of the battle raging around him, he stood up on top of his PICS, reached down to grasp the lever, and heaved up with his legs. Grudgingly, the lever moved—one millimeter, two millimeters, three—before suddenly giving way. The weapons pack was free. Ryck had to kick it up and over the PICS helmet before it fell to the dirt.

He scrambled back to it, pushing it over so it "faced" up. The battery was just under the left shoulder. It seemed fine. Ryck pushed the purple test button, and the test lights lit up the armorer's panel in the correct sequence and all green. The weapons pack was undamaged. Throw it on another PICS, and it would be good to go. But Ryck didn't have another PICS.

The question was how he could get the rockets or grenades to fire. The targeting system was in the PICS, not the pack, and his PICS was out of the equation. The firing signal was also generated from the PICS. Ryck couldn't figure out a way to target a weapons pack alone, but he could bypass the firing signal.

He worried out one of his longjohns' control wires, the interface between his body and the PICS. For all the high-tech aspects of the longjohns, the controller was essentially a copper wire. He pulled off the connector, revealing the bright bare metal. Taking out his combat knife, he cut the wire in two. An explosion less than five meters away erupted beside him, showering him with dirt, but he ignored that as he twisted one end of one wire around the HCL firing input positive, and the other around the common ground in the female connector in the pack. All the prongs were color-coded, and because of his work in the armory, he knew which prong was which.

He had to "fool" the pack into thinking a signal was coming from the PICS to fire. But the only power was from the pack's own battery. Using his combat knife, he dug through the silicon coating of the battery to reveal the terminals. He had to be careful. One slip, and the battery would short. He ended up making a small slit on the outside of both terminals. Stripping two more wires from his longjohns, he slid them into the two slits he'd made, trusting the silicon's elasticity to keep the ends of the wires in contact. He took the negative wire and twisted it around the wire that went into the firing input negative. All he would have to do, he figured, was touch the positive from the battery to the positive of the firing input, and the HTC should launch.

"Should," being the operative word.

The power from the battery was not the same as the power from the PICS. Ryck didn't know if the small output from the battery would be enough to activate the trigger mechanism.

All of this had taken a surprisingly short amount of time, maybe a minute at most. Ryck looked up in time to see a PICS off in the distance go down. One of the BAAAs was down as well, but there were three still in action. They were stationary targets, and Ryck didn't understand why the Marines were having issues with them, or why Marine or Navy Air couldn't take them out. He couldn't affect any of that, though.

Ryck had to get the weapons pack up and aimed somehow. The logical step would be to wear the pack, just as if it was on a PICS. The pack alone, with ammo, weighed in at a good 160 kg.

That was a pretty hefty load, and Ryck wasn't sure he could manage it, especially with a half-frozen butt. He turned it around so it was facing down and slid his body in. His head went through the opening easily. Too easily. The pack was designed to sit around the collar and on the shoulders of a PICS. Ryck's shoulders were not nearly as wide, and the collar ring of the pack came down right on the edge of this shoulders. There wasn't much he could do about that, though.

Ryck gathered his feet under him and tried to stand up. He actually lifted the pack off the ground before he fell forward, his neck slamming into the hard edge of the pack. Simply standing up was not going to work. He had to get his feet under him. That was easier said than done. It took some maneuvering and using his PICS hulk as an anchor, but he finally got it done. Taking a deep breath, he stood up.

In the gym, he'd squatted more than that before. But that was on a pad with the weight being a barbell. In this case, he was standing in the dirt of Luminosity, a battle was going full tilt around him, his right butt cheek and leg were numb, and the edge of the weapons pack was digging into his shoulders. With a grunt, he did it, though. He stood up.

He expected the B-Triple A in front of him to swing in his direction and let loose. He was surprised, but quite relieved, when it seemed to ignore him. The AIs or targeting computers evidently were not particularly discerning.

He staggered forward a few steps and stopped. The pack was digging unmercifully into his shoulders. The edge of the pack came down within a couple of centimeters from the edge of this shoulder, so a lot of weight was being supported by only a little of Ryck. And that hurt.

Fifteen meters or 10 meters wouldn't make much difference, so he stopped his advance. The bulk of the grenade launcher was in the pack itself, but the muzzle was normally "worn" on the gauntlet of the PICS. Ryck didn't have the PICS there, so he simply jammed his right hand into the dangling muzzle, then strained to lift it up. A gauntlet was much bigger than a naked hand, so the fit was not right, but at least he could still reach the thumb trigger. The firing trigger itself was electronic, but the switch to open the circuit was the mechanical trigger. With his left hand, he would have to reach to the loose wire to bring it to the other one, closing the circuit and (hopefully) firing the launcher. As he raised the weapon, though, with his right arm aiming and his left trying to reach back under the pack, his shoulders narrowed, and the pack almost slipped off. He had to tense up his left shoulder, keeping it in place as his fingers quested for the wire. He should have made them longer.

He couldn't really aim, so he simply pointed the HTC at the BAAA, hoping that it was on target. With his right arm trembling to hold the muzzle steady while keeping the thumb trigger depressed, he felt the wire and quickly yanked it and touched the end of the wire going into the firing controls.

The grenade launched, nearly ripping Ryck's right arm off, spinning him around and to the ground. The big PICS had the mass to withstand the recoil, but Ryck's 85 kg did not, especially when he had not been prepared for it. He should have been prepared for the recoil, but he hadn't considered that.

Ryck struggled to get up, looking back at the BAAA. The gun had stopped firing, and its movement seemed jerky. But it was still very much alive and very dangerous. Ryck managed to get up, moving toward the rear of the gun, where its armor was not as imposing. Whoever or whatever was controlling the BAAA finally figured out that there was a threat near it. The big gun turned to Ryck, but the cutout that kept the gun from firing back toward the center of the camp also kept it from hitting Ryck, who was not ten meters to the rear. The turtle hatch provided the gun with some cover from the rear, but it wasn't enough.

Ryck leaned forward, bracing himself. Carefully, he touched the wires again while depressing the thumb trigger. The recoil still felt like a mule kick, but Ryck stayed on his feet.

The BAAA started firing, the rounds whipping by five meters to Ryck's front. They couldn't reach him. Ryck fired again. And again.

After the fourth round, the BAAA canted up and to the left. The armor-piercing grenades had hit something vital. The BAAA was dead.

There wasn't a huge explosion, which was all well and good. Standing a mere 10 meters away and without armor, that could have messed up Ryck's day. To be honest, Ryck thought the kill had been somewhat anticlimactic. He had expected something more dramatic. But he'd done it. Without his PICS, he'd accomplished his mission.

No rest for the weary, though. Two more BAAAs were still hammering away. The nearest active gun was a good 100 meters from Ryck's kill. Ryck tried to shrug the pack into a better position, which was more of a "less horrible" than a "better," and staggered down the perimeter, hoping that no one would notice him. A simple rebel sniper farther inside the perimeter would have no problem taking Ryck out.

It took a good three minutes to advance just 50 meters, and Ryck was exhausted. He had to make sure that he could hit the gun ahead, so he limped forward another 10 meters, coming up on a wooden obstacle of some kind. Ryck knew a functional PICS could simply smash it down, but to him, in his present state, it was pretty impressive. It did, however, give him something he could use as a support. He gratefully leaned on it, taking some of the weight off of him. He laid the muzzle of the HCL across one of the logs, then fired. Pain lanced through his shoulder. He was pretty sure that he had dislocated it when firing at the first BAAA.

The grenade arched up and over the BAAA. He'd have to fire again.

Explosions started saturating the area. The rebels must have finally figured out that he was there and a threat, but for some unfathomable reason, they didn't seem to be able to pinpoint him. This puzzled Ryck, but he was not about to question his good luck.

He fired again, scoring a direct hit, but not taking the gun out. He sighed and touched the wires again. Nothing happened. There was a faint click, but the HTC did not fire. Evidently, the battery, which was not made for activating a firing mechanism, no longer had enough juice.

His only remaining possible weapon was his shoulder rockets. He didn't know if there was enough power left to fire them, but they should take less than the HTC, so it was a possibility. He pulled out the positive from the connector and twisted it around the positive from the battery.

More rounds landed around him, but he had to ignore them as he straightened up, aiming his shoulder launcher in the general direction of the BAAA. Of the 12 rockets, six had anti-personnel warheads, six anti-armor. The anti-armor rockets were semi-smart, that is, they could alter their course slightly to hit metallic targets within their acquisition cone.

Ryck didn't know of a way to fire the rockets separately as he could if he was in his PICS. This would be one salvo—that is, if he could even ignite them at all. He reached around with the free wire and started poking it into where he could feel the connector. He didn't have the time nor energy to bring the weapons pack back down, find the correct positive, and wire it. This would rely on blind luck.

Blind luck was with him. On this third poke, he touched the correct connection, the tiny rocket igniters sparked, and all twelve rockets took off. Ryck was glad that rockets had no recoil and their exhaust was too quick to burn him. He wasn't sure he could stand up to either.

Ryck wasn't sure how many rockets slammed into the BAAA, but it was enough. Flames erupted for a brief moment as the gun was blown off its gimbal. A few seconds later, a huge explosion, whether from ground forces or air, Ryck didn't see, knocked out the third BAAA another 200 meters from him. The perimeter was breached.

His shoulder was on fire, and the numbness in his ass was slowly transitioning to a pretty severe ache. Ryck looked inwards to the rest of the camp, but he knew his battle was over. He slumped against the wooden obstacle and waited.

Within moments, a PICS Marine made his appearance. From Ryck's perspective sitting down in the dirt, the suit looked immense. The Marine inside stopped the suit and turned toward him. The visor momentarily went clear, and King Tong's face looked out at him. The squad leader winked at Ryck before the visor went dark again and he continued his assault into the camp.

Prophesy

Chapter 25

"You be lookin' for a good time dere, sailor boy?" a heavily accented male voice came from behind him as he entered the passenger pickup.

Ryck spun around, took in the dark blue shirt of a Torritite, and took a step to hug the man.

"Hey sailor, we must be agreeing to price afore we be getting cozy-like," Joshua Hope-of-Life said, but returning the bear hug.

"Josh, good to see you. I thought we weren't going to get together until next week, though," Ryck said as they broke their hug.

"Eh, I've already been back for a week, and my sibs are driving me crazy. It's crazy and boring at the same time, so I told your sister I'd come into Williamson to pick you up. It gave me a good excuse to get out of the house for a bit," he said, back in the accent and manner of speaking he'd cultivated in the Marines, all trace of his Torritite drawl gone.

"Looking copacetic, there, Marine," he continued, eyeing the Silver Star on Ryck's chest.

Ryck was still self-conscious about the medal, which had been approved seven months after Luminosity. The citation read that Ryck's "ingenuity" and "courage" while "wounded" had cleared the way for the stalled assault to continue. Ryck had only participated in the war for an hour, really. He'd been picked up by a corpsman while sitting at the wooden obstacle, all fighting by then much farther inside the camp. He'd been casevac'd back to the *Prake* where they immediately began the regen on his dislocated shoulder and frostbit ass. The fighting on Luminosity took a little longer than expected due to the arms the rebels had acquired. Ryck tried to rejoin his platoon while they were supporting the recovery of the main mines, but even with his shoulder basically set, the Navy docs wouldn't clear him. The dead skin on his ass and leg evidently took longer to regen for some reason, and so he was stuck on the ship while the rest of the platoon fought.

It was a minor miracle, from Ryck's point of view, that no one from the squad was killed. Four PICS had been knocked out, but only the boot Prifit had been seriously hurt and put into long-term regen. All told, the battalion had lost 21 Marines and one Navy corpsman with 28 Marines, mostly from the light platoons, going into long-term regen. The fighting in the mines had been the fiercest of the operation, and the light platoons, in the skins and bones, had been the go-to Marines for that.

Two men, one of the Marines from India Company and the corpsman from Fox who had been killed, had been put in for the Federation Nova, which had been approved only a couple of months ago, while another two Marines had been approved for the Navy Cross. One of those was Sergeant Hector Phantawisangtong, King Tong, who had single-handedly blown the central bunker. Along with the two Platinum Stars, four Silver Stars, a Legion of Merit for the colonel, and more than a few Battle Commendations of all three classes, that made the battalion one of the most decorated for a single operation since the War of the Far Reaches. And Ryck missed most of it.

This was not false modesty. Ryck realized that what he'd done was pretty grubbing copacetic. But when the war stories on the two-week battle were brought out in the galley, at the club, out in town, he could just listen in. When they gushed over King Tong's one-man assault, with "Did you see when he . . ." or "What about when he blasted that . . ." no, Ryck hadn't seen. When they described the Helicon Mine going up, a suicide by the rebels inside of it just before the Marines of India entered, no, he hadn't seen that, either. He was already on his way back to the *Prake*. He stayed on the ship, getting three hots and a cot, while the Marines slugged it out on the planet below.

"Nice stripes, too," Joshua continued, pointing at the corporal chevrons on his sleeve.

"Shit, just in the right place at the right time," Ryck said, uncomfortable under Joshua's gaze.

Joshua had served his entire enlistment without one actual operation. He'd gone to First Division, yet nothing had happened. Ryck had three combat stars while Joshua had none.

"Hey, no more Marine shit for now. Let's get you home to your sister. You've got to see your nieces, cute as a grub in a rug. The big celebrations don't start for another two days, so you've got to get out of the uniform and decompress."

This was Ryck's first time home since he enlisted. "Home," though, didn't really fit anymore. It was where he grew up, and it was where his sister was, but not much else tugged at him. Barret had let him know that there was a place for him in his company, a well-paying job with room for advancement. If Ryck got out in another three months, he knew he could be set with a comfortable lifestyle. That was one of the reasons why he took his leave back on Prophesy. The timing also coincided with Incorporation Day. Even with PCDC bankrupt and out of the picture, the people of Prophesy still celebrated Incorporation Day, the anniversary of when they became a legal entity. This was a time for family and friends.

Ryck followed Joshua out into the parking and up to a brand new, shiny red Hyundai Tonora.

"Holy gubbing shit! This thing yours?" he asked.

"Hell no! You know my lowly lance corporal's salary. This is my baby brother's. Only 21, and his processing company is going gangbusters. The company is not even a year old, and look at this baby," Joshua said, pointing at the Hyundai.

"Damn! Sure looks like we picked the wrong line of work," Ryck said, stepping back to take in the sleek lines of the sports hover.

"Yeah, sure did. Caleb says he's got a job for me in the company if I don't re-up. I could get one of these for myself."

Ryck went quiet for a moment. Talking about reenlisting was something generally off the table. But Joshua was his friend.

"You going to take him up on that?" he asked.

"Me? In an office? Nah, I don't grubbing think so. I'm not a grubbing combat hero like you, but still, I like it, and if I stay in long enough, I'll see some action. Show you what a real warrior can do!" he said, punching Ryck in the arm.

Ryck was both relieved and disappointed to hear that, and he wasn't sure why. Ryck wanted to reenlist, and he had a good tour, but he wasn't sure yet. He'd lost friends, he'd had a miserable year plus in regen, but he had actually made a difference. On the other hand, if he took Barret up on his offer, he could make a good living, find a wife, settle down, and start a family.

He dumped his pack in the Hyundai's small trunk and slid into the passenger seat. It felt decadent, and Ryck was in love. That love deepened as the Tonora lifted off the pavement and slowly moved to the exit. He knew that the hover could be almost silent, but the sound engineers for Hyundai created a low rumble, more felt than heard, that reflected the power in the car. Lysa's home was on the other side of Williamson, so Joshua took the ring road around the city, opening the hover up at 240 KPH. This was better than a Stork!

Too soon, Joshua pulled off the ring road and onto the surface streets flipping the hover to auto. Within minutes, they pulled into Elysium Hills, the subdivision where Lysa and Barret had bought a house the year before. Ryck had been to their previous home, and he thought it had been rather nice. But with two kids, Lysa told him they needed someplace bigger, and Barret wanted to be in the capital city.

Bigger was an understatement, Ryck thought as Joshua pulled in front of a, well, a mansion. There was no other way to describe it. Easily twice as large as Barret's old home, it had all the architectural extras currently in fashion. The front yard was stately, with two huge trees of some sort as the main features. The water tax on those two trees alone would eat up a huge chunk of Ryck's corporal's salary. From one tree, a rope swing hung, out of place in the new construction, but a nice touch. Above the side wall, Ryck could see the tops of what looked like a jungle gym. This wasn't Barret's old bachelor pad. This was a family home.

"Here you go, my man," Joshua said as he pulled up.

"You coming in?"

"Nah, this is family time. Do your duty. We're all getting together on I-Day to watch the fireworks, so I'll see you then. Don't worry, we'll have some time together, just you and me," Joshua told him.

Ryck took his pack, watched Joshua pull out, and walked up to the front door. Before he reached it, the door opened, and Lysa ran out, colliding with him in a hug.

"Little brother, it's so good to see you. Come in, come in!"

"Uncle Ryck, Uncle Ryck, come here," a little voice said from behind Lysa.

Ryck had spoken with Kylee on the cam, but this was the first time he'd seen her in the flesh. She reached around Lysa to take his hand.

"Kylee! What did I tell you! Give Uncle Ryck a chance to breathe first. He'll see your room later," Lysa told her daughter. Lysa took Ryck's hand and led him into the house. Barret was waiting there, a beer in his hand that Ryck gratefully took, giving his pack to Barret in exchange.

"You look good, there, Ryck. I don't know what all those ribbons mean on your chest exactly, but your friend Joshua says they are pretty important. I know the girls want you to stay in your uniform, but I bet you'd like to get into something more comfortable," Barret said.

Ryck was towed to his room by Kylee as she pulled on his arm. He managed to get into the room alone and changed into shorts and a 2/9 t-shirt. As he opened the door, Kylee was waiting, and grabbing his arm, she dragged him back into the living room. Barret was sitting down, another little girl peeking out from behind his chair.

"Hi, Camyle," Ryck said to his youngest niece.

The two-year-old retreated back a little further behind her father's chair.

"Don't worry about her. She's a little shy, but she'll warm up to you," Lysa told him.

The next few hours were pure domesticity. Lysa cooked up some katsudon and yakisoba, Barret talked about the job he was offering Ryck, sports, and asked about Ryck's military operations, Kylee dragged him to her room for an introduction to over 30 stuffed animals, and Camyle even said a few words to him.

Ryck didn't have much time alone with Lysa. He managed to catch her while she was making the noodles for the yakisoba. She had flour on her forehead as she kneaded the dough. She was different. Not just the weight, which had crept on during the last four years. This woman was not the woman who left the house in skin-tight dresses for a night in the bars and night-spots. This was a woman who was at home.

"You look happy," Ryck told her, knowing it was true.

"Like this?" she said with a laugh, brushing the hair back off her forehead, leaving more flour.

"Yeah, just like that."

"You're right. I am happy. I'm not sure I deserve it, but I thank God every day for my two little girls, my husband. The only thing I am missing is you. If you take Barret's job offer, then that would complete me. Of course, then I'll be bugging you to find a wife and give me some nieces and nephews."

"And I'm happy for you, big sister. Really, I am."

Dinner was great, and the conversation was surprisingly interesting, even when initiated by a three-year-old. Three-and-a-half, that was, as Kylee took pains to remind everyone. Ryck had to watch his language a bit as some choice phrases and words almost leaked out. Little girls should not be faced with the same language as salty Marines and sailors.

To his surprise, Ryck was tired, and he went to bed early. He had to show up at his high school the next day to receive an award. He'd have liked to skip it, but he got three extra days of free leave for what the Marines considered a recruiting trip. In the afternoon, he promised he'd visit Barret at his office to check out the position being offered.

He had never been in Lysa and Barret's house before, and never in the guest bedroom. But as he lay down, with the little-girl shrieks of laughter coming from downstairs, it was feeling much more like home than he would have imagined.

Chapter 26

"This is your office," Barret told him, as they stepped into a good-sized, if barren, room. "Of course, you can personalize it as you want when you get here. But you can see it has a pretty good view. You don't get a private bathroom, I mean 'head,' but who knows?" he said with a laugh.

Water, or water reclamation and prospecting, had been good to Barret. With PCDC off the planet, water was scarce, and those who could find it were at a premium. Barret's company had done very well since the PCDC's charter was revoked. Barret was offering Ryck a position as vice-president of operations. Ryck didn't know the first thing about the water business, or any business for that matter, and he knew this was an offer based entirely on Barret's love for his sister. Still, as Barret said, the discipline Ryck had gained as a Marine would enable him to quickly grasp the ins and outs of his job.

The day had turned out better than he'd expected. Going back to school, this time in his dress blues, had been a rush. He felt like a flick star with all the attention. He was even moved by the Distinguished Alumni Award he'd received, much to his surprise. He'd received the extra three days of leave for meeting with his school, but frankly, he'd do it again even without the extra leave.

Barret had picked him up after lunch and taken him out to one of his projects in the area, which proved quite interesting. The company had dug several "lead wells" around what had once been a producing well but was now dry. With modern technology, the lead wells were able to "suck," as Barret explained in not so technical terms, the residual moisture from the area. The science was beyond him, but Barret assured him that the understanding would only take a bit of time.

During the long drive back to Williamson, Barret did most of the talking, and most of that was family-related. Barret would never fit in with a Marine platoon, and he had no idea of what Ryck had experienced, but he was a good man. Ryck felt guilty for not liking him at first. He would never be Ryck's best buddy, but he was good for Lysa and good for the girls. For that, he deserved Ryck's respect.

"Well, what do you think? I mean, do you like it?" he asked Ryck.

"I have to admit, it's kinda interesting. You've certainly done well with it," he said.

"You will, too. We'll talk about salary and perks later, but be easy on me, OK? No Marine combat attacks here. I'm not the enemy!" Barret said with yet another laugh.

Barret's sense of humor was not the most developed, and that fact alone made Ryck smile.

Chapter 27

"You ever get to Goa?" Charles asked as they looked out over the crowd.

"No," Joshua and Ryck said in unison.

"You've got to get there," Charles said. "Grubbing amazing! Better than Vegas or Pattaya, and I've been to both of them. We pulled into Goa, and as soon as you get off the spaceport, there's this line of bars with hot, and I mean hot mares . . ."

Ryck and Joshua had met up with Charles at The Park while waiting for the fireworks. He was obviously military, and he could tell both Marines were military, too. After introductions, they found out he was Navy, a petty officer second class. His ship was in the same sector as with First Division, and the talk drifted to bases in the area, then liberty ports. Ryck listened with half an ear while he watched Joshua's and his families. Joshua's dwarfed Ryck's in size, but for the little kids, Kylee was making her presence felt, bossing the other little ones around into playing her games.

She'd make a good DI, Ryck thought.

Ryck turned back to the two others. Charles was in the middle of a description of a very perverted, obscene, and frankly funny escapade he and another sailor had on Goa. Ryck found himself laughing along. Even Joshua got into the flow of it, with a few somewhat-risqué stories of his own. Ryck knew better now, but before he enlisted, he thought the Torritites were all pretty uptight prudes. In fact, he doubted that his family would be sitting there together with a Torritite family, sharing food and companionship, if Ryck and Joshua had not become friends. If nothing else, the Marines gave him the opportunity to have his eyes opened. If he got out of the Corps, he promised himself to stay in contact with Joshua's family.

His eyes roamed over the crowd. There were a lot of eligible women there, and Joshua had assured him that it was a good time to be in uniform. There was a new romance-flick that was all the rage, and the little-understood-but-noble-hero was a Marine lieutenant. Usually, the heroes, if they were military, were Navy or Legion, so this was something new, and Joshua was more than willing to take advantage of the current popularity if he could.

Joshua's own sister, Hannah, had grown into a fine-looking young woman. She had talked with Ryck for about 30 minutes as they set up the picnic dinner. Whether that was out of politeness to her brother's friend or something more, Ryck had no clue. He wouldn't mind finding out more about that, though.

He shifted his gaze to his sister just as Barret leaned over and kissed her. She accepted his kiss and laid her head on his shoulder as they sat on the blanket, waiting for the show.

Joshua's laugh brought him back to where he was. Charles had finished the sea story, and Joshua was hurriedly launching into his own. Ryck didn't really have any of his own such escapades. He had combat stories, but those were usually only shared with those who were there, too. He could discuss regen, but that was for other gen hens. Still, the very nature of the military made him part and parcel to the stories, even if he hadn't actually been there. If Ryck decided to get out when his enlistment ended, he would miss that. He would miss the brotherhood.

Down in front of him, there was family. Beside him was the brotherhood of the uniform. He had to make his choice.

His train of thought was interrupted when the first explosion showered the sky with color. The show was on.

Tarawa

Chapter 28

"Enter!" the voice ordered.

Corporal Ryck Lysander opened the hatch, then marched in to center himself in front of Sergeant Major Huertas.

"Corporal Lysander, reporting as ordered."

"At ease, Lysdander, at ease. You know why you're here. Your enlistment is up in seven days. It's declare time for you. As you know, you've been approved for reenlistment. It's yours if you want it. You can stay infantry, but there have been by-name requests for you from the armory and armor. Have you made your decision?"

"Yes, sergeant major, but first, can I ask you something, if I can get personal?"

That seemed to take the sergeant major back, but after a moment, he replied, "Sure, son. What is it?"

"Well, and please accept it if I'm getting too personal, but you never married. Why?"

Ryck half expected a blast with a "None of your fucking business!"

Instead, the sergeant major looked down at his fingers as if checking the nails for dirt, then said "I was married to the Corps, son. It wouldn't be fair for some young honey to be waiting for me, to wonder what was happening, to sit with me while I was going through regen. Hardly seems fair to me."

"Do you regret it?"

"Oh, I like women, you can be sure of that. And I've had my fun. Maybe I've had some regrets, but I made my choice."

"Was it worth it, though?" Ryck asked.

"Yes. Absolutely. You know I'm retiring next month. But if I could I would switch places with you in a heartbeat. To be a corporal in the Marines again. Things are happening now, things are heating up. If the shit hits the fan, I would want to be at the tip of the spear, son, the tip of the spear.

"But I'm just an old fart now, regened three times, and ready to be put out to pasture. Maybe I'll hook up with some honeywa and see what all those civvies think is so great about marriage. Maybe I'll just whore around until they bury me. But my time has passed. Now it's your time. So, it's up to you. What is your decision?"

"You know I went to my home planet two months ago, right? I saw my sister, her kids. I got a great job offer. I'd make more money in a year than I would in an entire career in the Corps. I could find a wife. I could have a family."

"And so . . . ?"

"But that was not my home. My home is here. My family is here. In the Corps. I want to reenlist."

Thank you for reading *Recruit*. If you liked it, please feel free to leave a review of the book in Amazon. Please continue with Ryck's story in *Sergeant*, the next books of the series.

If you would like updates on new books releases, news, or special offers, please consider signing up for my mailing list. Your email will not be sold, rented, or in any other way disseminated. If you are interested, please sign up at the link below:

http://eepurl.com/bnFSHH

Other Books by Jonathan Brazee

The United Federation Marine Corps

Recruit
Sergeant
Lieutenant
Captain
Major
Lieutenant Colonel
Colonel
Commandant

Rebel
(Set in the UFMC universe.)
Behind Enemy Lines (A UFMC Prequel)
The Accidental War (A Ryck Lysander Short Story Published in
BOB's Bar: Tales from the Multiverse)

The United Federation Marine Corps' Lysander Twins

Legacy Marines
Esther's Story: Recon Marine
Noah's Story: Marine Tanker
Esther's Story: Special Duty
Blood United

Coda

Women of the United Federation Marines
Gladiator
Sniper
Corpsman

High Value Target (A Gracie Medicine Crow Short Story)
BOLO Mission (A Gracie Medicine Crow Short Story)
Weaponized Math (A Gracie Medicine Crow Novelette, Published in
The Expanding Universe 3, a 2017 Nebula Award Finalist)

The Navy of Humankind: Wasp Squadron
Fire Ant (2018 Nebula Award Finalist)
Crystals
Ace
Fortitude

Ghost Marines
Integration (2018 Dragon Award Finalist)
Unification
Fusion

The Return of the Marines Trilogy
The Few
The Proud
The Marines

The Al Anbar Chronicles: First Marine Expeditionary Force--Iraq
Prisoner of Fallujah
Combat Corpsman
Sniper

Werewolf of Marines
Werewolf of Marines: Semper Lycanus
Werewolf of Marines: Patria Lycanus
Werewolf of Marines: Pax Lycanus

To the Shores of Tripoli

Wererat

Darwin's Quest: The Search for the Ultimate Survivor

Venus: A Paleolithic Short Story

Duty

Semper Fidelis

Checkmate (Originally Published in The Expanding Universe 4)

THE BOHICA WARRIORS
(with Michael Anderle and C. J. Fawcett)
Reprobates
Degenerates
Redeemables

Thor

SEEDS OF WAR
(With Lawrence Schoen)
Invasion
Scorched Earth
Bitter Harvest

SENTENCED TO WAR
(with JN Chaney)
Sentenced to War
Children of Angels

Non-Fiction

Exercise for a Longer Life

The Effects of Environmental Activism on the Yellowfin Tuna
Industry

Author Website
http://www.jonathanbrazee.com

Printed in Great Britain
by Amazon

61750493R00122